To Rosemary
Happy Birthday
From Margaret

4 . 5 . 61 .

THE FARM ON THE DOWNS

F.D.

Joanna and Louise unpacked the picnic basket.

(*See page* 79)

THE FARM
ON THE DOWNS

by

GWENDOLINE COURTNEY

COLLINS
LONDON AND GLASGOW

FIRST PRINTED IN THIS EDITION 1961

CONTENTS

CHAPTER ONE

A FAMILY CONCLAVE

"OH, GOOD! You're all here!"

As the door burst open with a violence that could only portend an earthquake or the entrance of Joanna, the second daughter of the house of Lister, the three occupants of the sitting-room betrayed a singular lack of interest. Louise, who was manicuring her nails, barely glanced up; Paul, apparently, was not even aware of the interruption; and Sarah, who was sharing the hearthrug and an apple with Woggles, a small, woolly, black-and-white dog that was the pride and joy of the family, paused for a thoughtful bite before inquiring, somewhat inarticulately, the cause for this particular rejoicing at their presence.

"Mummy wants to hold a family conclave," Joanna announced, seating herself comfortably, if ungracefully, beside Sarah. Louise looked up; it was a different matter if their mother wanted them.

"What is it?" she queried, and then gazed at Joanna in faint disapproval. "You *are* creasing your dress."

"Oh, bother my dress," Joanna said comfortably. "I don't know. She wouldn't say."

"£ s. d., I expect," Paul said coolly. "It always is."

"I suppose there is rather a crowd of us," Joanna said in an almost apologetic tone. Financially things had been very difficult since their father's death some six years before.

"Well, as long as we're here, I suppose we're here,"

7

Paul said philosophically, if a trifle cryptically, stretching out his long willowy form more comfortably and once again becoming absorbed in his book.

Fifteen months his senior, Louise at seventeen and a half was an attractive looking girl, for, added to a good figure, a fair skin and regular features, were a pleasant manner and a neatness quite alien to her two younger sisters. So far Joanna, at fifteen, was showing no signs of ever rivalling Louise in looks, being decidedly at the leggy stage. Her features, too, were not so regular; her mouth was too wide, and her hair, several shades darker than Louise's, instead of curling and waving at the whim of its owner, as the latter's did, persisted in going its own stubborn, heavy way; neither did her nose please her; but to discerning onlookers her face was redeemed by its expression of vital interest in whatever she was doing, and a pair of fine grey eyes, which she mournfully complained—whenever she stopped to think about her looks, which was not often— were her one redeeming feature. Sarah, aged ten, was the baby of the family, a small but, on occasion, imperious young lady with Louise's curly, fair hair, Joanna's wide grey eyes, and a guileless expression difficult to resist.

"Mummy's been looking worried for days," Louise volunteered, and Paul forgot his usual indolence and jumped up as his mother appeared.

"Come and sit down and get it off your chest," he commanded. "What's the demned total this time, as Mr. Mantalini would say?"

Mrs. Lister laughed as she sat down. Fair like Louise and Paul, but small, with a vivacious, alert face, she certainly did not look her forty years.

"It isn't money," she said, almost breathlessly, a little

dimple peeping out wickedly, as if amused at some secret joke, and her family stared at her, almost aghast.

"Not money!" Louise exclaimed incredulously.

"But it must be," Joanna protested. "Unless you've come into a fortune unbeknownst to us."

"Well, primarily I suppose it's money," Mrs. Lister admitted, and Joanna looked almost relieved.

"I knew it must be. We'd be lost if we hadn't got to worry about the state of our finances."

"Come, it's not quite as bad as that," Mrs. Lister laughed. "Though I must admit the last few years have been difficult. Keeping four of you at school——"

"Never mind, you won't have me to worry about now," Louise declared comfortingly. She had never been much good at lessons, and she was now rejoicing that her schooldays would end in a few days' time.

"I know," Mrs. Lister said, "but that's only a drop in the bucket. My being able to do part-time teaching has helped quite a lot—but last week Miss Cartwright told me she was getting another full-time mistress, and so——"

"Mummy! She hasn't given you the sack?" Joanna exclaimed tragically.

"Well, I suppose that's what it amounts to," Mrs. Lister said reluctantly. "At least, she did ask me first if I could go full-time, but I knew I just couldn't manage that and keep the home going decently."

"Wait till next term!" Joanna said darkly. "I'll make her rue the day!"

Mrs. Lister let her glance rove from one face to another, and then to a letter she held in her hand. She had not dropped her bombshell yet.

"When she broke the news to me last week I suddenly felt I couldn't struggle along by myself any longer," she confessed, and immediately remorseful exclamations came from all round her.

"Mummy! You poor little thing!" Joanna exclaimed, catching her mother's free hand in a jealous clasp.

"You weren't alone. You had us," Sarah said in a matter-of-fact tone, and her mother laughed, a little tremulously.

"I know, dear. But it was you four I was worrying about—and so I gave in and wrote to your Uncle John."

"But I thought you didn't want him to know we were having a rather difficult time," Paul protested, with rather more decision than usual. His mother's brother, although a couple of years her junior, and quite a favourite with them all, was of a somewhat dogmatic disposition, and Mrs. Lister had rather feared that if she took her troubles to him he would insist on applying his own solution (whatever that might be) whether she liked it or not.

"I didn't," Mrs. Lister confessed. "And I still don't. But I just couldn't struggle on any longer by myself."

"What does he say?" demanded Joanna, eyeing the letter apprehensively, and Mrs. Lister looked round from one to another almost as if she feared to tell them.

"I know it's something ghastly," Paul groaned.

"No, it isn't really," his mother protested. "John has been splendid—even better than I'd dared to hope."

"I like Uncle John," Sarah observed in thoughtful approval. "He likes Woggles."

"Go on, Mummy!" Joanna urged.

"Well, after scolding me thoroughly for not telling him before, he suggests that, as his housekeeper has just let him down and left, we should all transplant ourselves to Long Barrow, and that I should keep house for him."

"What!"

It was a breathtaking suggestion. Just over a year before, that old farmhouse, lying amongst the downs on the borders of Wiltshire and Dorset, had been left to John Eldon by an old uncle, and he had, to the great surprise of Mrs. Lister and her children, almost immediately thrown up his practice at the Bar and taken possession of his new estate, where he was now trying his hand at farming on a small scale.

"It sounds rather fun," Joanna said thoughtfully.

"I don't know about that. What do you think Uncle John would be like to *live* with?" Paul asked apprehensively. "He's horribly energetic."

"Do you good," Joanna said unsympathetically.

"Do you think we'd like living in the country?" Louise asked doubtfully. "Wouldn't it be dreadfully slow?"

Sarah looked round with eyes full of perplexity.

"What is the difference between a *long* barrow and an ordinary one? I thought they were always the same shape—like the one Mr. Prescott has for his garden——"

There was a shriek of laughter from her more knowledgeable elders.

"Bless the child, she's thinking of a wheelbarrow!" Joanna exclaimed.

"Well, isn't it?" Sarah demanded, undaunted.

"Of course not. It's a *barrow*—the places where people were buried in the Neolithic Age," Paul explained, but Sarah only looked more puzzled.

"But surely Uncle doesn't live in one of those——"

"No, the house is called that because it's near one of these barrows," Mrs. Lister hastened to explain, laughing as much as the others at Sarah's obvious fear that they would have to share their home with a Neolithic corpse.

"I think Woggles would like to live in the country," Sarah observed, calmly changing the subject with an aplomb many an older person would have envied. She seldom was perturbed by having displayed her ignorance. "Wouldn't you, Wogs?"

A pink tongue shot up on to her nose, apparently in approbation.

"Well, that's one in favour," Joanna said. "What do you feel, Mummy?"

Mrs. Lister glanced down at the letter again.

"John warns us that it is in rather a lonely spot, and his suggestion is that, before committing ourselves irrevocably, we should let this house furnished for a few months so that we shan't be burning our bridges behind us, and can always return here if we don't like it there."

Louise looked relieved. Having none of Joanna's adventurous spirit she was by nature opposed to any drastic change, and she did not appreciate the thought of being uprooted from the home she had always known. Judging by his expression, Paul shared her relief. Obviously he did not expect that country life would appeal to him to any great extent.

"I believe you'd like to try it," Joanna said, looking up searchingly into her mother's face. "Own up now."

"I believe I should," Mrs. Lister confessed. As she had been brought up in the country the suggestion rather appealed to her. "And the change would help a lot financially. We should be able to get quite a big rent if we let this house furnished, and our expenses would be very few at Long Barrow."

"Have you ever been there?" Louise asked curiously.

"No. Uncle James quarrelled with my father when I was still a child, and we didn't know he'd ever got over

it until we found he'd left everything to John. He was a
very eccentric man, I believe."

"So it would be just as fresh to you," Joanna said
musingly. "I believe I should like to give it a trial."

"What about schools?" asked Paul suddenly.

"I don't know. John hasn't mentioned them, but he'll
arrange something. You can rely on that."

"Does Hugh still go to school?" inquired Sarah, and
consternation sat on every face.

"I'd forgotten clean all about him," Paul exclaimed.
"I suppose he's still with Uncle John?"

"Yes, he mentions him somewhere," Mrs. Lister said,
fluttering over the pages of her letter.

"How old is he?" asked Louise, wrinkling her brow.

"Same age as Paul, isn't he?" Joanna said. "I wonder
how he'll take our all going there?"

Hugh was their cousin, who had been orphaned at the
age of ten and adopted by their Uncle John. Hitherto they
had seen very little of him, for he had always lived in the
south, while their home was in Liverpool, but they had
faint recollections of a silent, rather surly-looking boy.

"I don't suppose he'll be very pleased," Paul said
lazily. "Wouldn't be human if he was. At present he
probably has things all his own way——"

"Not with Uncle John," Joanna chuckled. "He'll make
you toe the line, Paul."

"He can try," Paul said equably, and Mrs. Lister shot
him a swift glance, unnoticed by her children. She had
been feeling of late that Paul needed a stronger hand
than hers, and one of her reasons for writing to her
brother was the hope that he could help her in this. Not
that Paul was overtly troublesome in any way; he was
too indolent for that; but she felt that the time was fast

approaching when she should be able to lean on him a little, an idea that had certainly never occurred to him.

"Then you would like to try it?" she asked, looking round the circle. "Joanna, I can see you would——"

"Johnny will try anything fresh," Paul remarked.

"Variety's the spice of life," Joanna retorted.

"And Sarah?" Mrs. Lister went on, smiling down at her baby.

"*And* Woggles?" that young lady amended. "Mummy, Wogs would go, too, wouldn't she?"

"Of course. Woggles is one of the family just as much as the rest of us," Mrs. Lister declared, stooping to pick up that spoilt little animal, which reached up to give her ear a hasty but affectionate lick before settling down on her knee with a blissful grunt.

"Louise?" Mrs. Lister went on, glancing across a little more doubtfully at her eldest daughter.

"As long as we can retreat if we want to," Louise added hastily, and then laughed at herself. "I know I'm a coward, but I do hate committing myself to the unknown."

"I know how you feel," Mrs. Lister said, remembering her own feelings on leaving her home in a country village for a busy port on her marriage. "Any big change is always rather frightening. Don't worry, Louise, if we don't like it we'll come back here, I promise. Paul?"

"Oh, if the rest of you want to," Paul said carelessly. "Though changing schools now won't do us any good."

"No, I agree I don't like the prospect of that very much," Mrs. Lister admitted. "But it can't be helped. You've no other objections?"

"No, whatever you want," Paul said easily, and a little frown creased his mother's forehead. He never would trouble to make decisions himself. A moment later, however, the frown was chased away by a laugh as Joanna exclaimed blissfully:

"Won't we have to do a lovely lot of packing!"

"Speak for yourself," Louise said hastily. "I'm dreading it. Mummy, when do we go?"

"We shouldn't have any difficulty in getting a tenant, so I suggest as soon as you break up, if we've fixed up about the house by then. We mustn't leave it too long, you know, if John is having to fend for himself without a housekeeper."

"Couldn't we start packing now?" Joanna asked impetuously. "There must be something we can start doing at once!" and the conference broke up with a laugh.

Mrs. Lister went off to do some shopping, and the others proceeded to discuss the astounding news.

"Staggering is the word!" Joanna declared.

"A bit too staggering," Paul commented. "I'm not at all sure what Uncle John will be like to live with."

"I'm not looking forward to all the work," Louise groaned. "Think of the packing!"

"Yes, it's almost like emigrating, isn't it? Even like going to an unknown land," Joanna remarked.

"I suppose Uncle John in his more energetic moods could be regarded as nearly as much of a menace as hostile Indians," Paul agreed, remembering, as the others well knew, the last time their uncle had spent a few days with them, when he had insisted on dragging his nephew off on a cross-country walk from which Paul had returned in a state almost of complete collapse.

"Paul will never forgive Uncle for that walk," Louise laughed.

"I'll certainly never forget it," Paul agreed feelingly.

CHAPTER TWO

HUGH

AT LAST the great day arrived when they took a last glance at their home as the taxi bore them from the door *en route* for the station.

"It's queer to think that to-night we'll be over two hundred miles away," Louise said soberly.

"I feel as if we're setting out on a real adventure," Joanna said, while Sarah hugged Woggles and beamed with anticipation. Paul was already deep in a book he had drawn from his pocket.

The first part of their journey passed swiftly enough, but the last part, on a slow train that stopped at every tiny station, dragged and dragged until they began to think they would never arrive at their destination.

"And according to Uncle John we've got quite a long drive after we leave the train, haven't we?" Louise said, turning to her mother.

"Yes, apparently Long Barrow is far beyond the reach of civilisation—as far as trains are concerned, anyway," Mrs. Lister said.

At long last they found themselves scrambling out on to a small country platform, and Sarah gave a cry of excitement as a tall, broad-shouldered figure came striding down the platform towards them. The young Listers always declared they could never understand how anyone as large as their uncle and as small as their mother could be brother and sister.

There could be no doubting the fact that Mr. Eldon was pleased to have them, and Mrs. Lister's secret qualms vanished before his warm welcome.

"I've been feeling horribly guilty at landing such a crowd on you, even though it was your own suggestion," she confided to him, as they all made for the station exit.

"Long Barrow will be all the better for having you," he returned. "It's much too large just for Hugh and me."

It was some time since they had seen him, and his nieces and nephew were all glad to see the twinkle in his grey eyes as he surveyed them. His sense of humour did much to alleviate his sometimes too dogmatic manner.

"I hope you're not going to be too bored out in the wilds," he said, as he packed them into his car. "Ruth, if you, Louise, Joanna and the dog——"

"Uncle John!" Sarah's outraged voice pulled him up. "You mustn't just say *the dog* like that. She'll be awfully hurt. You must say Woggles—or Wogs if you're feeling very affectionate."

"I beg her pardon," her uncle said gravely, picking up Woggles and dumping her on Joanna's knee. "There, if you're all tucked in at the back, perhaps Paul can have Sarah on his knee in front. Now, are you all ready?"

Feeling at last that they really were approaching their destination, the Listers all looked round eagerly as they left the station behind them and made for a long range of downs that lay before them. They were mounting now, after flashing through a couple of villages, a long gradual climb out of a tree-lined lane up on to the bare top of the downs, and *Oh's* and *Ah's* came from all the newcomers as they found themselves gazing across miles and miles of green downs, fields golden with corn, and dark woods, all lit by the glow of the evening sun. Then they began to go down again, down until the lane seemed to go through a tunnel of trees, then a quick swing round to the left, and they were in the loveliest village they had yet seen, a tiny place with a gracious old church with rounded Norman arches, and small, mellowed stone cottages, covered with roses, and with lichened roofs of old red tiles.

"Fontroy Magna, our nearest village," their uncle said, taking a sharp turn to the right by the church.

"Are we nearly there now?" Joanna asked regretfully.

"No, not quite yet," her uncle said, and Louise began to look a little apprehensive as they again mounted under an archway of trees and ran out on to the open downs. "There!" He pointed down on their right, to where a lichen-covered roof showed amongst some trees below them in a fold of the downs. "That's Long Barrow."

"Oh!" Louise made no attempt to hide her dismay as she realised for the first time just how isolated their destination was, and even Mrs. Lister glanced anxiously at her brother. If he was aware of their feelings, however, he did not show it, but calmly turned down a narrow lane that was little better than a cart track, and which led to the house.

For a moment Joanna had been as appalled as the others; then her natural spirit of adventure reasserted itself. This was quite as good as emigrating to the back-woods.

"I'm so glad you've got one of those lovely old red roofs," she exclaimed as the house itself came into view, a grey stone building, with outhouses built of the same material.

Mr. Eldon drove in through an open gate into a garden gay with flowers and, getting out, helped his sister and the two elder girls to alight, while Sarah tumbled out excitedly.

Louise looked as if she was very near to tears, and Paul could not suppress an expression of dismay, but Joanna's quick eyes were sweeping round with indomitable curiosity.

For a moment their uncle studied with interest the expressions of the three elder ones, and then he turned to the house.

"Come and see your new home. I'm afraid since Mrs. Shaw left we've been living entirely in the kitchen to save work, Ruth, but we'll soon settle down to a more civilised life again now you're here."

He opened the front door and led them through a square hall, past two closed doors and a staircase, and through a door at the back of the hall into a big, stone-flagged kitchen with a low raftered ceiling. One wall was entirely occupied by a huge built-in dresser and cupboards, and the old-fashioned kitchen range filled part of the wall opposite, while in the centre of the room was a large kitchen table, already laid for a meal. Near the range stood a rocking-chair and a wooden arm-chair of considerable age, while the rug between them was shared by a large ginger cat and a big collie in amicable concord.

At the sight of Woggles the cat arched his back and, leaping for safety on to the rocking-chair, proceeded to swear violently, while the collie treated Woggles to a benevolent inspection and then lay down again, evidently having decided in her favour.

"Sam seems quite ready to be friendly and Nero will soon get used to Woggles," Mr. Eldon said, as Sarah snatched up her favourite in case the cat should decide to exchange words for deeds.

"Nero?" Joanna repeated. "Why d'you call him Nero?"

"Because he's so fond of a fire," her uncle said. "That was Hugh's idea."

"Where is Hugh?" Sarah asked the question that was in all their minds, for everyone felt he might have come to welcome them.

"Oh, he'll be working somewhere," her uncle replied casually. "We don't have much time for idling here, you know."

Joanna's eyes met Paul's with a wicked twinkle, and he gazed at her in dismay, but before anyone could speak the outer door opened and a fresh figure stood regarding them in silent curiosity, the figure of a well-built boy of sixteen, with dark hair and greenish, rather sulky-looking eyes, and a square chin that promised a firm will. At the moment the hair was ruffled, the face was smeared, apparently with mud, while his ancient clothes, equally ancient boots, and his hands were in an even more bespattered condition.

The collie sprang up with wagging tail to greet him, but the Listers stared in silence—some almost in horror—at the apparition, while he, for his part, let his eyes sweep from Mrs. Lister's dainty little figure to Paul, leaning indolently against the dresser, on to Sarah's wide-eyed, frank amazement, to Joanna, whose eyes were beginning to gleam mischievously, and finally to Louise, who, almost as neat and attractive as when she started her journey, was eyeing him in a shocked astonishment she could not hide.

As he felt the horrified disapproval or amusement of his cousins, the boy's face took on a sulkier expression, and he took an instinctive step backwards as Mrs. Lister, pulling herself together, turned to her brother, who was surveying the scene with considerable amusement.

"Is—is this——"

"This is Hugh," Mr. Eldon announced, the twinkle in his eyes becoming more pronounced.

Hugh glanced at his aunt with doubtful suspicions as she stepped towards him with outstretched hand, and backed again.

"I'm sorry—I didn't realise you'd come. I've been cleaning the pigsties. I couldn't get round to them earlier—I'd too much to do."

"Cl—cleaning pigsties!" Louise echoed in horror, and Hugh eyed her dainty figure in its city-made clothes disapprovingly, instantly deciding that she would never fit into life at Long Barrow.

"Yes. Someone's got to do it," he said bluntly.

"I like pigs," Sarah remarked, eyeing her cousin with greater favour as he automatically stooped to pat Woggles, who was sniffing round him. "Can I help you, Hugh?"

Her cousin looked decidedly taken aback as she confidently stepped forward to join him.

"No, it's finished—thanks," he added somewhat belatedly, and Sarah's face fell. Then she cheered up.

"Never mind, I'll help you next time."

"Regard that as a threat," Paul said dryly, as Hugh flashed a glance at his uncle that was comical in its appeal.

"I think that's really more a job for Paul," their uncle said casually, and Paul's face was a study. "Someone's got to do it," Mr. Eldon added, repeating Hugh's words, and Joanna suddenly laughed as she slipped an arm through her uncle's.

"We're far too tired—and hungry—to be teased now," she said chidingly and her uncle gave a swift, amused glance at his sister, who was looking a little apprehensive.

"All go and get a wash—you particularly, Hugh—and then we'll have supper," he ordered in his old familiar tone of unconscious command. "I'll show you your rooms," he added, and led the way upstairs, stopping at a room at the front of the house with good but old-fashioned furniture. "This is yours, Ruth. Paul, you'll have to share Hugh's room." He paused at the foot of a smaller staircase. "Would you three girls be nervous about sharing a large room up here?"

"Of course not," Joanna exclaimed, setting off up the stairs at once.

"Especially as Woggles always sleeps with us," Sarah added, scrambling after her.

"Oh, she does, does she?" her uncle said. "I hope she won't put ideas like that into Sam's head. I refuse to have him in my room—there's rather too much of him."

"Oh, I like this!" Joanna exclaimed, as he opened the door of a large attic which ran right across the front of the house, with a double and a single bed covered with gay patchwork quilts, and three dormer windows looking out on to the downs, where purple scabious was waving lazily in the wind.

"There's water in all your rooms," Mr. Eldon said, indicating an old-fashioned toilet set on the washstand, and Louise stared at him blankly.

"But—where's the bathroom?"

"There isn't one," her uncle said calmly, and Louise gave a gasp of dismay.

"No bathroom?" she repeated faintly, and Sarah gave a squeak of excitement.

"Ooh! and look, we've got to have a candle," she said.

"Good gracious, yes!" Joanna exclaimed, glancing up at the ceiling and suddenly realising that no familiar flex and bulb hung from it. "Isn't there electric light up here, Uncle?"

"There isn't any in the house," her uncle answered, looking as if he were deriving considerable amusement from their consternation. "We have lamps downstairs. Now don't be long, girls. I'll soon have supper ready."

Mrs. Lister retired to her own room, and Paul rather unwillingly went to the room indicated by his uncle on the first floor. He was glad to find he had it to himself, as Hugh, apparently, was endeavouring to get the worst dirt off somewhere downstairs, and only came to change just as Paul was going down again. Like the other rooms, it had good but old-fashioned furniture, with two single beds, and two chests of drawers.

"Cold water!" Louise said expressively, investigating as soon as the girls were left alone.

"I think I'm rather glad. I feel so hot and sticky," Joanna said, pulling off her hat and tossing it on a bed.

"But I never feel as clean if I don't use hot water," Louise complained, sounding very near to tears.

"We're in the wilds now, my dear," Joanna said cheerfully. "You must learn to rough it."

When the three girls finally went downstairs—rather shyly on the part of the two elder ones—they found their mother cutting bread and butter, their uncle frying eggs, and Paul, in a corner near the window, making the most of the last few minutes of daylight, deep in a book.

"Come along in," their uncle said hospitably. "Would one of you mind making the tea? The kettle's boiling."

As Louise did so, the door opened again and Hugh

came in, looking very different from the disreputable figure they had first seen, for he had changed into flannels and a fresh shirt, while his hair was still damp after being washed. He glanced round curiously, but rather uncomfortably, at his cousins, almost shied from Mrs. Lister's quick, warm smile, and retired into the darkest corner of the kitchen—unavailingly as it happened, for Sarah immediately followed him up.

"How many pigs are there?" she demanded, evidently still deeply interested in that entrancing subject. "And are they big ones or little ones?"

"Supper!" Mr. Eldon announced rather hurriedly, to his nephew's relief. Small girls of ten were a completely unknown quantity to Hugh.

Joanna crossed to the student by the window and gently but firmly gripped his left ear.

"Supper, Paul!" she announced. "Wake up!" She chuckled as she caught her uncle's eye. "He's always like this. Just speaking to him is no use whatever."

Certainly her method appeared to be efficacious. With an annoyed grunt Paul dropped his book and rubbed his maltreated ear.

"One of these days, Johnny, you'll do that once too often," he said threateningly, and Joanna beamed at him seraphically.

"Of course, if you're not hungry, I don't mind helping out with your share——"

"Sorry to disappoint you," Paul returned, "but I am." He put his book on the window ledge and joined her at the table, while Hugh, who had also left his corner, eyed them curiously, though not without a slight smile as he shot a quick glance at his uncle.

"Do you still read as much as ever, Paul?" Mr. Eldon

inquired, as he lit the big lamp in the centre of the table, and glanced from Paul's thin, rather pale face to Hugh's sunburnt, rugged features.

"More," Joanna said feelingly. "I wonder he ever stops to eat or sleep."

"He *eats*, anyway," Louise said as Paul, not a bit perturbed by this discussion, proceeded to make a good supper.

"Must keep my strength up somehow," he said equably. "I need to, to cope with a family of four females. They need some keeping in order."

"I expect they do," his uncle agreed. "But you won't be standing alone now."

"He doesn't need any support," Joanna laughed. "He just looks at us—and then goes on reading and forgets we're there. We might just as well talk to the poker."

"Just as well," Paul agreed, while Hugh looked from one to the other, knitting his dark brows as if he were not sure in what spirit these exchanges were made.

When the travellers' appetites were appeased, and even Sarah, the least affected by their strange, lamplit surroundings, was content to sit back with a sigh of repletion, Mr. Eldon looked round the table with a pleased air he made no attempt to hide.

"This looks like a real family," he declared appreciatively, "and not just Hugh, Joe and me."

"Who's Joe?" demanded Sarah, who never let politeness interfere with her desire for knowledge.

"Joe is our staff—indoor and outdoor. He's spending this evening in the village," her uncle added, as Sarah opened her mouth to ask another question. "He sleeps in a room over the stables, and he'll turn his hand to anything, Ruth. You'll find him him just as willing to do the washing up for you as to wash the car or do the milking."

"Is this a real farm, then?" Joanna asked hopefully.

"No, not exactly," her uncle said. "We just dabble in various branches of farming on a small scale—more as a hobby," he added, and Hugh shot him a queer look that his cousins could not fathom—a strange mixture of respect and—something else they could not identify.

"An energetic hobby," Paul commented.

"But great fun, I should think," Joanna said quickly as her uncle glanced sharply at Paul. "I like energetic hobbies."

"I don't," Paul said frankly. "It's quite wearing enough having one energetic person in the family——"

"Mummy's just as bad as Joanna," Louise said. "And Sarah——"

"Let's leave Sarah out of it," Paul begged hastily, with an apprehensive glance at his youngest sister, who had until now been happily engaged in slipping surreptitious titbits under the table to Woggles and Sam, the collie.

"I'm going to help," she announced, her attention drawn to the conversation, and Paul groaned.

"Why couldn't you let sleeping dogs lie, Louise? Uncle, take my advice. If you value your farm, lock Sarah up."

"Why, is she as bad as that?" his uncle laughed.

"She *will* help," Paul groaned. "I know her intentions are most laudable, but the results——"

"Are usually lamentable," Joanna finished for him. "But, Uncle, why did you decide to give up being a barrister to become a farmer?"

"Yes, you've never told me, though I've asked you nearly every time I've written," Mrs. Lister said, and her brother pushed back his chair and got up abruptly.

"I suppose I felt I needed a change—I didn't want to spend my whole life buried in legal documents—and inheriting this place gave me a chance to get away—so I thought I'd try my hand at farming."

"I don't blame you," Joanna said, though Paul's face showed plainly which life he would prefer. "But it must be rather fun to stand up in Court in a wig and gown and dazzle everyone with your eloquence."

"Even allowing the dazzling, there's a lot of hard spade work to be done before you go into Court," her uncle said with a laugh, as he filled his pipe.

"Well, I should think there's a lot of hard spade work to be done here, too," Joanna retorted quickly, and Hugh gave an unexpected chuckle. He was finding her more amusing than he had expected. "Uncle," she added, slipping her hand coaxingly through Mr. Eldon's arm. "Can I help?"

"I hope you all will," her uncle said quickly, with a glance at Paul. "A place like this is no good unless everyone pulls his weight. And I'm afraid your mother will want help, too. This is quite a big place to run."

"Oh, we always helped at home," Joanna declared. "Mummy couldn't go out and teach *and* do all the housework."

"I'm glad to hear it—I mean that you helped," Mr. Eldon said, smiling down at her eager face.

"Though I'm sure I'd rather do outdoor work," Joanna went on naïvely, and he laughed.

"We'll have to try to arrange a judicious mixture of the two. But I believe Sarah will be asleep in another minute or two."

"No, I won't," that young lady declared, opening her eyes wide with a painful effort.

"Yes, you will! Come along!" her mother said, rising. "We're all tired to-night. Come on, girls. Paul, you mustn't start reading to-night."

"He won't read in bed, if that's what you're afraid of," Mr. Eldon said, eyeing Paul with grim amusement. "Hugh is generally up by half-past five, so he won't want a light in the room longer than is absolutely necessary."

Louise stared at her cousin incredulously.

"Half-past five!"

"Yes. Uncle's usually up then, too," Hugh said, speaking for the first time since supper started, although he had not missed a word or gesture on the part of his cousins.

"We *have* emigrated!" Joanna said with conviction, and went up to bed, leaving her mother to explain to her highly amused brother that his home had been likened to the backwoods.

"Well, what do you think of it?" Joanna asked as the girls undressed.

"It's *dreadful*!" Louise exclaimed, looking round distastefully at the flickering shadows thrown on the walls and sloping ceiling by the candle. "I never, never imagined anything quite so—so uncivilised as this. And I shall never feel clean washing in cold water."

"What do you think of Hugh?" Joanna asked curiously and Louise rubbed her nose disapprovingly.

"Didn't he look *terrible*? I felt absolutely ashamed to think he was our cousin. He's an awful boor, isn't he?"

"He looked better later," Joanna said fairly. "Look here, Sarah! Who said you could have the single bed?"

"No one," Sarah answered promptly, having taken advantage of her seniors' preoccupation to take her choice. "But I'm in it now."

Joanna hesitated, wondering whether to evict her by

force, but decided that she was too tired to bother, so she climbed into the other bed, and Louise, after carefully extinguishing the candle, got in beside her.

For a while they were silent, but Joanna found everything too strange to sleep, and realising after a time from her steady breathing that Sarah was safely in dreamland, she whispered cautiously:

"Are you awake, Louise?"

"Yes," and to her sister's dismay Louise's voice sounded suspiciously tearful.

"Cheer up," Joanna murmured, slipping her arm round her. "It probably won't be half as bad as you think. Personally, I believe I'll enjoy it."

"But you always did like an outdoor life," Louise demurred. "I think it's going to be awful—and dreadfully lonely and dull."

"Not with all of us here," Joanna said with a chuckle. "But what I was going to say is, I don't believe Uncle and Paul are going to get on too well together."

"Why?" Louise forgot herself in this fresh cause for anxiety.

"I don't quite know, but I just feel it," Joanna said, a trifle vaguely. "I don't think Uncle likes Paul reading so much."

Louise gave a little laugh—a shaky one, it is true, but it was a laugh.

"Then he'll just have to put up with it. No power on earth could keep Paul from his books."

"I know. We know that, but Uncle doesn't," Joanna said, and Louise gave a sigh.

"I hope you're wrong."

CHAPTER THREE

LONG BARROW

JOANNA WAS the first of the girls to wake the following morning. It was still quite early, but the sun was shining in so enticingly that she could not resist it and padded across to the open window, where she stood, delightedly sniffing the fresh country air.

"You are an idiot!" Louise's sleepy voice roused her from a pleasant reverie. "You'll catch cold standing there."

"I won't," Joanna said, disagreeing almost as a matter of course, though hastily suppressing a slight shiver, for the morning air was keen. "It's glorious, Louise. Do get up, and come and explore."

"What time is it?" asked Louise suspiciously.

"Half-past six," Joanna said blithely, and Louise promptly snuggled down again.

"You must be mad. Come back to bed again."

"No fear!" Joanna declared. "And you needn't prepare to hibernate. You're coming to explore, my dear." And Louise groaned as firm hands were laid on the bedclothes. "Besides," Joanna added cheerfully, "we're not the first. Someone's at work out there already."

Louise groaned again and reluctantly sat up. Being now most effectively awakened, there was not much point in staying in bed.

"Well, don't wake Sarah," she said warningly, and, pulling her dressing-gown around her, she too crossed to the window and looked out. Away beyond the garden a single figure was hard at work with a scythe, and she watched the rhythmical movement with interest.

"Surely that's Hugh," she exclaimed. "Fancy being at work already!"

"Didn't Uncle say he gets up at half-past five?" Joanna said, scrambling into her clothes. "If you don't get dressed it will be you who'll be catching cold."

Thus adjured, Louise hastily dressed, though she nearly forgot all about the glorious morning when she realised they had only cold water to wash in, and her wail of woe wakened Sarah, who stared round in sleepy perplexity at her strange surroundings.

"Oh! Wait for me!" she exclaimed, as she remembered where she was.

"No, you stay in bed," Joanna ordered, but Sarah was already sitting up, drawing a sleepy protest from Woggles, who was lying curled up on her feet.

"Where are you going?" she demanded.

"Only to explore," Joanna said. "Are you ready, Louise?"

"Almost," Louise said, hastily, combing her hair. "Sarah, do wait until Mummy is up."

Sarah sniffed as she clutched Woggles firmly and watched her two seniors depart. Then she slipped out of bed herself, made a perfunctory toilet, and set off on an exploring expedition of her own with Woggles. While she was dressing, the two elder girls paused on the first floor landing and looked at each other questioningly. Everything was silent.

"I'm sure a walk before breakfast would do him good," Joanna murmured solemnly.

"As you've dragged me out of bed, I don't see why he shouldn't suffer too," Louise agreed, and they marched determinedly into the boys' room, where Paul had his dreams rudely shattered when Joanna descended like a ton weight on his feet, and Louise tweaked a lock of fair hair that was hanging over his face.

"Go away," he grunted. "It's still the middle of the night."

"Rubbish!" Joanna declared. "Hugh's out working. He must have been up for ages."

Paul gave an expressive snort as he rolled over and pulled the bedclothes more firmly round him. "Hugh's mad! He must be!"

"How have you got on?" asked Joanna curiously.

"We haven't," Paul said briefly, without opening his eyes, and Louise looked worried.

"Paul! You haven't been quarrelling?"

"Oh, no! I never quarrel. He just showed me which drawers and cupboards I could use, and that's all we said to each other," Paul said coolly, abandoning his useless pose of sleep.

"Was he—unpleasant?" Louise asked anxiously.

"No, just not effusive," Paul said. "He doesn't seem a very sociable soul."

"Were you rude?" Joanna asked bluntly, and Paul looked pained.

"Good heavens, no! I don't usually go round being rude to people. That's your little habit—if they happen to annoy you."

"You don't always bother to talk to people if there's a book anywhere near," Louise said frankly. "And that's tantamount to being rude."

Paul grinned lazily. "If you're so fussy, My Lady Airs and Graces, go and be polite to him yourself."

"You *are* going to have a nice sociable time in here,"

Joanna laughed, but Louise looked anxious. She always hated discord of any kind.

"If we're all going to live here together we must try to be friendly," she demurred.

"Oh, I'm quite willing to be friendly," Paul said, "but I'm not going round forcing my friendship on anyone who doesn't want it."

"Well, never mind Hugh now," Joanna said briskly as Louise sighed. "Get up and come and explore with us."

"At this hour of the morning!" Paul exclaimed. "No fear!" Nevertheless, he watched with a cautious eye as Joanna crossed meaningly to the washstand. "All right," he said resignedly, and Joanna put back the sponge she had just picked up.

"We'll wait for you downstairs," she declared. "But if you go to sleep again, we'll come up to you."

Paul grinned. He could quite believe that.

"I'll get up this morning, but I warn you, I'm not doing it regularly," he added, as the girls retired.

He did not keep them waiting long, and then they set off to explore. They located the pigsties easily enough, just beyond the stables, and from there they skirted the hen runs, while Sarah, who had slipped out of the house while the girls were persuading Paul to get up, was still exploring behind the stables, where great boughs of trees waited to be converted into fuel.

Beyond the hen runs was a paddock occupied by a roan pony and a bay horse, while beyond the paddock was a field occupied by ten or a dozen cows, and near here they found Hugh busy with a scythe. When he saw them he suspended operations for the moment, and pushed his hair back out of his eyes while he regarded them in sombre silence.

"You've more energy than I have," Paul commented.

"Is it difficult?" Joanna asked.

"Not when you're used to it," Hugh returned briefly, and began work again, showing no desire to continue the conversation.

"I do hope you don't mind our coming here," Louise said, eyeing his sombre face anxiously. "I mean——" she added, a little uncomfortably—"as you've lived with Uncle for so long, and—and, well you must feel this is your home."

Hugh gave a slight shrug. He had not forgotten their expressions when they first saw him the previous evening.

"It's Uncle's home. He can do as he likes," he said ungraciously, and as Louise flushed at the snub, Joanna gave an indignant gasp. She might not always agree with her sister herself, but she would not let anyone else be rude to her.

"Does anyone ever slap you?" she demanded abruptly, and Hugh, surprised by the unexpectedness of the question, stopped work to stare at her.

"No. Why?"

"Because people must want to—often. And it would do you all the good in the world," Joanna declared hotly.

"Johnny!" Louise gasped, while Paul grinned. Hugh flushed, then, to their surprise, suddenly laughed.

"There's no one here to do it—except Uncle and Joe."

"There is now," Joanna said darkly, and Hugh looked amused as he glanced at her indignant face.

"Is that a threat? he inquired.

"Yes—if you're rude to Louise again," Joanna said frankly, and Louise looked anything but grateful.

"Johnny!" she protested again, and Paul laughed.

"Leave her alone," he advised. "If we're going to live

here, Hugh will have to get used to her highly belligerent temperament——"

"Belligerent yourself!" Joanna retorted, while Hugh looked from one to the other as if he did not quite know what to make of them. "Oh, there's Uncle!"

Mr. Eldon, with Sam, the collie, at his heels, joined them and leaned against the gate.

"Getting acquainted?" he asked, glancing round at their tell-tale faces.

"Getting exasperated," Joanna corrected him with a snort of disgust. "Is Hugh always so—so awkward to talk to?"

"Well, as he scarcely ever speaks to a girl from one year's end to another, you've got to give him time to get used to you."

"Don't you really ever talk to girls?" Joanna demanded, staring at her cousin in astonishment.

"I very seldom see any," Hugh grunted, as if he did not particularly want to.

"You're lucky," Paul sighed. "I frequently see far too much of them. Look! Here's another!" he added resignedly.

Hugh turned, and Sarah, attended by Woggles, treated him to a beaming smile as she approached.

"Can I help?" she inquired, sensibly not wasting her breath on useless greetings.

"No!" Her brother and sisters spoke together before Hugh could reply.

"I won't try to patch you up if you chop your foot off," Paul added.

"I shouldn't," Sarah returned calmly. "Hugh isn't hurting his. Hugh, can't I——"

"Not this job, Sarah," her uncle said hastily as Hugh

turned a goaded look on him. "You need to have the knack of using a scythe."

"I could learn," Sarah returned, with a simple confidence that seemed almost unassailable. "Hugh could teach me an'——"

"I haven't time," Hugh said gruffly.

"How wise you are!" Paul sighed, and Hugh cast a doubtful glance at him, as if not at all sure whether his imperturbable cousin was making fun of him.

Mr. Eldon laughed and strolled away, deciding that the cousins would probably get acquainted sooner without him. Hugh, however, returned to his work, and the other three walked on, leaving Sarah gazing at him in awed fascination.

"You might let me try," she begged, and Hugh frowned as he eyed the small, determined figure before him with its half-combed fair curls, wide grey eyes, and resolute little chin. Sarah was an attractive child, and people outside her own immediate family usually found it difficult to harden their hearts against her until they, too, had suffered from her never-failing desire to be helpful. Hugh certainly did not know how to deal with her, and as he gazed at her in perplexity Sarah smiled up at him seraphically.

"I want to help with *everything*," she announced, waving a vaguely descriptive arm. "So you must show me how."

"But I—I haven't time—and besides, you're too small," Hugh protested helplessly.

"I'm *ten*!" Sarah objected in an outraged tone she knew only too well how to assume. "Children used to go to work when they were ten. I heard Paul say so once."

Hugh felt strongly that Paul should be far more careful what he said in front of his youngest sister, and gazed round for inspiration. To his relief he saw his uncle returning, and Mr. Eldon took compassion on him.

"I'm just going to the orchard to see if the plums are ripe," he said. "Like to come with me, Sarah?"

Such an invitation was not to be resisted, and the next moment Hugh found with relief that he had been completely deserted.

Despite their cousin's churlish attitude, Paul and the two girls laughed as they wandered on beside a little stream that flowed through fields until, just beyond a large copse, it ran into a wide pool fringed with rushes and irises that formed part of the boundaries of Long Barrow.

"I believe Sarah's going to adopt Hugh," Louise said, pausing to watch a host of minnows darting to and fro.

"Not if he can help it," Joanna returned with a chuckle. "He looked terrified of her."

"If he only knew it, he has need to be," Paul remarked, for Sarah's habit of attaching herself with doglike devotion to people was a byword in the family.

"Serve him right," Joanna said callously. "I've a good mind to do all I can to encourage her."

"Do you think that's fair?" Louise protested. "She's worse than a burr."

"He was rude to you when you were trying to think of his feelings," Joanna declared in the tone of a judge passing sentence. "I say, I'm hungry! Let's go back."

They retraced their steps and found their mother busy preparing breakfast. The two girls began to help her, and Paul extended his long limbs in a chair and drew a book out of his pocket. He was still deep in it when his uncle came in, and Mr. Eldon flashed a quick glance from him to the girls, who were busy setting the breakfast table, though he did not pass any comment.

"Where's Sarah?" asked Mrs. Lister of her brother.

"With Hugh," her brother said, and the two girls laughed.

"Oh dear!" Mrs. Lister said ruefully. "Is he the latest victim?"

"Why victim?" asked Mr. Eldon, and then smiled when the girls explained. "It looks rather like it," he agreed. "Oh, here's Joe!"

Joe was a big, loose-limbed man with a thatch of fair hair, pale blue eyes, and the most amiable expression the Listers had ever seen. He beamed round at them with a sheepish friendliness, and volunteered the information that Hugh and the "little 'un" were just coming.

Mrs. Lister's face crinkled up in a mischievous smile, and Joanna and Paul wore broad grins as the outer door opened and Hugh appeared, a harassed expression on his face, and Sarah at his heels.

"Hugh's been showing me the pigs," she announced cheerfully. "There are some lovely baby ones."

Hugh glared at his grinning cousins and retired hastily into a corner, uncomfortably conscious of his ancient clothes as Louise stepped forward to the table, the teapot in her hands, and, as usual, with not a hair out of place.

"Don't let her worry you," she said, still trying, despite his earlier snub, to be friendly, but Hugh merely grunted inarticulately and not very gratefully.

Mrs. Lister laughed—her usual merry, infectious laugh.

"It's no use telling him that, Louise. If Sarah wants to, no power on earth will keep her away. Hugh, I'm very sorry, but I'm afraid you'll have to reconcile yourself to your lot. If Sarah's adopted you, nothing can be done about it."

Hugh stared at his aunt with surprise in his eyes. This

small, vivacious, impetuous creature was so different from the aunt he had pictured.

Quite used to opprobrious remarks from her family, Sarah treated them with the silent scorn they deserved, and proceeded to drag two chairs to the table.

"Come an' sit by me, Hugh," she ordered imperiously, and her uncle suddenly began to laugh.

"I see now why you use the word *victim*. Sarah reminds me very much of you at an early age, Ruth!"

"I know," Mrs. Lister said resignedly. "I quite appreciate that it's my own sins being visited upon me——"

"But at the moment they're being visited on Hugh," Joanna pointed out with a chuckle. "Paul, do put that book away and come and have breakfast. Sarah, you can come and sit between Paul and me."

"But I can sit by you any time," Sarah said in a tone that betrayed her opinion of that treat. "An' I want Hugh to tell me about the pigs."

"Hugh doesn't want you," Joanna said flatly.

Paul said nothing but, reaching out a long arm, his hand firmly caught hold of Sarah's abbreviated skirt and pulled her down between Joanna and himself, and Mr. Eldon laughed again as she gave a snort of protest.

"You must have your hands full sometimes."

"Oh, between us we can usually manage her," Paul said. "Joanna's the real problem. Now when *she* gets the bit between her teeth——"

"And I suppose your mother's the biggest handful of all?" Mr. Eldon remarked, as Paul stopped expressively.

"Oh, she's quite incorrigible," Paul nodded. "We gave her up two years ago."

Mrs. Lister glanced across at Hugh, who was looking

from one to another in astonishment, and laughed.

"Don't take any notice of them, Hugh. They always talk a great deal of nonsense. It's a family failing."

"Inherited from the distaff side," Joanna proclaimed, making a hearty breakfast. "Uncle, may we explore round the house after breakfast, please?"

"Explore where you like," her uncle returned promptly.

"I'm going to help Hugh," Sarah announced, and her cousin gazed at his uncle in desperation.

"Surely you want to see your new home?" Mr. Eldon said tactfully, and Sarah hesitated.

"All right," she capitulated. "I'll explore first, an' help Hugh afterwards."

"A reprieve!" Mrs. Lister laughed, turning to her nephew. "Escape while you may!"

Hugh took her advice, wondering somewhat dazedly just what he really thought of his aunt and cousins, and bitterly regretting his old quiet life at Long Barrow.

Paul grinned as he disappeared. "Sarah's put the fear of death into him," he confided to Joanna, who chuckled, while Sarah eyed them both disapprovingly.

"I like him," she said decidedly. "He likes Wogs, and he isn't too lazy to look what he means," she added cryptically, but with a dignity beautiful to behold, and their uncle glanced thoughtfully across at Paul's indolent figure. Sarah, with a child's critical eye, had seized at once on the difference between the two boys; Hugh threw his whole self into everything he did, while Paul apparently never took anything very seriously.

"Anyway, what about this exploring?" demanded Joanna the energetic. "Come along!"

"I must just put some water on to boil for the washing up," Louise said, looking round with a puzzled frown.

"Uncle, where's the sink?" she asked. "I couldn't find it before breakfast. Or even a tap."

"I'm afraid we don't possess such a luxury," her uncle said, looking at her quizzically as her face fell. "We're very primitive. We've only a well."

"A *well!*" Louise echoed in stark horror, her forebodings of the previous night returning a hundredfold.

"I'm afraid so," her uncle said apologetically, although his twinkling eyes belied his tone. "It's one of Hugh's jobs to draw the water every morning. Of course, we use rainwater for washing."

"Cheer up, Louise!" Joanna exclaimed encouragingly. "Think how ravishing you'll be. Rainwater is awfully good for the complexion."

Despite this consoling thought, Louise still looked a picture of woeful despondency. So far things had looked more cheerful in the brighter light of morning, but now she suddenly remembered Long Barrow's isolated position, and the dim, lamplit kitchen of the previous evening —and Hugh snubbing her when she tried to be pleasant and friendly.

"Come and explore," Joanna said firmly, seizing her arm. "That will cheer you up. After all, you'll survive, even if you can't have five baths a day!"

This reference to Louise's passion for cleanliness brought a chuckle from Paul and a reminder of Sarah's presence.

"I'll help Hugh to get the water," she observed.

"You won't!" Her family spoke as one.

"We don't want any drowning fatalities here," Paul added hastily. "Uncle wouldn't care for it."

"You'd resus—resusperate me, wouldn't you?" Sarah remarked in the tone of one conferring a favour.

"No, I jolly well shouldn't," Paul retorted promptly,

"that is, if you mean resuscitate. I'd leave you drowned, and then we shouldn't have to worry about you any more."

"And Hugh would be your debtor for life," Joanna added with a grin to her brother. "I believe if she did insist on helping him he'd end by pushing her down himself."

"Well, you couldn't blame him if he did," Paul argued fairly, and Mr. Eldon laughed as he went out, wondering afresh how Hugh, completely unused these days to companionship of his own age, was going to fit in with his cousins.

Long Barrow was an old building with stone walls about two feet thick, and the first door they opened led the Listers into the dining-room, a large room with good, heavy furniture of a past age, and rather a fine fireplace, but it was so dark that it was almost impossible to see its better points.

"It's this dreadfully dark tapestry paper," said Mrs. Lister. "It must be like eating in a mausoleum."

"Or the catacombs," suggested Paul, who had lounged in after the girls. "I feel there ought to be a row of skulls on the shelf in that alcove."

Sarah gave a startled squeak and retired precipitately from that corner, and Louise turned to her mother despairingly, her beauty-loving soul revolted to its very depths.

"Mummy! Did you *ever* see such a room!" she wailed.

"There's nothing wrong that can't be rectified," returned her mother, looking round the room with a calculating eye known only too well by her children.

"She's off!" Paul said resignedly to Joanna.

"I shall speak to John," Mrs. Lister said decisively. "A

tin or two of distemper—Louise, do you remember, we made quite a good job of that back bedroom?"

"Do you think we could do anything with this?" Louise asked, gazing round doubtfully.

"Of course we could," Mrs. Lister said briskly. She was beginning to enjoy herself. "I shall suggest that for the time being we go on having meals in the kitchen and keep this room shut up until it's finished. I've got all sorts of ideas for it already."

Louise began to look interested. Like her mother, she enjoyed making beauty out of ugliness.

"If you really think it could be done, I should like to help," she said, though not too optimistically.

"I'll help, too—oh, no, I can't if I'm going to help Hugh," Sarah said regretfully. "And I promised him first."

"He won't hold you to it," Joanna assured her; but Sarah's word once given—even if not wanted—was her bond.

With a last look round, as if to impress the room on her mind—the girls felt there was no need to do that so far as they were concerned; it was a room to be forgotten as soon as possible in its present state—Mrs. Lister crossed the hall to the sitting-room, and her children followed curiously. This was much better. The pale pink wall-paper was sadly faded in places, but at least the room looked light enough with its cream paint, and the old mahogany furniture showed up quite well on a good but faded pink carpet, while the odd pieces of china scattered here and there were both old and valuable, and Mrs. Lister murmured blissful and slightly cryptic comments of *Famille Rose*, *Crown Derby* and *Sèvres* as she passed from one piece to another, though the girls took more delight in a quaint china candlestick, or a cup and saucer made in one piece, than in the firms that had fashioned them.

A second door led out of the sitting-room, and Joanna, ever curious, opened it, half-expecting to find a large cupboard, but to her delight it led into another, smaller room, a cosy little den with a couple of easy chairs and a small table and bookcases full to overflowing, while two or three whips graced the walls, together with an ancient shotgun.

"I like this room best of all!" she exclaimed, as the others crowded in after her, and Louise laughed.

"At least we'll always know where to find Paul now."

He was already selecting two or three volumes from the shelves, and proceeded to bury himself in a chair with them, obviously intending to remain there until forcibly removed at dinner-time. Mrs. Lister shook her head at him.

"Don't you want to see any more?" she asked, though the twinkle in her eyes betrayed that she already knew what answer she would get.

"No, thanks," Paul said promptly, and Joanna slipped her arm through her mother's and led her to the door.

"Why bother about him—you know what he is," she declared. "Come and see the rest of the house."

Actually there was very little else to see. Apart from the bedrooms there were three extra attics and a small dressing-room opening off their uncle's room. One of the attics was nearly as large as the girls' bedroom; here seeds were drying for the garden, and here, too, they were to discover later, their uncle kept stocks of apples, hazel nuts, bunches of herbs, and everything else that might be required for the winter. Next to it, a smaller attic was obviously intended as an extra bedroom when one was needed, but the third attic was securely locked, and there was no sign of the key anywhere. As soon as this was discovered, of course, the girls' desire to see inside increased a hundredfold.

"You don't think Uncle is a modern Bluebeard, do you?" demanded Joanna in blood-curdling tones, "who lures unsuspecting relatives to this isolated spot and then does away with them?"

"Don't be so horrible," Louise protested, while Sarah's eyes grew as round as saucers. "You do say the craziest things."

"My personal opinion is that that room contains skeletons," Joanna proclaimed in thrilling tones, "rows of them—mouldering away to dust——"

"You idiot! Even if Uncle were a Bluebeard, the skeletons couldn't be as old as that," Louise said practically. "But I should like to see inside."

"We need to call on the Ingoldsby Legends," Joanna said with ghoulish enjoyment. "What's that incantation from *The Hand of Glory*?

> *Open lock to the Dead Man's knock!*
> *Fly bolt, and bar, and band!—*
> *Nor move, nor——*"

"Joanna!" her mother protested. "Look at Sarah! Even if her eyes ever get back to their right proportions, she'll refuse to sleep up here——"

But Sarah gave a deep sigh of delight. "I love it when Joanna makes my back shiver," she remarked ecstatically.

"I don't," Louise said flatly. "She's making me dislike the place more than ever."

"Well, as we can't get in, I think we'd better go down and see about preparing lunch," Mrs. Lister said hastily, and gave Joanna a silencing nudge.

CHAPTER FOUR

AN UNFORTUNATE REMARK

THE SUN was shining gloriously as Joanna ran out of the house later in search of her uncle, and she paused to gaze round in delight on rolling green downs, chequered here and there with great squares of waving corn, while she breathed in the fresh country air laden with the scent of hay, honeysuckle, and all sorts of other exciting perfumes—including, it must be confessed, that of pigs. At the hen runs she came across Hugh engaged in mending a hole in the wire netting, while Sarah watched with grave interest, and as she came up to them Hugh glanced up, and at the mischievous light in her eyes an almost answering gleam showed for a moment in his.

"You've just got to be quite blunt and rude," Joanna said cheerfully, and Hugh sat back on his heels and wiped a hand across his heated forehead.

"I have been. Both blunt and rude. *Very!* But she still wants to help," he said wearily.

"I could if you'd let me," Sarah said with dignity. "Couldn't I, Johnny?"

"No," Joanna said unequivocally. "If you did we'd wake up to-morrow and find all the birds had flown."

"Are you always so downright with each other?" Hugh asked, looking amused.

"You've got to be with Sarah. It's sheer self-defence. But you needn't talk! Are you always so terse and—and monosyllabic?" Joanna finished with a rush, borrowing one of Paul's favourite words, and as Hugh grinned

46

suddenly she was astonished to find just how attractive his usually somewhat sulky face could become.

"I'm out of practice. I seldom talk to anyone but Uncle and Joe."

"Well, you won't have much chance to talk now—not with Joanna about," Sarah suddenly declared, quoting Paul with deadly effect, and Hugh laughed.

"Oh, they always say I'm the chatterbox of the family," Joanna said cheerfully. "I take after Mummy. But I'm looking for Uncle. Do you know where he is?"

"Over there," Hugh said, and Joanna found her uncle busy amongst the vegetables.

"Mummy wants some vegetables for lunch," she announced as he suspended work to smile at her cheerfully.

"How about some of those beans?" Mr. Eldon suggested. "You'll find a basket in that shed."

When she had picked the beans and taken them in to her mother, Joanna hurried out again to her uncle, and settled herself on a gate near where he was working.

"I want to talk to you—seriously," she announced, and her uncle laughed as he looked across at her.

"This sounds bad. What have I been doing?"

"It's not you—it's us," Joanna said. "I've been thinking —it's awfully good of you to give a home to such a crowd of us, and we must be making a lot more work——"

"As your mother is taking over the housekeeping, she'll have to shoulder that," her uncle began.

"Oh, I expect Louise will help her," Joanna said easily. "Louise rather likes cooking, and making things look tidy and attractive——"

"And Joanna doesn't?" her uncle guessed with a twinkle.

"Not much," she confessed. "And so I was thinking— do you and Hugh and Joe do all the outside work here?"

Her uncle nodded, looking as if he could guess what was coming.

"Well, couldn't I take over an outside job, and really do it myself?" Joanna begged, and her uncle looked pleased.

"Would you really like to?"

"*Please!*"

Mr. Eldon laughed at her enthusiastic tone, and then looked round thoughtfully until his eyes rested on Hugh's distant figure, still with Sarah in close attendance.

"How would you like to take over the care of the poultry?" he asked, and Joanna's face lit up.

"Would you really let me?" she demanded breathlessly.

"If you'd like to," her uncle returned, and Joanna gazed with pride of possession at the hen runs.

"I'd love it. What should I have to do?" she demanded with a businesslike air.

"Feed them, and collect the eggs——"

"*And* do repairs when necessary?"

"Do you think you could?" Mr. Eldon asked, laughing again at her enthusiasm.

"Of course!" Joanna declared. "If I really got down to it. If I do a job, Uncle, I like to do it *properly*—not just the easy bits."

"Well, if you take over the poultry you'll find it's a job that must be done regularly. They must be fed at their set times—and if you're going to be away from home, you must be sure to arrange beforehand for someone else to do it," her uncle said, liking her earnestness.

"I will," Joanna promised. "And I can really feel they're my own particular job—and that no one else will interfere? Because if they do I shan't feel it is my job, and then I'll lose interest."

"I'm sure they won't," her uncle declared with a smile. "They'll be only too relieved to have the poultry off their hands—unless, of course, Sarah decides to help you."

"I can deal with Sarah," Joanna said firmly. "It was Hugh and Joe I was wondering about. Uncle, do tell me what I must do. I'm dying to start."

"I think you'd better ask Hugh—he's been chiefly responsible for them until now," her uncle said, basely deciding that this was a good opportunity to make Hugh better acquainted with at least one of his cousins.

"Will he mind, then?" Joanna asked, with a rather anxious glance at her cousin's distant figure.

"I'm sure he won't," Mr. Eldon said, also glancing across, but with a smile. "He'll be glad to have a little more time to himself—even if he won't own it," he added, half to himself, but Joanna was too thrilled by her new responsibilities to take much notice of this last remark.

"All the same, I don't think I'll ask him at the moment," she said reflectively. "I'll wait till Sarah's not there. I don't want all the eggs smashed before I begin."

"I'll remove Sarah," her uncle said. "That's easily done."

He strolled across to where Hugh was getting on with his work while endeavouring to ignore the expression of wistful earnestness on Sarah's small face.

"Sarah, I wonder if you'd like to come and help me?" he suggested, and she looked round with a pleased smile.

"Of course—if Hugh doesn't really need me," she added, gazing round at her exasperated cousin with eyes full of doglike devotion, and as Hugh looked up and glared his eyes caught Joanna's, brimful with mischief.

"Come on, then," and Mr. Eldon imprisoned Sarah's hand firmly in his. "Joanna wants to talk to you, Hugh," he added over his shoulder as he led his prisoner away.

"What about?" Hugh inquired abruptly.

"Uncle says I may look after the poultry," Joanna said, with an abruptness worthy of her cousin, and waited to see the effect of her pronouncement on him. "Completely," she added, so that there should be no misapprehension, and rather to her surprise, Hugh grinned.

"Do you realise what you're taking on?" he asked.

"Of course!" Joanna snapped. "A job to help Uncle."

A queer light—almost of unwilling admiration—flickered for a moment in Hugh's greenish eyes, and then he looked amused again.

"It'll be me you're helping chiefly," he said warningly.

"Well, of course, I mean generally," Joanna retorted.

"It's a big job," Hugh said slowly, "and not always pleasant."

"I don't mind that," Joanna said, her chin jutting out at a determined angle, and for a moment a certain likeness was apparent between them. "I know I'll have to feed them regularly, and collect the eggs, and——"

"And clean the hen houses out," Hugh added obligingly, and for a split second Joanna wavered; then she nodded determinedly.

"Of course! I'm not afraid of messy, dirty jobs."

"Then, of course, when we want any for the table, you'll have to kill and pluck and draw them——"

At last Joanna really blenched.

"No!" she wailed. "I couldn't *kill* one. I just couldn't. Anything else, but not that. I'd feel like a murderess," she finished, so tragically that Hugh could preserve his gravity no longer, but threw back his head and roared heartlessly, while Joanna abandoned her wails and eyed him grimly.

"You—you beast!" she gasped. "You were just pulling my leg!" and before Hugh knew what was happening a handful of his thick, dark hair was seized and tugged.

"Ow!" he gasped, not as used as Paul to such treatment. "Here! Stop that!"

Joanna desisted, and for a moment they stood eyeing each other, Joanna searchingly, and Hugh with a lurking grin about his mouth.

"You didn't mean it?" she demanded, but to her dismay he nodded.

"Yes, I did. It's definitely part of the job."

"I couldn't," Joanna repeated, appalled, and Hugh grinned.

"Well, you needn't. No one will want you to, but you said you were going to take over the job completely."

"Well—except for that," Joanna capitulated. "Everything except killing them."

"It's quite easy if you know how," Hugh said obligingly.

"I don't want to know, thanks," Joanna declared hastily.

"Well, how about plucking and drawing?" asked Hugh, and again Joanna hesitated, while to her cousin's amusement she looked a trifle green.

"I——" She saw the amused gleam in his eyes, and made up her mind swiftly. "I'll do *everything*—except kill them," she declared, and Hugh eyed her with approval.

"Good girl!" he exclaimed. "I'll show you anything you want to know."

Dinner was ready when Joanna, after placing a basket of eggs in the dairy with a delightful sense of importance, came into the kitchen, where Louise was putting the last touches to the table.

"Johnny!" Louise gazed at her reproachfully. "Whatever have you been doing? Look at your shoes—and your hair's a sight!"

Hugh, who had just come in behind Joanna, eyed Louise disapprovingly. He felt that even a town-bred girl should have more sense than to think anyone could do farm work and remain spick and span. Joanna, however, was not at all put out by Louise's elder-sisterly tone.

"Oh, I've been collecting eggs," she said casually. "It's great fun."

"An' I've been helping Uncle," added Sarah, presenting a muddy face to harrow Louise's tidy soul even more. "An' Joe," she added, as her uncle came in followed by his faithful henchman and Sam.

"Have you been busy, too?" Mr. Eldon asked, smiling at his eldest niece.

"Very busy—baking," Mrs. Lister said. "You'll find she's a very good cook."

"I'm delighted to hear it," Mr. Eldon said, turning to eye a tempting plateful of cakes with such interest that Louise hurried to remove them from danger, announcing firmly that they were for tea.

"Where's Paul?" asked Mr. Eldon as they sat down at the table, and the Listers looked at each other blankly.

"I haven't seen him for a long time," Mrs. Lister said.

"I know!" Joanna exclaimed. "He's——" she broke off suddenly as something in her uncle's eye made her feel he would not approve of Paul's way of spending such a beautiful morning.

"Well?" her uncle asked. "Go on, Joanna. After all, if we don't know where he is, we can't call him to his lunch—and I'm sure he'd hate to miss it."

Hugh looked across at his uncle quickly, and Joanna

stared at Mr. Eldon in dismay as she suddenly realised what he meant.

"But, Uncle——" She broke off and jumped up. "I'll go and find him."

"No!" Her uncle, who was still standing by the fire, shook his head. "Sit down, Joanna. Just tell me where to look, and I'll fetch him."

Joanna hesitated. There was a note in her uncle's tone she did not understand.

"Well?" he said again, and Joanna realised he meant to be obeyed.

"I—I expect he's still in the little room off the sitting-room. We left him there reading——"

Mr. Eldon went through to the sitting-room, and as they heard him exclaim: "Come along, lunch is ready!" Joanna gave a faint sigh of relief. She had feared that he was going to be angry with Paul. Delightful as he usually was with them, one always felt that he would not stand any nonsense, and she suspected, from her cousin's quick glance at him, that Hugh had expected trouble, too.

Paul, obviously, was troubled by no such apprehensions as he followed his uncle into the kitchen and slid into his chair at the table.

"You've got some fine books there, Uncle," he said appreciatively. "I shan't want to do anything but browse through them."

"That's nothing new," Louise laughed, and Joanna, more observant than her sister, wished Louise had not said it. She was positive that for some obscure reason their uncle did not like the idea of Paul's being such a bookworm. For the moment, however, Mr. Eldon changed the subject.

"Do you usually help your mother in the house, Louise?"

"Yes," Louise answered, looking surprised at the sudden question. "I like cooking, and making things look nice."

"That reminds me, John," Mrs. Lister said. "That dreadful dining-room——" She broke off as her children gave a shout of laughter and her brother chuckled.

"Always the soul of tact, Ruth!" he murmured. "But never mind, the decorations were Uncle James's choice, not mine. What do you want to do with it?"

"Distemper it," Mrs. Lister said promptly, dimpling mischievously at her *faux pas*.

"Can you?" her brother asked doubtfully.

"I'm sure I can, and Louise says she'll help. So if you don't mind——"

"I give you *carte blanche*. Do anything you like in the house," Mr. Eldon declared, smiling upon both would-be distemperers. "And if you'll let me know what materials you need, I'll order them for you. It looks as if you two are going to be busy for a while——" His eyes travelled round the table. "And Joanna certainly is——"

"Why?" asked Louise curiously.

"She's taken over the poultry side of the establishment—lock, stock and barrel."

"But she doesn't know the first thing about poultry," Paul protested.

"Hugh's teaching her," Mr. Eldon said, and Hugh grinned wickedly across at Joanna.

"Yes—even plucking and drawing——"

"I notice you don't add *killing*," Mr. Eldon commented with a laugh.

"No, she leaves that to us," Hugh said. "We're more brutal."

"How horrible!" Louise exclaimed with a shudder. Joe spoke for the first time, smiling across amiably at Joanna's bright face.

"You've no call to do the mucky jobs—leave 'em for me."

"No, let her do them, Joe," Mr. Eldon said pleasantly but nevertheless firmly. "I believe she'll be happier."

"Trust Johnny to enjoy anything messy," Paul said, as Joanna gave her uncle a glance of gratitude.

"And as for you, Paul," Mr. Eldon went on in a calmly reflective tone, and Paul looked startled, "I expect you'd like to help as well as the girls——"

"If you want me to," Paul said reluctantly, trying to hide his dismay.

"There's a pile of logs behind the stables waiting to be sawn up, and some of the smaller ones need splitting into firewood to light the kitchen range," his uncle went on coolly. "If you do some of those each day, you should have a good supply ready by the time we start needing fires properly. And then in addition I'm going to hand over the horses to you entirely."

If Paul's face had been a study before, no words could have described it now. So far as he was concerned, his uncle might just as well have set him the entire labours of Hercules.

"But—I don't know the first thing about horses—and I've never sawn wood in my life!" he protested.

"You'll learn," his uncle said heartlessly. "Joanna doesn't know anything about poultry, but she's taking the job on all the same."

"But—but——"

"Would you rather not do it?" Mr. Eldon asked coolly and for a moment Paul was tempted to tell the truth, but he could not admit that he did not want to do his share.

"Oh, I'll—I'll have a shot at it," he said gloomily, "but I don't suppose I'll be much good. And I've never even met a horse to speak to."

"You will," his uncle said cheerfully, and Paul slumped back in his chair, a picture of despair.

"I'll help—when I'm not helping Hugh," Sarah offered, and Paul was too crushed even to respond to this offer with the usual snubbing and emphatic negative.

"Cheer up!" Joanna murmured consolingly. "It might have been the pigs."

Paul revived enough to sit up as he realised his narrow escape, and everyone else laughed.

"Ye gods, yes!" he exclaimed. "Thank you for that, Uncle! By the way," he added thoughtfully, "what does one do with horses?"

"Joe will initiate you," Mr. Eldon said as he got up. Paul had taken it better than he had expected. "But don't forget, in dealing with livestock you've got to keep to regular hours—no going off and forgetting about them!"

"I suppose this is where I should look guilty," Paul remarked, obviously knowing his own weakness. "Or if not now, I shall have to in the future."

"If you'll come along with me I'll show you round the stables, and teach you how to keep them clean, and everything else," Joe said after lunch, lumbering to his feet.

"And introduce him to the horses," Mr. Eldon suggested.

Hugh slipped away unnoticed, and Joanna and Sarah went with Paul to see the horses, leaving Louise clearing the table, and Mrs. Lister looking rather anxiously at her brother, who laughed.

"A bit of work won't kill him," he said consolingly,

"and if he does forget the horses occasionally Joe will see they don't suffer."

"I wasn't thinking of the horses," Mrs. Lister said naïvely.

"I didn't really think you were," her brother said, smiling down into her upturned face. "I'm going to make a man of that boy, Ruth, whether you like it or not. There's good stuff in him, and he's going to be given a chance to show it. You must have known when you asked me——"

"Yes, I know," Mrs. Lister said, with a hasty glance at Louise, who had just come in with some cold water to cool the washing-up water. "But don't be too drastic!"

Her brother laughed as he slipped his arm round her shoulders. "Trust me, Ruth. He may not be my son, but he's my nephew—and you can't say Hugh looks as if I beat him, does he?"

"Hugh looks as if he worships you," Mrs. Lister returned unexpectedly, and her brother looked uncomfortable.

"I owe that boy more than you can realise—and all I've ever done for him was to give him a home to save him from going to his mother's people, whom he hated."

"I do know that he was left almost penniless, and that if it hadn't been for you he'd have fared badly for education," Mrs. Lister said softly. "His mother's people wouldn't have bothered with him much."

Louise listened with interest as she quietly got on with the washing-up, and later, when she managed to tear Joanna away from blissful contemplation of her feathered charges, she told her of it as they scrambled up the side of the down, bent on exploring.

"I believe Hugh's really quite human underneath,"

Joanna said thoughtfully. "He was actually teasing me this morning about the poultry."

"I'm sure he doesn't like me," Louise said in perplexity, for she usually got on well with people. "And oh, he does look so—so boorish—as if he doesn't care what he looks like—when he's working! Surely he needn't look quite so like a tramp—Oh!"

She broke off with a gasp as they approached a glowing clump of purple willow herb, and a figure that had been lying there, book in hand, rolled over and sat up almost at their feet, pushing back its dark hair with a gesture they were already getting to know.

"You gave us a fright," Joanna said severely.

"Sorry," Hugh said briefly, closing his book and thrusting it into his pocket as he glared at Louise. "You should look where you're going."

"We were talking——" Joanna began.

"I heard you," Hugh said, glowering at Louise's crimson cheeks. "Sorry I'm not fine enough to please you. But you can't do dirty jobs and remain immaculate—as you'll soon learn here."

Springing to his feet he set off down towards the farm, leaving Louise, who never willingly hurt anyone's feelings, on the verge of tears, and feeling she could never face him again.

"You *have* done it!" Joanna exclaimed, not exactly improving matters.

"He'll never forgive me for that," Louise wailed. "Oh dear! I do wish we hadn't come here. We were so happy at home, but here—Hugh's horrid, and we can't have proper baths, and there's only horrible lamps, and candles, and Uncle's making Paul work, and——"

As her sobs threatened to increase Joanna suddenly

began to laugh. The last of Louise's list of woes was too much for her sense of the ludicrous.

"I don't see that you need to worry about Paul having to work. It's for him to worry——"

"It will stop him studying," Louise protested, for Paul's future meant much to all his family.

"Rot!" Joanna said forcibly if inelegantly. "He isn't studying half the time—he's only reading. And anyway, I really think a little outdoor work will do him good. Hugh looks twice as strong and healthy, even if he does look like a tramp. And I believe I like boys who don't fuss too much about their appearance," she added reflectively, remembering how pleasant Hugh's face could become when he really laughed. She chuckled as she looked down at the farm buildings. "There's Paul now. He doesn't *look* as if he's overstraining himself."

Even Louise smiled a little as she gazed down at the tall, slender figure disconsolately contemplating the pile of boughs waiting to be converted into logs, and even as they watched Paul shrugged his shoulders in a gesture they well knew, drew a book out of his pocket, sat down on one of the larger branches and began to read.

"He really is the limit!" Joanna said, with a quick frown. Tremendously energetic herself, she understood better than Louise just how her uncle would view Paul's indolence. "There's going to be trouble if he isn't careful—and I believe Hugh knows it. Haven't you noticed how he always glances at Uncle when Paul's caught reading while everyone else is working?"

When they returned to the house Hugh was vigorously attacking a mound of decaying vegetable matter, with the intention, Joanna suspected, of getting into as much of a mess as possible, just as a matter of principle. Louise, less shrewd than her sister, merely looked pained, and Hugh directed a glare of disgust after her retreating figure. However, he did come into tea looking tolerably clean and tidy, having apparently worked off most of his annoyance on the rubbish heap, and found himself immediately adopted by Sarah.

"Come and sit here by me," she commanded. "I looked for you," she added reproachfully, "but I couldn't find you."

"For which I hope you're suitably grateful," Paul remarked.

"How did you get on with the horses?" asked his mother.

"I didn't. At least, I looked at them from across the paddock, but they didn't seem keen on a closer acquaintance."

"Oh, look!" Joanna exclaimed. "It's raining! And I was going exploring this evening!"

"As it's looking so dismal, shall we light a fire in the sitting-room?" Mrs. Lister asked, turning to her brother.

"Couldn't we have it in the little room?" Joanna begged. "Then we could look at all the books."

"In what Uncle James always called the snuggery?" her uncle asked. "Yes, of course."

"Uncle, why is that room upstairs locked?" asked Sarah suddenly.

"Oh yes, I've been meaning to ask you all day," Joanna said. "You know, the one by our bedroom."

"Oh, that's Hugh's own particular den," his uncle said, glancing almost questioningly at his nephew, who, however, was looking his most forbidding. "He keeps all his odds and ends in there."

"There's no need to lock it," Sarah observed with

dignity, obviously assumed to hide her intense curiosity. "We shouldn't hurt anything."

"I'm not so sure," Paul remarked. "I shouldn't leave it open, Hugh——"

"I shan't," Hugh said brusquely, and his three elder cousins all looked a little taken aback.

"You needn't bother," Joanna said hotly. "We don't want——"

"Joanna says it's probably full of skeletons," Sarah observed conversationally, unconsciously saving the situation, and Hugh sat up with a jerk.

"*What?*"

"Oh, she was only talking rubbish as usual," Louise said hastily. "Her imagination runs away with her."

Hugh looked doubtfully from one to the other, but said no more, and Mrs. Lister glanced round the table with a faint frown. It was clear that all was not well between the cousins. Louise had been looking very subdued ever since she came in, Hugh had certainly been ruder than he need have been about his room, Joanna looked ready to snap at the slightest excuse, and Paul was leaning back with an amused smile well calculated to aggravate further anyone who was already slightly ruffled.

After tea they all scattered; Joanna to see to her poultry, Joe to light the fire in the snuggery, Paul to settle there with a book, and Hugh to some unknown destination out of doors. Sarah would have followed, but Louise caught her just in time.

"You can't go out in that rain," she pointed out.

"Hugh did," Sarah said in an aggrieved tone.

"He'd got an old mackintosh round him," Louise pointed out. "And I really can't see why you're so keen to follow him when he shows plainly he doesn't want you."

This from Louise was astonishingly plain speaking, and Mrs. Lister turned to stare at her, while Mr. Eldon, who was standing in front of the fire, filling his pipe, suspended operations for a while.

"Trouble?" he asked, and Louise looked shamefaced.

"I'm afraid it's really my fault," she confessed. "He overheard something I said to Joanna, and he's annoyed."

"I expect he'll get over it," her uncle said consolingly, though, knowing Hugh, he wondered. Mrs. Lister, too, looked worried. For all her impulsive ways, she saw more than most people realised, and she was afraid Hugh was not the type to forget easily.

"What did you say?" she asked, rather anxiously.

"I—that he didn't seem to care if he looked like a tramp," Louise said reluctantly, and her uncle glanced at her quickly while Mrs. Lister hid a smile. Hugh's working clothes would offend the dainty Louise.

"*Au fond* Hugh is scrupulously particular about cleanliness," her uncle said thoughtfully, "but he always does every job he undertakes so thoroughly that he is apt to get—well rather begrimed and bespattered. But it's all top dirt. And he's a wonderful worker."

"I wouldn't have said it for him to hear for worlds," Louise said, nearly crying with mortification, "but I didn't know he was anywhere near. I nearly trod on him before I saw him."

"That must have added insult to injury," her uncle remarked, looking amused. "Well, it can't be helped."

"I hate hurting people's feelings," Louise said regretfully, "but I don't see what I can do about it now."

The tea-things were washed and put away, and the three girls had retired to the snuggery before Hugh came in again, his old mackintosh dripping wet. He started on seeing his aunt still in the kitchen, while she gave an exclamation of horror at the sight of him.

"My dear boy! You're drenched! Take those wet things off at once."

"I'm all right," Hugh muttered. "I'm often as wet as this."

"Whatever have you been doing?" his aunt went on, firmly removing the dripping mackintosh and forcing him down in a chair by the fire. "Take those wet boots off at once. Now you must have slippers somewhere. Where are they?"

"In that cupboard," Hugh said tersely, his eyes following Mrs. Lister's small figure curiously as she hurried across to get them. It was a new experience for him to be mothered and waited on like this, and he was not sure whether he liked it or not.

"I'm sorry I—I look such a sight," he said gruffly, as she returned with the slippers and set them down beside him. "I—I——"

"My dear boy, you don't need to explain to me. Remember I was brought up in the country. Although your grandfather was a doctor, John and I—and your father—spent nearly all our spare time on a neighbouring farm, and you've no idea what sights we used to be."

Hugh's face lightened considerably. "I thought—I thought you'd look down on me because——"

"I didn't think you could be so stupid," Mrs. Lister said quickly, without waiting for him to finish. "How could I look down on you when you're simply doing your work properly—though I don't really believe it was necessary for you to get as wet as this," she added with a twinkle in her eyes, and a grin spread over Hugh's face.

"No—I was just feeling fed up—and—and——" he

went red— "please don't think I'm—I'm beastly, but I—
I don't know how to deal with Sarah when she follows
me round, and——"

Mrs. Lister threw back her head and laughed.

"No one does! Don't worry about that. Haven't you
heard the others trying to discourage her?"

An expression of relief spread over Hugh's face.

"I know they do, but they're her brother and sisters,
and I was afraid you'd think I should——"

"I'm not one of those doting mothers who can't see
wrong in their own children, if that's what you mean,"
Mrs. Lister laughed, as he faltered. "I'm only too ready to
admit that Sarah, bless her heart, can be a veritable Old
Man of the Sea, and I don't blame you for trying to dodge
her in the slightest. But come and join the others now.
They're all looking very cosy and comfortable."

Hugh would have drawn back, but he did not want to
hurt his aunt's feelings, so he reluctantly followed her
into the snuggery, where Louise and Paul were sunk back
in chairs, Joanna was extended along the hearthrug, and
Sarah was sitting on the floor in front of one of the bookcases with a large volume full of pictures open on her
lap.

"This is my sociable family," Mrs. Lister laughed.
"Look at them! We won't hear a word from any of them
for the rest of the evening."

Hugh looked rather relieved at this information, but
Paul revived sufficiently to drag his length out of his
chair and gently but firmly push his mother down into it.

"You might as well sit and rest for once," he remarked
and, sitting down at the table, immediately became
absorbed again.

"What a group of students!" Mr. Eldon commented,

looking in on them as Hugh settled in a corner with the book he had stuffed into his pocket on the downs, and they all looked up.

"You needn't talk!" Joanna exclaimed. "You're as bad as any of us. So come and join us."

To her surprise her uncle hesitated a moment, and then shook his head.

"Not now, Joanna. I've one or two things to see to." As he turned away Hugh glanced up at him questioningly and half-rose, but Mr. Eldon shook his head. "No—I want to see to the lamps."

"Can't one of the boys?" Mrs. Lister asked, and her brother smiled down at her.

"No, that's a job I always do myself."

He shut the door and left them, but after a short time Hugh quietly closed his book and went out after him.

"I'm sure there's something up between Uncle and Hugh," Joanna declared, looking up. "Didn't you notice Hugh when Uncle was in here?"

"I can't say I did," her mother remarked. "But I've been lazy long enough. Would you like to get my darning from the kitchen?"

Joanna jumped up willingly, and burst into the kitchen, to find her uncle sitting beside the fire in a state of most unusual idleness while Hugh was just settling down opposite to him with a newspaper.

"Well!" she gasped in frank disgust. "You unsociable people! Why can't you come and sit with us?" She looked curiously from one to the other, and was surprised to find that both looked a little confused. Suddenly a new thought struck her, and she coloured hotly. "Oh, I didn't think—I suppose we are—I mean, I suppose you do want to be together without all of us sometimes—at least—I mean——" As she floundered more and more her uncle jumped up.

"Joanna, you mustn't think that. You're quite wrong. I'm really and genuinely delighted to have you all here— and I was coming in in a few minutes—only——"

"Well, when you came in before, Hugh looked at you— and then he followed you out——"

"Joanna those eyes of yours are much too sharp, and your imagination is much too vivid," her uncle said, holding out his hand to her. "It was nothing like that. Hugh merely wanted to know if he could do a little job for me—that was all. Go on back to the others, and we'll be with you in a few minutes."

Joanna could not do anything else but obey, and the rest of her family listened curiously as she told them what had happened.

"I don't see anything very strange in it," Mrs. Lister observed, rather pessimistically surveying a large hole in one of Sarah's socks. "After all, John probably does look on Hugh almost as a son, and they're so used to each other that he's bound to call on Hugh rather than one of you."

"I'm quite content to let him," Paul remarked, but Joanna was still convinced that she was right.

It was nearly half an hour later when the other two joined them, and then, while Hugh returned to his corner and his book, Mr. Eldon sat down and looked round, evidently more inclined for conversation than a book, and his sister, still busy darning, was quite ready to enjoy a chat with him, while the young people read or listened as they felt inclined.

CHAPTER FIVE

JOANNA'S IDEA

"WHAT'S THE matter with Wogs?" Louise paused in the pleasant—to her—task of unpacking and arranging her clothes to eye that animal somewhat apprehensively. It was deeply occupied in the darkest corner of their bedroom sniffing and snorting where the wall joined the floor. "You don't think it's rats, do you?" she added nervously.

"Might be," Joanna said casually. She did not happen to be troubled by a fear of those rodents. Not being as interested in unpacking as her sister, however, she willingly suspended operations in order to watch, while Sarah, who had been making a general nuisance of herself trying to help, ran across to investigate.

"Ooh!" she exclaimed, after peering at the scene of Woggles's operations. "There are cracks in the wall-paper, and the wall bulges out. Do come and look!"

Joanna went very willingly, followed more slowly by Louise, who still feared they might be attacked at any moment by rats.

"I believe it's a door!" Joanna exclaimed, trying to insert a finger in a crack. "Have you some scissors or a nail file or something?"

Louise fetched a nail file, while Sarah hopped excitedly on one foot as the only way of truly expressing her interest in the proceedings.

"Thanks!" Joanna inserted the file in the crack, and slowly levered the bulge outwards until the opening was

67

wide enough to get her fingers in. "It is a door!" she exclaimed triumphantly. "But I believe it's stuck with the damp. No, keep away, Sarah, I can do it."

She gave a firm tug, and then staggered backwards as the door opened outwards, disclosing a large closet—or what might almost be a tiny room—lit by the smallest window the girls had ever seen. A strong odour of camphor filled the musty air, and the floor space was almost completely taken up with ancient trunks, dress baskets, and boxes of various kinds.

"Phew!" Joanna gasped. "I wonder if that window opens?" She crossed, struggled with its rusty fastenings, and then flung it open, while Louise retreated into the purer air of their bedroom, and Sarah began to rummage amongst the trunks like an inquisitive terrier. Woggles had already possessed herself of a black and purple late Victorian bonnet that had been lying there loose, and was beginning to worry it when Louise cornered her and rescued it. "Treasure trove!" Joanna exclaimed joyfully, opening trunk after trunk, and displaying suits, dresses, petticoats and other underwear dating from earliest Victorian days—or even before—some almost in tatters, and some in very good condition. "Just look!" she exclaimed, brandishing a pair of corsets that narrowed ominously at the waist. "Fancy being laced up in those, Louise! That's what fashion does for you!"

Louise, looking more interested than she had yet done since their arrival at Long Barrow, took the corsets and tried them on over her dress, while Joanna exclaimed delightedly at finding a peculiar framework that she identified in great excitement as a crinoline, and Sarah paraded round with a bonnet, much too large for her, enveloping her head and face, and with difficulty holding up in front of her a dress whose skirt must have contained between ten and twenty yards of material.

"Whatever have you got there?" Mrs. Lister stood in the doorway of the bedroom staring at them in astonishment.

"Look what we've found!" Joanna exclaimed excitedly.

"Oof! This is heavy!" Sarah sighed, letting the dress fall at her mother's feet.

Mrs. Lister examined their find with almost as much excitement as they had shown, and cast envious eyes on a box of feathers and another of beautiful old lace.

"This must have been used as a store-room for years and then completely forgotten," she exclaimed, as Sarah, still burrowing in a large trunk like an excited rabbit, brought to light a beautifully carved fan, and when Mr. Eldon was told of their find he confessed that he had had no idea that the closet existed, although, as he admitted, he had only been in that particular room once or twice.

"And the door's in such a dark part of the room that it could easily be missed," Joanna explained, closing the door to demonstrate, as they told Mrs. Lister how they had made their find. "Isn't it marvellous! Think of the fun we could have dressing up in them."

"You baby!" Louise laughed, even while she eyed wistfully an evening dress of white satin and lace that Sarah had just unearthed, so full in the skirt that it was obviously intended to be worn over the crinoline.

"You know you're just as much of a baby as me," Joanna retorted. "And as far as I'm concerned, I shall still go on loving dressing up when I'm ninety."

Mrs. Lister laughed and then drew the two elder girls across to the far end of the large bedroom, leaving Sarah happily engaged in the closet and Woggles sniffing round for non-existent rats.

"It's a wonderful find," she agreed. "But, girls, I want to talk to you—about Hugh."

"Why spoil everything," protested Louise, the interest dying out of her face. "I'd managed to forget him for a moment."

"Because we can't and mustn't forget him," Mrs. Lister said soberly. Something about the unsociable, self-reliant boy had touched her the previous evening during their short talk in the kitchen. Perhaps she felt vaguely that his curt, abrupt manner was really a means of defence because he did not know or understand his cousins. "After all, this was Hugh's home before we came——"

"Then surely it was up to him to welcome us," Joanna said quickly.

"You couldn't blame him being a little resentful," Louise said, trying to be fair.

"And you must remember this," Mrs. Lister pointed out, "I am your mother, and you can't be called upon to share me—as a mother—with anyone. But John, who is the only person Hugh can feel really belongs to him, is the same relation to you that he is to him——"

"I see," Joanna said quickly. "You mean Hugh might be feeling that there is a chance we might take Uncle away from him? I hadn't thought of that."

"I do wish he hadn't heard that stupid thing I said yesterday," Louise remarked, looking troubled. "I don't believe he'll ever forgive me—and it's one of those awful things you can't undo——"

"Three things come not back," Joanna quoted solemnly. "The sped arrow, the spoken word, and the——"

"Don't, Joanna! Louise feels bad enough about it," Mrs. Lister said. "The only thing you can do, Louise, is to try to let him see by your future behaviour that you no longer think it——"

"But she does," Joanna put in, with a quick glance at her sister's face, and Mrs. Lister gave a little sigh.

"Louise, you must try to realise that no one doing farm work can look as if he's just come out of a bandbox. But, with people like your uncle and Hugh, it's only top dirt. Although Hugh looked such a sight when we first saw him, he didn't when he'd washed and changed, did he?"

"No," Louise said reluctantly. "But he doesn't like me——"

"Because he thinks you look down on him," Mrs. Lister said promptly. "And the only way that idea can be eradicated is for you to prove to him that he's wrong. I warn you that he'll take a lot of convincing, but I believe you can do it if you're patient enough." She hesitated a moment, and then added: "I feel you owe it to John to get on as well as possible with Hugh. After all, your uncle has taken us all into his house, and if you knew the ridiculously small amount which is all he will let me pay towards our keep—and that's only because I insist on giving him something——" She smiled at Joanna. "He says that if you and Paul help out of doors and Louise helps me, we shall be more than earning our keep."

Joanna's eyes lit up. That pleased her independent spirit.

"I'm glad he looks at it like that," she declared. "We will do our best with Hugh, Mummy—and I've got an idea already."

"You and your ideas!" Mrs. Lister laughed as she got up from the bed on which she had been sitting. "Louise, don't look so tragic."

"I can't help it." Louise gave a deep sigh. "First Hugh

—and then this place! It's so dreadfully far away from everywhere."

Mrs. Lister looked from one to the other thoughtfully. "I admit you can't go to a cinema for entertainment every evening, but if my children haven't enough in them to make their own pleasures and entertainments—I give them up! There are four of you—five with Hugh! Are you so empty-headed that you can't amuse yourselves?"

"Of course we can!" Joanna exclaimed, much moved by her mother's stirring appeal. "You'll see! In fact, that's what my idea's about. I knew Louise needed cheering up, and Hugh looks as if he doesn't know how to do anything but work—but wait till I've taken them both in hand!"

"I will," Mrs. Lister promised, looking relieved. Past experience had taught her that Joanna was the one to handle the present difficult situation. "What is your idea?"

"I must discuss it with Louise and Paul first," Joanna said, shaking her head. "Then, if they agree, I'll approach you, Mummy. So mind you're in a really good temper, because I shall want something from you."

"You usually do," her mother laughed. "Well, don't forget to tidy the closet before you come down. It looks now as if there's been an earthquake in it."

"That's Sarah!" Joanna said grimly. "So she can jolly well tidy it while we finish our unpacking."

It was nearly as hard work making Sarah tidy the closet as doing it themselves, but this task achieved, and the unpacking finished, the two elder girls ran downstairs in search of Paul, whom they eventually ran to earth in the orchard, perched on the low bough of an apple tree, deep in a book, but coming to the surface now and again to eat one of a handful of plums with which he had provided himself.

"How are the logs and the horses?" asked Joanna with suspicious gravity, and Paul gave her an expressive glance.

"If you hadn't put ideas in Uncle's head about the poultry——"

"I believe the ideas were there even before I said anything," Joanna said, thoughtfully helping herself to one of his plums. "I noticed the night we came that he didn't seem to like your reading so much while everyone else was helping. But we didn't come to talk about that."

"Johnny says she's got an idea," Louise said, and Paul grinned.

"I've never known the moment when she hadn't," he remarked, nevertheless putting his book aside, for Joanna's ideas were usually worth listening to. "What's inspired it this time?"

"Some things that Mummy said," Joanna explained, and went on to repeat all her mother had said. Paul listened in silence, and then nodded.

"I can see her point about Hugh. This *is* his home, and he probably does resent our coming. And what Louise said wouldn't help matters."

"Don't rub it in," Louise begged. "I just cringe every time I think of it."

"I suppose we will have to try to be friendly with him," Paul went on, "but whether he'll consent to be friendly with us is another matter."

"We can try," Joanna said eagerly, thinking of her cousin when he was teasing her about the poultry. "I believe he's probably quite nice underneath."

"And as to what Mother said about entertaining ourselves, I'm not worrying," Paul remarked, and Joanna gave a sigh of exasperation.

"You never care about anything as long as you can read."

"I'm afraid it is going to be horribly lonely and dull here," Louise said, looking depressed.

"All the more reason why we must do something about it," Joanna said briskly. "For the first part of my idea, I'm going to call a meeting this evening. I should think that copse near the pond would be a nice spot. So will everyone assemble in the kitchen at seven p.m.—sharp, Paul!"

"All right," Paul said, grinning good-humouredly at this dig at his unpunctual habits. "If someone will remind me. Is Sarah in this?"

"Everyone—including Hugh," Joanna said firmly.

"He won't come," Paul said with conviction.

"He will," Joanna affirmed out of the depths of her knowledge of human nature. "Curiosity will bring him. Louise, will you tell Sarah, if I go and tell Hugh?"

Louise nodded. As it had always been a custom of the Lister family to discuss every problem in open meeting, neither she nor Paul was at all surprised by Joanna's suggestion.

"There'll be no difficulty about her," she agreed. "But what's it all about, Johnny?"

"I'm not telling anyone yet. Then Hugh can't feel we've been discussing it together first," Joanna said, displaying unusual tact, and, leaving Louise to tell Paul of their find, she went off in search of Hugh, whom she ran to earth in the stables.

"Want me?" he asked, and she nodded.

"Yes, I've asked the others to come to a meeting this evening—and I want you to come, too," she said, suddenly feeling uncomfortable before his steady gaze. Somehow he seemed older than she had realised, and for the first time she doubted if he would come. "I—we always hold meetings when there's anything to discuss," she added, feeling vaguely that some explanation was necessary.

"What are you going to discuss?" asked Hugh.

"Oh, I'm not telling anyone until the meeting," Joanna returned, gaining a little more confidence as she realised that so far she had not met with a direct refusal. "There'd be no need for the meeting if I told everyone beforehand."

To her relief Hugh, after staring at her for a moment, suddenly laughed.

"Where's the meeting to be held, and what time?"

Joanna was just about to blurt out: "Then you will come?" when once again unusual tactfulness stopped her betraying her doubt that he would come, and instead she merely said: "Near that copse by the pond, but I want everyone to meet at seven o'clock in the kitchen."

"Why not at the copse?" asked Hugh.

"Because I want you all to help carry things," Joanna returned swiftly. "And now I must go and talk to Mummy. Don't forget! Seven o'clock in the kitchen."

"Just a minute!" At last Hugh was beginning to look really curious. "What are we to carry?" he demanded, and Joanna smiled mischievously.

"You must wait and see about that, too!"

At seven o'clock Hugh strolled into the kitchen, not without considerable curiosity, and found Joanna guarding three baskets, their contents mysteriously covered by clean tea towels, while Sarah, whom he had managed to avoid for an hour, was trying to poke the coverings in order to guess at the contents. Paul was leaning against the dresser and Louise was stroking Sam's silky head as he sniffed at the baskets, while Woggles, furiously indignant because she could not reach them, dodged from side to side in vain attempts to jump up. Neither Paul nor

Louise could quite hide their surprise at seeing their cousin, for neither had really believed that he would come, but they tactfully refrained from passing any comment.

"Have we got to take all this junk?" Paul asked, as he tested the weight of one of the baskets.

"Yes. I'll take this one because it might spill," Joanna said, thereby raising Sarah's curiosity to fever pitch.

"What *is* all this?" asked Louise, but Joanna refused to be drawn.

Hugh picked up the other basket and followed in silence as Joanna led the way out. On the far side of the copse she called a halt by the trunk of a fallen tree that overlooked the pond, and Louise sank down on it, while the two dogs, who had accompanied the party unasked, showed a remarkable interest in the baskets when they had been set down on the grass.

"Now!" Joanna said, when she and Paul had joined Louise on the tree trunk, and Hugh sat down on the grass, while Sarah seated herself beside the baskets, as curious as the dogs.

"Yes, go ahead, Johnny," Paul remarked. "If you've dragged us here for nothing you'll hear about it."

"Well, the point is that, as Mummy remarked this morning, Long Barrow is such an awfully isolated spot that we'll have to make our own amusements."

"Yes, but what?" asked Louise rather despondently, while Hugh looked at Joanna with a doubtful frown, wondering just what he had let himself in for by attending the meeting.

"Personally I'm not worrying," Paul said lazily.

"You wouldn't be," Joanna retorted, and Paul grinned.

"Well, out with it! What frightful thing are you going to wish on us?"

"My idea," Joanna said slowly and impressively, "is that we form a society—just the five of us—and that we hold a meeting once a week, and that we take it in turns to arrange what shall be done at each meeting. F'rinstance, I've arranged something for to-night——"

"You have, have you?" Paul murmured, with a glance at the baskets. "And who does it next time?"

"If you like, we could draw lots to arrange the order," Joanna suggested, and Louise, leaning forward with her chin in her hands, nodded thoughtfully.

"It's an idea," she conceded.

"But—what could we do?" Hugh asked in dismay, and a mischievous smile flashed across Joanna's face at the implication of that unconscious *we*. Hugh was not refusing forthwith to join in, anyway.

"That's up to you when it's your turn," she said. "After all, you know Long Barrow and this countryside, so you should have more ideas than us. You could take us exploring to somewhere interesting, or—oh, heaps of things!" she finished, but Hugh did not look at all happy.

"It might be quite interesting," Paul admitted, "and it would be something to look forward to."

"Then you all agree?" Joanna asked.

"I do," Sarah said promptly. "What's in the baskets?" Evidently her main concern was to get the business part of the programme over as quickly as possible.

"Yes, as Paul said, the meetings would be something to look forward to," Louise said with a sigh, as she remembered how bare the prospect seemed as far as entertainment was concerned.

"Hugh?" Joanna glanced across at her cousin, not sure even now that he would agree.

Hugh hesitated, the doubtful frown still on his face. He would have preferred not to be included in the plan, but he did not quite know how to get out of it.

"I—I suppose we could try it," he said dubiously. "Though I shouldn't know what to do——"

"You'll think of something," Joanna said encouragingly.

"But look here," Paul said suddenly. "Suppose, for instance, someone had arranged an out-of-doors programme, and it poured with rain?"

For a moment everyone looked blank; then Joanna delivered a ruling.

"You must arrange an alternative programme. After all, you can always use it again later."

Loud groans greeted this suggestion, and Hugh, appalled though he was, could not suppress a laugh at Louise's and Paul's expressions.

"Saw logs, look after the horses, prepare two programmes—one of which won't be needed," Paul murmured. "Someone will have to invent a thirty-six hour day for me to get through everything."

"Lazy animal!" Joanna said scathingly. "It will do you the world of good."

"What about Sarah?" asked Hugh, speaking for the first time of his own accord.

"Oh, she'll be all right," Joanna and Paul spoke together.

"I've got all sorts of ideas," Sarah said with dignity.

"She's used to our queer ways," Joanna explained.

"An' now, what's in the baskets?" demanded she of the one-track mind, and Paul groaned.

"For the love of mike, satisfy her curiosity," he begged.

"No, business first," Joanna said firmly. "Paul, you

usually carry a notebook and pencil. Write your names on four slips, and we'll draw lots at once."

Paul obediently did as she ordered, and having folded the slips, shook them up in his hand, and then held them out to Sarah.

"You can do the drawing," he remarked, and, duly impressed with her importance, Sarah obediently drew a slip and opened it.

"Louise," she announced with some disappointment. Evidently she had hoped to draw her own name. Then she drew again. "Hugh!" she read out, and all his cousins laughed at his expression of sheer horror. Sarah drew again. "Me, an' then Paul!" she declared. "Oh, I wish I was sooner."

"I'll change," Hugh said with obliging haste.

"You won't," Joanna said firmly, in her *rôle* of mistress of the ceremonies, as she leaned over and drew the baskets towards her. "Now, can you boys collect some wood and make a fire? Here are some matches." Carefully unpacking the basket she had carried, she drew out a kettle and a bottle of milk. "I don't fancy pond water, so I brought some from the well," she announced, as she set the kettle down carefully. "Buck up with that fire!"

By the time the kettle was precariously balanced on some stones over a small fire, she and Louise had spread a small tablecloth on the smoothest piece of turf they could find, and were drawing from the baskets five cups, plates and teaspoons, a tin of cocoa, some sugar, a bag of fresh scones, another of small fairy cakes—which Louise recognised as some she had made that morning—a loaf of bread and some butter, and lastly some hard-boiled eggs, salt and pepper.

"I love picnics," Sarah sighed, having clapped her hands

at each successive thing that was brought out. "An' supper's more fun than tea."

"I suppose because you can stay up later," Paul remarked, assiduously feeding the fire, while Louise mixed the cocoa, sugar and milk in the cups, Joanna cut bread and butter, and Hugh, having gathered enough wood for two or three fires, stood a little apart looking on as if he felt—as indeed he did—strange amongst them.

"There! Now all come and sit down," Joanna ordered, as Louise added boiling water to the cocoa. "I didn't know your tastes, Hugh, so I hope you like what I've brought."

"Oh—yes, thanks," Hugh said rather awkwardly, as she handed him an egg.

"You do get good ideas occasionally, Johnny," Paul said approvingly, tackling his supper with a hearty appetite. "Hugh, I've been meaning to ask you ever since we came. Didn't Uncle share a house in London with Robert Temple, the surgeon?"

"Yes," Hugh said. "Though he's Sir Robert now. He received a knighthood in the last Honours List."

"I suppose you know him quite well?" Paul went on, almost enviously.

"Yes, of course," Hugh said in a matter-of-fact tone. "Why?"

"Oh, I just wondered," Paul said thoughtfully. "Mother knew him well when they were children, you know. What's he like?"

Hugh smiled to himself as if at some amusing recollection.

"I like him," he said cautiously.

The sun was setting now behind the downs, and everything seemed strangely hushed when the boys stopped speaking.

"Isn't everything peaceful!" exclaimed Joanna, her expression unusually quiet and content.

"It's almost frightening," Louise said with a tiny shiver. "I believe I should be afraid if I were alone."

"You always get that curious sense of remoteness on or near the downs," Hugh said thoughtfully. "As if the world's very far away. I like it."

"So do I—as long as I can get back to the world," Joanna said. "Who'll have one of these cakes?"

This prosaic question met with exclamations of protest from the more aesthetic members of the party, but nevertheless, no one refused, and as the conversation grew more general Hugh began to find, to his surprise, that he was actually quite enjoying himself, and his usually sombre expression gave place more and more frequently to his much pleasanter smile.

When it was finally time to pack up and return home there were general sighs of regret, and Joanna had the satisfaction of knowing that her efforts had met with success.

"I've enjoyed this," Sarah said, gravely licking her fingers. "I'm so glad we're having more meetings. What are we going to do next week, Louise?"

"I don't know yet," Louise said absently, and then came back to the present with a start. "Sarah, don't lick your fingers like that. If they're sticky, go and wash them in the stream."

"And don't fall in," Paul added as Sarah chose the steepest part of the bank, and Hugh, looking amused, caught hold of her dress and held her firmly. He was beginning to think there might be points in favour of being a member of a large family.

CHAPTER SIX

SOME PLAIN SPEAKING

JOANNA PLACED her basket of eggs on the floor of a hen house and retired in good order. Safely outside, she gave a sigh of relief as she saw her cousin approaching. "Hugh! Do come and help me," she called, and Hugh grinned as he obeyed. Since the picnic supper he had been much more approachable, though he still fought shy of Louise.

"What's the matter?" he asked.

"What *do* you do when they won't come out of the nests?" Joanna demanded.

Hugh's grin deepened and, plunging into the hen house, he firmly evicted one broody hen after another while Joanna watched admiringly as they scuttled round, squawking wildly.

"I'd never dare to do that," she declared.

"Oh, yes, you will, once you're used to them," Hugh said, as she picked several eggs out of the recently vacated nests. "Call me again next time, and I'll show you just how to handle them."

"Thanks," Joanna said gratefully, picking up her basket and accompanying him out into the open air. "Look, aren't there a lot of eggs?"

"Yes," Hugh said, a trifle absently, and then seemed to come to a sudden decision. "Look here," he said, turning to her abruptly. "Can't you give Paul a tip?"

"What about?" As Joanna eyed him a trifle suspiciously, Hugh looked uncomfortable.

"About the way he isn't doing his work. If there's

anything Uncle hates, it's someone falling down on a job. I've tried to give Paul a hint, but he won't listen to me."

"He is an idiot!" Joanna said in exasperation. "Uncle's being so good to us that the last thing we want to do is annoy him. All right, I'll tell him not to be such an ass."

Hugh grinned to himself as she walked off. He had asked her as a last resort, but he could not help wondering how much notice Paul usually took of her admonitions.

It took Joanna some time to find her brother, but at last she ran him to earth on the fallen tree by the pond, as usual deep in a book.

"You are the limit!" she exploded.

"What is it now?" he queried.

"You!" Joanna said firmly. "Hugh's asked me to warn you not to scamp your work——"

"I'd like to know what it's got to do with him," Paul exclaimed in unwonted exasperation.

"He says Uncle will be annoyed," Joanna said.

"Oh, rot!" Paul said easily, his exasperation fading already. "Hugh takes everything too seriously."

"I'm not so sure," Joanna remarked thoughtfully. "I've thought all along——"

"Oh, you're as bad as Hugh," Paul said carelessly. "Run away and stop worrying. I'll go and see to the stables when I've finished this chapter."

With this Joanna had to be content, but as she wandered thoughtfully away she ran into her uncle, who was looking unusually grim.

"Where's Paul?" he asked, and then smiled at Joanna's startled expression. "Don't look so scared. I only want him to saddle Shamus for me. I've got to ride to the village. Will you go and tell him?"

Much relieved that he had not asked what Paul was doing, Joanna hurried back and delivered her message, and Paul gave a grunt of disgust.

"Oh, bother! All right, I'll come!"

He sauntered stablewards, and Joanna saw, with a sinking heart, that her uncle was watching, his face still grim, as he gave Joe some last-minute instructions.

"You must learn to groom them, Paul," Mr. Eldon remarked as he mounted. "Shamus is looking very dusty."

Paul made a grimace as Shamus trotted away up the lane, but Joanna frowned anxiously. Her uncle was clearly annoyed.

Joe usually lit the kitchen fire in the mornings for Mrs. Lister to cook the breakfast, but to the surprise of Louise and Joanna when they came down the following morning there was no fire blazing away in the kitchen range, and their uncle was engaged in getting out an oil stove.

"What's the matter?" asked Louise.

Her uncle looked at them quizzically.

"Your brother, for reasons of his own, no doubt, has omitted to supply us with any firewood."

"Oh, dear!" Joanna exclaimed in dismay, and made for the door. "I'll go and chop some at once."

"No, Joanna!" Her uncle's voice arrested her. "That's Paul's job, and you're not to do it for him. Instead you can go upstairs and tell him what has happened."

"Isn't he up yet?" Louise asked, glancing rather apprehensively at the clock, for they had come down a little later than usual themselves.

"Apparently not," her uncle said, intent on the oil stove, and Joanna ran upstairs to the boys' room, where Paul was still sound asleep.

"Wake up!" she exclaimed, shaking him violently, and Paul opened his eyes and gazed at her in sleepy wonder.

"What's the excitement now?"

"There's no wood to light the kitchen fire, and I believe Uncle's frightfully annoyed," Joanna gasped, and for once a look of dismay came over Paul's face.

"Oh, bother! I'd forgotten all about it."

"Look here, Paul, you're letting us all down," Joanna said in exasperation. "I do think you might try to help a bit."

"I didn't deliberately leave it," Paul said, looking a trifle ashamed. "I just forgot all about it."

"That's what I mean," Joanna declared. "Hugh must have known this was going to happen."

"Oh, bother Hugh! He's too good to be true," Paul grunted. "All right! You can tell Uncle John I'm coming."

He dressed at top speed, but by the time he got downstairs his mother was already frying their breakfast on the oil stove.

"Uncle wants you outside," Louise murmured, and watched anxiously as Paul strolled to the door in his most nonchalant manner. "What do you think Uncle wants him for?" she asked, turning to her mother when Paul had gone, and Mrs. Lister, a little frown between her eyes, shook her head.

"I've no idea. But I trust John, and I don't intend to interfere."

Louise looked dismayed. Things were serious if their mother was prepared to abandon Paul to his fate.

Mr. Eldon was standing watching Joanna feeding the poultry, but he turned as Paul reluctantly approached.

"I'm sorry——" Paul began, but his uncle interrupted.

"It's rather late to be sorry. Come along!"

Joanna gazed after them apprehensively, and then turned impulsively as Hugh came towards her.

"What's going to happen? Is Uncle very angry?"

"He's not very pleased," Hugh said thoughtfully, as if he knew the signs. "Did you warn Paul?"

"Yes, but he wouldn't listen," Joanna said gloomily.

"Well, you did your best," Hugh said consolingly. "You'd better come and have breakfast now."

"I don't think I want any," Joanna began, and Hugh grinned.

"Anyone would think Paul was going to be whipped at the cart's tail, or flogged or something. What do you think Uncle is? Come on!"

Paul himself wondered just what was going to happen as he accompanied Mr. Eldon to the pile of logs behind the stables. It seemed to him that his uncle's attitude was out of all proportion to his trivial offence.

Arrived at the logs, his uncle turned and faced him.

"Look here, Paul. I gave you two jobs—neither of which have you attempted to do properly. Joanna took over the poultry, and she's really doing it thoroughly——"

"Joanna likes being energetic——" Paul began.

"I quite understand that," his uncle said gravely, and Paul's face assumed an expression of obstinacy.

"I didn't do it deliberately, but I got hold of a book I wanted to study——"

"Hugh also wants to study—which is why I hoped that you would help to take some of the work off his shoulders and give him more free time," Mr. Eldon said. "You're both my nephews, Paul, and I want to treat you both absolutely fairly—therefore I can't let you scamp your work while Hugh does his. In fact, there is more reason why you should help me."

Paul looked at him in surprise.

"I don't want any thanks, because I'm delighted to be able to do it, but I do think you should remember that I'm not only giving a home to you—as I'm also doing to Hugh—but to your mother and sisters as well. All being well, in time it will be your responsibility to look after them and see that they are all right, and the least you can do is to start now by doing a little to help."

Paul stared at him, his face slowly crimsoning.

"I—I hadn't looked at it like that," he muttered.

"No, I thought you hadn't." The gravity of his uncle's face began to relax. "Look here, Paul, now you have thought of it, suppose we start afresh?"

Paul nodded uncomfortably. "I—yes——"

Mr. Eldon smiled suddenly, and Paul grinned back in a shamefaced way.

"Now in order to impress the fact on your memory, I feel that as you nearly made the whole family miss their breakfast—after all, you didn't know that I keep an oil stove for emergencies—you should ensure that there is enough firewood ready for, say, a week, before you have your breakfast," Mr. Eldon suggested, the twinkle in his eyes becoming more pronounced as Paul stared at him in dismay. "Then, if you keep up a regular supply after that, you should always have some in hand.

Paul stared at the pile of logs in horror. He was already hungry, and the thought of having to do so much before he could appease his very healthy appetite was appalling. Despite his twinkling eyes Mr. Eldon watched him shrewdly. He thought the boy would take it well, but if he didn't——to his relief Paul suddenly stooped and picked up the axe, which was lying against a log.

"*Peccavi! Mea culpa!*" he observed, with a touch of his old manner. "All right, Uncle, I will. And—I'm sorry I forgot, but it honestly wasn't intentional."

Mr. Eldon nodded, and returned to the house and his own breakfast, well pleased as he heard the sound of the axe behind him. In the big kitchen the whole family, already at the table, turned to eye him questioningly.

"Paul——" Mrs. Lister began rather anxiously.

"Paul's just doing something for me," Mr. Eldon said equably as he sat down. "He'll be in later for his breakfast. Can you keep it warm?"

"I'll try," Mrs. Lister said dubiously. "But it won't be as nice."

"I'm afraid that can't be helped," Mr. Eldon remarked, attacking his own breakfast with a good appetite.

Joanna's eyes wandered to Hugh, who was looking at his uncle as if he had a very good idea of what had happened, and as soon as the meal was over and Mrs. Lister had followed her brother through to the front of the house, she pounced. Catching his arm as her cousin made for the door, she pulled him up short.

"No, you don't! Just what has been happening? Why hasn't Paul come in to breakfast? What's Uncle done with him?"

Hugh grinned as he looked down at the determined hand clutching his sleeve, and Louise suspended her clearing-up activities to listen.

"I don't know, of course, but I suspect Uncle's making him chop the wood before he has any breakfast. He's rather fond of making the punishment fit the crime." He grinned at Joanna. "So you'd better be careful. In his opinion it doesn't matter whether you've been given a job to do, or taken it on of your own accord—the main thing is that if you have a job to do, you must get down to it and do it thoroughly. He's no time for anyone who's half-hearted about anything."

"Isn't that being rather too particular and severe?" Louise asked.

"I don't know," Hugh said thoughtfully. "After all, if you let a thing slide it's your own fault. At least, that's how I've always felt when he's caught me out and made me make up for it."

"You!" Joanna fell back in surprise. "I can't imagine you ever leaving your work like that."

Hugh grinned. "Oh, I have done—before Uncle cured me. But now I realise that the sooner I get my work done, the more leisure I'll have, so I get on with it."

"Well!" Joanna said expressively, and then turned to the door as Paul came in with an armful of firewood. "Paul! You poor thing! Are you starving?"

"Completely," Paul said expressively, looking a little shamefaced and uncomfortable as he felt them all watching him.

"Here's your breakfast," Louise said.

"Did Uncle make you do it before you had your breakfast?" Joanna asked curiously, with no respect for her brother's feelings. "Hugh says he's done that to him a couple of times."

"What?" Paul, who had been hiding his face as he put the wood down, straightened up and stared at his cousin. "Do you mean to say you're not perfect after all?" he demanded incredulously, and Hugh flushed angrily.

"What do you mean by that?" he demanded, and Joanna sighed.

"Now don't start quarrelling——" she began, but neither boy took any notice of her. Hugh was glaring angrily at his cousin, while a slow, appreciative grin was slowly spreading across Paul's face.

"If you're trying to be rude——" Hugh began, and then stopped to stare at Paul's expression in surprise.

"No, I'm being complimentary," Paul said, his grin assuming larger proportions. "I'd thought you were too good to be true, the way you sweated away at your work, but if you, too, have been a shirker and backslider in your time——"

Hugh's angry expression faded as he suddenly laughed.

"Oh, I've often been in Uncle's bad books. He sets an unpleasantly high standard at times—only somehow it does keep you on tiptoe doing your best."

"I believe I know what you mean," Joanna exclaimed. "I rather like it myself."

"I'm afraid I shall find it a trifle wearing," Paul admitted frankly, as he set to work on his neglected breakfast. He eyed Hugh appraisingly. "I believe life's going to be much more bearable here now that I know you won't be held up before me as a Shining Example."

"I'm sorry," Hugh grinned faintly. "I didn't know you were feeling like that. I thought it was the opposite——" he broke off and glanced round uncertainly, as if not sure how to express himself, and then suddenly bolted out, leaving his cousins staring after him in perplexity.

"Obviously *non compos mentis*," Paul said, looking round for more to eat.

When he had finished his breakfast he strolled thoughtfully out and stood contemplating the pigs unseeingly as he tried to think things out—probably for the first time in his life. After always taking everything for granted his uncle's plain speaking had shaken him considerably. His mother and sisters had always been so wrapped up in his future career that it had never occurred to him that sooner or later he ought to shoulder the responsibility of being the only man in the family, and certainly, until this morning, it had never occurred to him that he owed his uncle any particular debt for open- ing his home to them all. Despite his natural indolence— where physical exertion was concerned—Paul had an essentially fair mind and, far from bearing a grudge against his uncle, he could not help conceding that Mr. Eldon had been right, and that he had been shirking badly, though if he had not discovered that Hugh, too, had offended in the same way, it is doubtful if his pride would have allowed him to admit being in the wrong. As it was, however, he saw the amusing side of the situation, which enabled him to carry it off with a better air than might have been expected.

Having come to a definite decision, he strolled round to the log pile and eyed it thoughtfully for a few minutes. Then, glancing down at a badly blistered hand that bore witness to the unaccustomed work it had done that morning, he decided that he had done enough in that direction for the time being, and wandered off in search of his cousin, whom he found repairing a fence, while Sarah and Woggles investigated in a ditch nearby.

"Are you very busy?" he inquired, after watching in silence for a moment or two, and Hugh glanced round at him curiously.

"I've nearly finished this. Why?"

Paul grinned, as if amused at himself.

"Well, as one about to turn over a new leaf—until next time I get immersed in a book—I wondered if you'd show me how to groom those equine quadrupeds for which I'm supposed to be responsible," he said airily, and Hugh, after glancing at him sharply, grinned too.

"Of course! I'll only be a few minutes."

"I'll help," offered a kindly voice from the ditch, and Hugh groaned.

"I've given up trying to suppress her. It's beyond me."

"It's a family fable that I'm the only one who can do it," Paul sighed. "But I feel too crushed to-day."

Hugh laughed as he eyed Paul's whimsical face.

"You don't look very crushed."

"Oh, I am," Paul said cheerfully. "I must be, to be contemplating physical toil."

"We'll probably have a job to catch the horses," Hugh said, putting the finishing touches to the fence. "Do you think Joanna would like to come and help?"

"Johnny will seize any opportunity of being energetic," Paul said confidently, "and for once, no doubt, we can make use of Sarah's superabundant zeal."

As he had prophesied, both girls came willingly, and when they had finally captured Shamus and Jessamy, Hugh proceeded to instruct all three Listers in the art of grooming.

Mr. Eldon, coming back to the house some time later, wondering thoughtfully how Paul had reacted to his little homily, heard the unusual sound of laughter and excited voices issuing from the stable and, crossing quietly to the door, stood looking in, unobserved for a moment.

Sarah, squeaking with excitement, and clutching firmly at the pony's mane, was seated on Jessamy's shining back, while in the next stall Joanna was carefully combing Shamus's long tail, Paul was rubbing away at his bay coat, and Hugh, superintending generally, was listening in obvious amusement to his cousins' comments as they worked.

"I must admit they repay grooming," Paul said, as he stepped back, breathing a little heavily, to survey his handiwork while he surreptitiously massaged his hand.

"They're beautiful!" Sarah said firmly, and then gave a squeak as her mount side-stepped.

"Hadn't you better lift her down?" Paul said, glancing at Hugh. "I know it seems incredible, but Mother might object if she fell off and got spoilt—you know, if Jessamy trod on her face or something."

"I shan't fall off," Sarah declared, with another squeak.

"At least she can't help while she's up there," Hugh remarked.

"There's something in that," Paul conceded gravely. "Well, now that's done, I feel I might venture to relax for a few minutes."

"How about helping me with my henhouses now I've helped you with your horses?" Joanna suggested wickedly, and Paul looked pained.

"I didn't *ask* for your help. You *chose* to come and butt in——"

"Anyway, what about Hugh's work?" Joanna asked triumphantly. "You dragged him away from that."

"Ye gods, yes!" Paul looked guilty. "What should you have been doing, Hugh?"

"What's the matter with your hand?" demanded a voice from Jessamy's back before Hugh could reply, and Paul jumped guiltily at the sudden question, and then hesitated uncomfortably.

"I—oh, nothing." His right hand dropped instinctively to his side, as if he wanted to hide it, but Joanna jumped forward and seized it, turning it palm upwards before he could stop her.

"Oh!" she gasped, as he tried to drag it away, but Hugh's hand caught his wrist, and they all looked down at where the blisters had been torn away in places, exposing the raw flesh underneath.

"You idiot!" Hugh said forcefully. "Uncle didn't want you to do that."

"Gives me away, doesn't it?" Paul said ruefully. "Shows how much manual labour I do as a rule."

"Come indoors and I'll see to it for you," Hugh said.

"No, thanks. I'll deal with it myself," Paul said, but not ungratefully, as he pulled his hand away. "I'm used to patching myself up."

"But——"

"Oh, let him," Joanna said easily, as Hugh would have objected. "He likes messing round with bandages and things."

Hugh looked at Paul rather queerly as they turned to the door, but the sight of their uncle stopped any further discussion.

"Let me look," Mr. Eldon said, and Paul very reluctantly held out his hand, while a squeal from Sarah reminded Hugh to go and lift her down. Mr. Eldon's mouth twitched as he examined the maltreated hand. At least it proved that Paul had taken his words to heart. "Watch it carefully for a day or two," he ordered. "And you'd better not use it again to-day."

"But I must help Hugh to make up for the time he's lost——" Paul began.

"I'll soon catch up," Hugh said hastily. "Now that you and Joanna have taken over some of the work it's making quite a lot of difference."

"Besides, I'm helping him," Sarah said firmly, and Hugh ran a despairing hand through his hair while the others laughed. Then he came to a sudden decision. If he really took her at her word and kept her perpetually busy, she might soon get tired of following him around.

"Yes, you can help," he said unexpectedly. "Come on!"

"What are we going to do?" asked Sarah happily as they set off, and Hugh grinned.

"You can do some weeding while I start turning over some ground for autumn planting. Look, weed between those rows."

Having seen her safely at work, he began digging and worked steadily for a while, until a sudden query from her made him drop his spade and hurry to see what she was up to.

"What are these with the thick roots?" she inquired innocently. "There are lots of them, and they look so like radishes."

"They *are* radishes," Hugh groaned, beginning to think that his idea was not so good after all. "I said *between* the rows!"

"Oh!" Sarah's small face looked so downcast that his annoyance fled.

"I suppose I couldn't expect you to know," he said brusquely but not unkindly. "Look, concentrate on this stuff——" and he pulled up some groundsel. "It spreads like wildfire, so if you just pull out all you can find, you'll be helping a lot. Now don't touch anything else, even if you're sure it's a weed."

"I won't," Sarah promised, and set to work happily again, while Hugh ruefully reflected that the family would have a surfeit of radishes for a few days.

CHAPTER SEVEN

THE SECOND MEETING

FAR FROM being put off by the fact that Hugh kept her busy, Sarah apparently decided that he was the only person who really appreciated her well-meant efforts, and as she thereafter followed him like a small but faithful shadow, he found he had to accept her allegiance with philosophical resignation. Her efforts to assist were often comical, and occasionally almost tragic when she threatened to ruin the result of some hard work by her well-meant intervention, but fortunately her cousin had a well-developed sense of humour under his rather brusque exterior, and actually began to derive a certain amount of amusement from the situation.

In the meantime Louise was busy helping her mother in the transformation of the dining-room, and while she worked she racked her brains for an idea for the next meeting of the Society. At first she was unable to think of anything, but then, all of a sudden, an idea came, and she promptly deserted the dining-room and shut herself in the snuggery, where she did some hard thinking, and used up many sheets of paper before she was satisfied. The finished sheets she took upstairs and hid in her best gloves, as the only place safe from her sisters' eyes.

At tea-time on the day of their next meeting four pairs of curious eyes surveyed her.

"Got anything ready?" asked Joanna, and Louise nodded with a smile.

"Everything's ready," she announced. "Meet here at seven."

"Anything to carry this time?" asked Paul suspiciously.

"No, nothing."

"Then it's not a picnic," Sarah said with some regret, and even Hugh looked interested as they all tried to guess what form the entertainment was to take. Louise, however, refused to be drawn, and confined her conversation to her mother and uncle, both of whom had heard of the new society with amused approval, and followed its progress with interest.

At seven o'clock every member was at the meeting place, and watched curiously as Louise proceeded to pin up a slip of paper. As soon as she stepped back there was a rush to read it.

> To-night you'll have to be, I fear,
> Quite energetic—Paul, don't grunt!
> We start from fountain crystal clear,
> And go upon a treasure hunt!

"Oh, lovely!" Joanna exclaimed, while Paul chuckled at the ridiculous rhyme. "I love treasure hunts!"

"But none of you must think aloud," Louise said warningly. "It spoils it completely if you do."

"The first one's easy," Paul said, and led a rush to the well, where, sure enough, there was another clue.

> Where great god Pan rules undisputed—
> Naiads, dryads, frolic free—
> There in sacred place reputed
> Lies our next clue—Number Three!

"Shades of the Muses!" Paul groaned, while Joanna gazed round despairingly.

"Naiads! Dryads! Some kind of heathen goddesses, weren't they?" she asked vaguely.

"Hugh! I'm coming with you," Sarah exclaimed, her mouth drooping pathetically. "I've never heard of them."

"I'm sorry," Louise said guiltily. "I found that if I tried to keep them easy enough for you, they were too simple for the others. I spent hours trying to work these out. I'm afraid I'm not a natural poet."

Paul grinned and, without a word, quietly left their group.

"Someone's got it!" Joanna said enviously, and Hugh suddenly glanced round at Sarah.

"Come on!" he exclaimed, holding out his hand, and with a gasp of excitement she trotted off with him, while Joanna stood racking her brains.

"Dryads—aren't they something to do with trees?" she said, gazing vaguely at Louise, who was watching with the amused air of one in the secret. "And naiads—weren't they—fountains or rivers or—something to do with water, anyway? Water—trees——" She suddenly stared at Louise. "I believe you mean the copse and the pond! Oh, the boys will be well ahead of me by now!" She turned and set off at top speed, while Louise followed more leisurely. When she reached the fallen tree, however, the other four were all still there, frowning over the next clue.

> A nest on high, inhabited
> By cooing doves of whom 'tis said
> None gentler ever lived in nest
> Or rough rude quarrels more detest.

"Completely beyond me," Hugh said, but Joanna gave a sudden chuckle as she glanced at Louise's twinkling eyes.

"Cooing doves! On high! I believe I've got it!" she

exclaimed, and tore off through the copse, while the boys looked at each other blankly.

"Are there any doves or pigeons here?" Paul demanded, and Hugh shook his head.

"Not that I know of, but——" He broke off as something in Louise's expression caught his attention. "None gentler!" he exclaimed. "I suppose you're speaking of Joanna! Come on, Sarah!"

Paul looked blankly at Louise.

"Where does Johnny come in?—Ye gods! ' A nest on high'—I'll wager it's your bedroom!"

Louise's mirth bubbled over as, without waiting for a reply, he bolted off. Up in the bedroom he found Joanna, Hugh and Sarah still searching for the next clue.

"If it is here she meant, she's hidden it well," was Joanna's greeting as Paul burst in.

"Here it is!" Sarah exclaimed before Hugh could stop her, and there was the clue neatly hidden in a fold of one of the curtains.

> A kingly robe now guides us—oh!
> To habitation strange!
> Though fashions come and fashions go,
> Its occupants ne'er change.

Joanna sank down weakly on one of the beds.

"This is too much!" she exclaimed. "A kingly robe! Habitation strange!"

"Occupants never change!" Paul repeated thoughtfully, while Hugh stood and frowned blankly at the clue.

"What on earth can she mean by kingly robe?" Joanna demanded, but neither of the boys could answer, and Sarah, content to leave the thinking to her partner, leaned out of the window.

"Ooh! Here's uncle in the car! And look, there's some-one with him!"

Three heads popped out round hers, and four pairs of eyes watched critically as a plain, rather dowdily dressed woman, who might have been any age between thirty and fifty, got out of the car and waited while Mr. Eldon lifted out two suitcases. She had a pleasant, if somewhat non-descript, face, and the Listers felt there was something vaguely familiar about her.

"Looks as if she's come to stay," Paul commented.

"Who is she?" demanded Joanna, turning to Hugh, who was frowning in a puzzled manner.

"Annie Harris—Joe's sister," he answered. "She's house-keeper to a farmer out towards Fontroy Royal—an old beast of a man who comes home drunk and in raving tempers. She's always threatening to leave him."

"It looks as if she has," Paul said.

"Let's go and find out," proposed Joanna, the treasure hunt forgotten for the time being, and they all raced downstairs and into the kitchen, where Mrs. Lister was just welcoming the new arrival, while Joe stood grinning in the background.

"Well!" The newcomer turned to beam at Hugh as they all burst in. "So here I am! I've done it at last!" she exclaimed, almost proudly.

"What? Walked out on old Philips?" Hugh asked.

"Yes. I said I wouldn't stay there a moment longer, so I went and rang up Joe, and Mr. Eldon said he'd come for me at once, and that Mrs. Lister would be glad of help here," Annie said, almost in one breath. "I've put up with a lot, but when it comes to throwing things at me——" She stopped, at a loss for words to express her feelings, and Mr. Eldon laughed.

"Never mind, Annie! You've left him now, and no one will start throwing things at you here—I hope," he added, laughing again.

"Did they hit you?" asked Sarah, surveying Annie with deep interest.

"The joint did," Annie said, rubbing her cheek ruefully. "I'm glad I was standing near the scuttle and it fell in on the coal."

"Where's Louise?" asked Mrs. Lister, as everyone laughed, and the young ones looked at each other in amused dismay as they remembered the neglected treasure hunt.

"I don't know. She didn't come after us this time," Joanna said in perplexity, missing her sister for the first time.

"I saw her climbing up the down past that great patch of willow herb," Joe volunteered, and Joanna and the boys stared at each other in wild surmise.

"That great purple patch—a king's robe!" Joanna exclaimed excitedly, forgetting that she was giving away the clue to her fellow competitors. "But *habitation strange!* There are no houses up there."

"*Occupants never change——*" Paul said thoughtfully. "Here, I've got it!"

"So have I!' Hugh exclaimed, grabbing Sarah's hand.

"The barrow! Of course!" Joanna gasped, and to the amused astonishment of their elders, all four raced out.

"Well I never!" Annie exclaimed. "Master Hugh's altered, hasn't he?"

"It was time he had companions of his own age," Mr. Eldon said.

"That's what I've always told Joe," Annie said, nodding sagely. "What are they up to now?"

"I believe that it's a treasure hunt," Mrs. Lister said.

"They'll be good and hungry by the time they've raced up to that barrow and back," Annie declared. "I'll just get my hat and coat off, and then I'll start getting supper for them." She and Mrs. Lister stood looking at each other for a moment, and then, as Mrs. Lister laughed happily, a slow beam spread over Annie's face. "I like young 'uns," she declared. "They make all the difference to a house."

"They certainly do," Mrs. Lister agreed, laying her hand on Annie's arm in a warm, friendly gesture. "Come upstairs and see your room—it's next to the girls'. Joe will bring up your cases."

It was a long, stiff climb up the sloping face of the down, and the treasure hunters were too breathless to talk much as they scrambled up. Joanna and Paul could have got ahead, for Hugh had to wait for Sarah with her shorter legs, but they held back, and all four arrived together at the great tumulus that crowned the top of the down. As they had expected, Louise was already there, her hands filled with a great bunch of scabious, and her cheeks pink with the fresh breeze that blew unobstructed across the green uplands.

"What a time you've been!" she exclaimed, but as between them they poured out the story of Annie's arrival, she was not sorry to hear that she and her mother were to have help with the more humdrum parts of the housework.

"But where's the next clue?" asked Paul.

"Here," she answered, fishing in her pocket. "I didn't dare put it down anywhere in case it blew away."

They all gathered round and read the couplet.

Where sage proclaims his presence sere,
'Tis time you'll find the treasure near.

"I gather this is the final one?" Hugh asked.

"Each one's worse than the last," Joanna said despairingly. "There isn't a sage near here—unless you mean Uncle? And he's anything but sere."

Paul thoughtfully read the couplet out aloud, and Hugh's eyes suddenly brightened.

"Come on," he murmured to Sarah, and together they stole away, only Louise seeing them go, for the other two were still poring over the paper.

"A sage," Joanna repeated. "Who can you mean, Louise?"

" 'Tis time—time—oh, I believe you mean *thyme!*" Paul exclaimed, a great light flashing upon him.

"Of course she means time," Joanna protested, but Paul had gone. "Time—a sage—Oh! Aren't I an idiot! Thyme, of course! and sage—sere—*dried sage!*" she exclaimed excitedly, and turned to run down towards the house, Louise beside her. "Though it's no good hurrying," she exclaimed. "The others will be there long before me."

"They may not realise about the *sere*," Louise said cheeringly. "Oh, look! Paul's gone to the kitchen garden!"

"Oh, goody!" Joanna exclaimed. "I may be in time yet, if Hugh did the same."

As they approached the house they saw Paul coming towards them, and Annie, busy laying the table for supper in the kitchen, looked round in pleased amusement as Joanna flew through and up the stairs, closely pursued by Paul, while Louise followed in a slightly more decorous manner.

They were too late, however. Up in the big attic used

as a storeroom, Hugh and Sarah, seated on the floor, were
busy unwrapping an interesting-looking parcel that had
been hanging from a rafter close to a bunch of thyme,
while the smell of dried sage pervaded that part of the
room.

"What is it?" demanded Joanna, gasping after her run
upstairs, and Sarah pulled off the last wrapper, displaying a cardboard box.

"Whatever can it be?" asked Paul, as interested as
anyone, and Hugh threw back the lid, displaying one of
Louise's sponge cakes, always popular with her family,
covered with white icing.

"Ooh!" Sarah said blissfully.

"You must all have some," Hugh said, taking a pen-
knife out of his pocket.

"No, you won it," Joanna protested.

"Yes, I think the winners should eat it," Louise agreed.

"Well, we'll just have a small piece each, and you and
Sarah can share the rest," Paul compromised, for Hugh,
ignoring their protests, had already begun to cut it, and
so, sitting on the bare but well-swept floor of the attic,
the whole party risked spoiling their supper by eating the
cake with hearty appetites before returning to the kitchen.

"That was good fun while it lasted," Paul remarked.

"Yes, I've never taken part in a treasure hunt before,"
Hugh said, eating his share with evident appreciation.

"Then you don't think my idea was too bad?" Joanna
asked.

"Not so far—but I'm afraid it won't work so well
when it's my turn," Hugh said, suddenly looking gloomy.

"You'll think of something," Paul said. "If all else
fails, fall back on food in some shape or form. That
always goes down well with the Lister family."

"So I've noticed," Hugh said with a grin as Joanna jumped up with alacrity on hearing their uncle calling them to supper.

"I wonder what Uncle's arranged about schools for us," Joanna remarked thoughtfully to Louise a few days after the treasure hunt. "He's never mentioned it, and Paul's beginning to get worried." She chuckled as she added: "Sarah isn't."

"I'm afraid none of the female members of our family are keen students," Louise laughed, a little guiltily.

"Oh, school's all right," Joanna remarked. "Anyway, Paul and I are going to tackle Uncle to-night—if he comes into the sitting-room with us. I say! Have you noticed how he's altered?"

"Who? Uncle?"

"Yes. When he used to come and stay with us he was an awful bookworm—nearly as bad as Paul—but now he never settles down. He's always pottering round doing odd jobs. He's much more restless than he used to be."

"Yes, now I come to think of it, he has altered," Louise agreed, nodding thoughtfully, and Joanna turned round impetuously as Hugh came into the kitchen and began rummaging in a drawer of the dresser.

"Hugh, why has Uncle altered so? He never seems to read now, and he used to be an awful bookworm. Is he worried about something, that he's so restless?"

Hugh dropped a ball of string on the floor, retrieved it from under a chair, and then hesitated a brief moment before answering.

"Oh, I suppose he's too busy," he said vaguely, and was gone before either of the girls could stop him.

"Oh, and I wanted to ask him about one of the geese

that's looking queer," Joanna said in some annoyance. "I'll go after him while I think of it."

Out in the garden Hugh was cutting great shaggy pink dahlias, while Sarah stood beside him, taking each bloom as it was cut. As he caught sight of Joanna approaching he thrust the last bloom into Sarah's arms, asked her to take them in to her mother, and then made for the stables, while Joanna glared indignantly after him, suspecting strongly that he was trying to avoid her. For a moment she stood stock still, and then, deciding not to take any notice of his moods, she turned and followed. Inside the stables, however, she came to a halt, for there was no sign of him anywhere. Then she heard the sound of footsteps in the room above. Joe was out in the fields, she knew, so without any hesitation she made for the precipitous staircase that led up to his room and climbed up. An ancient door barred her progress at the top, but she flung it open, and then stood staring. The room itself was plainly but comfortably furnished, but what surprised her was the sight of her uncle standing by the window, while Hugh was standing near a small table with an open letter in his hand. They both started guiltily at her abrupt entrance, and then her uncle, recovering himself, smiled.

"Were you looking for me?" he asked.

"No—no, I was looking for Hugh," Joanna stammered, while her cousin frowned in annoyance he did not try to hide. "I saw him come to the stables—and then I heard someone up here." She looked curiously at the letter, which Hugh was slipping back in an envelope. "I—I didn't know you were here."

"I'm just going," Mr. Eldon said. "I was merely giving Hugh directions about something."

"I'm going, too," Hugh said, slipping the letter in his pocket, and somehow or other Joanna found herself scrambling down the steep steps with her uncle and cousin following, more convinced than ever that there was something they were keeping secret from her family. Her uncle, however, was his usual pleasant self as they walked away from the stables, though Hugh was still frowning gloomily.

When Mr. Eldon left them, Joanna turned abruptly to her cousin, who was looking very much as if he wanted to lose her.

"Hugh, I wanted to ask you about one of the geese. I'm sure it isn't well," she said, and was surprised to see his face clear, as if he had feared she was going to ask him something else. He went with her willingly to see the goose, but had to advise her to consult their uncle, and then he hastily made his escape. Something in his manner made her turn and look after him, and somehow she was not surprised to see him making for the stables. In the doorway, however, he came to an abrupt halt, for Paul was now there working.

Rather to his own surprise, as well as everyone else's, Paul was sticking to his work with astonishing assiduity. He did not enjoy sawing logs, but as he began to get used to the horses he found them an interesting charge, and one which promised to become more interesting still now that he—like Joanna and Sarah—was learning to ride. Louise was too nervous to try.

Hugh hesitated in the doorway for a moment, and then went and took down a bridle. "I'm just going for a canter. Like to come?" he asked.

"Rather!" Paul returned, and abandoned his work forthwith.

When they returned Annie met them with a beaming smile. She had quite adopted the whole family, and might indeed have been an old family retainer.

"If I were you, Master Hugh, I'd keep out of Miss Sarah's way," she warned him. "She's quite sure you sent her in with those flowers on purpose to get rid of her while you went off without her."

"Oh!" Hugh's face assumed an expression of comical consternation. "I'd forgotten all about her. But I *can't* take her everywhere with me."

"Leave her alone," Paul advised. "She'll come round."

"Where is she?" asked Hugh, feeling curiously guilty.

"Miss Louise has taken her out," Annie answered, as she went back into the house.

Paul went off to finish his work, and Hugh wandered round the house to where Mrs. Lister was lying back lazily in a deck-chair on the lawn.

"I'm sorry about Sarah," he said abruptly. "I didn't really sneak off—I just forgot all about her."

Mrs. Lister's face dimpled attractively.

"I couldn't have blamed you if you had done. You're wonderfully patient with her—in fact, almost too patient. That's why we've had such a scene with her this afternoon."

"A scene?" Hugh repeated in dismay.

"A second Alice and the Pool of Tears," his aunt assured him. "As a matter of fact, I think it's probably good for her to be crossed occasionally. As there are no children here of her own age she's getting far too much of her own way."

"I haven't noticed the others giving in to her," Hugh said, smiling a little.

"Oh, they do," Mrs. Lister said. "They often just don't

bother to argue, she's so quietly persistent and obstinate. Look at the way she clings to you whatever we say."

"Perhaps she won't after this afternoon," Hugh said, suddenly feeling oddly sorry.

"She'll get over it," Mrs. Lister said shrewdly. "She isn't put off as easily as that." She looked round as Woggles came frisking up to her. "Here they come!"

Sarah, her small face covered by a most successfully forlorn expression, came to a halt beside her mother.

"Had a nice walk?" Mrs. Lister asked, her eyes bright with amusement, and Sarah nodded solemnly.

"Well, I must go and get on with the milking," Hugh said casually, and the amusement in his aunt's eyes deepened as Sarah took a half-step forward. Hugh turned and glanced at her, and half-held out his hand. "Coming to help?" he queried.

It was an invitation not to be resisted. In a second Sarah's hand was in his, and with a beam of joy she accompanied him to fetch the cows.

That evening, when the younger members of the family had settled down round the sitting-room fire, Joanna looked up at her uncle as he stood by the door for a moment looking at them.

"Uncle, do stop and talk to us for a bit," she begged. "You always run away in the evenings, and I'm sure you haven't *got* to be working all the time."

Mr. Eldon allowed himself to be pulled down into a chair, and Joanna plumped down on his knee.

"What do you want to talk about?" he asked, smiling across at his sister.

"School," Joanna said, and a groan came from the hearthrug.

"No!" Sarah protested. "We don't."

"Yes, we do," Paul said, looking up and putting his book aside. "What are we going to do about schools, Uncle?"

Mr. Eldon smiled across again at his sister; it was evident that they had already discussed that question.

"Well, the nearest schools are at Shaftesbury, and transport would be very difficult—especially in winter," he began, and Paul's face fell.

"Then what——"

"So I've been wondering if you would like to go on working at home," Mr. Eldon went on with a calmness that took their breath away. "There are enough of you for a little healthy competition, and your mother and I can help you. After all, your mother is a B.A. and a qualified teacher, and I have a few degrees and qualifications myself. I think between us your education wouldn't suffer."

For a moment no one was ready to speak. Paul and Joanna looked at each other questioningly, and Louise put down her sewing. Only Sarah betrayed complete approval.

"No school! Oh, goody!" she ejaculated.

"But that doesn't mean no work," her uncle warned her. "Well, what do you others say? Hugh has been doing that ever since we came here. I expect you two boys are at about the same stage, so you could work together, and Joanna would probably give you a run for your money in some subjects."

"I'd do my best," Joanna declared, her eyes lighting up with the joy of battle. "I like the idea, Uncle."

"Louise!" Mr. Eldon turned to his eldest niece. "I know you've left school officially, but if you'd like to join in some of our classes——"

"Anything except maths," Louise agreed, suddenly feeling that she did not want to be left out altogether.

"All right! No maths for Louise," Mr. Eldon laughed. "Well, Paul?"

Paul hesitated for a moment. The decision meant far more to him than any of the others. Then he nodded.

"We could try it," he agreed, cheered by the thought that his uncle had always had the reputation of being a brilliant scholar.

"Good!" Mr. Eldon said briskly. "We'll turn the snuggery into a schoolroom, and your mother and I will work out our curriculum."

"*Easy* lessons," Sarah begged.

"No, we want to get on," Paul protested.

"You will," his uncle promised in a tone of dire warning, and Joanna groaned as she tweaked his hair.

"We're for it now. I know! You'll prove a regular Dr. Blimber!"

"I think we'll start by endeavouring to inculcate a little respect for your teachers," her uncle returned, pinching her ear. "Ruth, we must concentrate on discipline."

Joanna chuckled as she glanced across at Paul, who grinned sheepishly.

"I'll toe the line," he promised. "It's Joanna who'll be the rebel."

"Not at this school," Joanna said promptly. "Uncle, let's start now."

"No!" Sarah wailed, while the others laughed at Joanna's enthusiasm.

"I'll get you some books," Joanna began, jumping up. "What do you want?"

"I don't want any books now." Her uncle pulled her

down on his knee again. "Tell me what history you've been doing."

Everyone spoke at once, and Mr. Eldon laughed.

"I can see we're going to have difficulty in fitting you all in together. Sarah will definitely have to have separate lessons, I'm afraid, but you other four must try to fit in together."

"I don't mind in subjects like history and geography or English," Joanna said decidedly, "but I cannot and will not try to reach Paul's standard in Latin."

"There you are!" Paul proclaimed triumphantly. "I said she'd be the rebel. Where's your disciplinary action, Uncle?"

"She shall start the ball rolling by opening our history class. You all seem to have reached the end of the seventeenth century—except Sarah, of course—so tell me all you know about Queen Anne's reign, Joanna."

Joanna settled herself more comfortably on his knee, and then gave a chuckle.

"This isn't a bit like school, is it? Now let me think— she came to the throne in 1702, and——"

Before they knew where they were, the whole class was swept in, even that lukewarm scholar, Louise, putting aside her sewing, and finding a new interest in Lord Bolingbroke's intrigues with the Stuarts and Marlborough's campaigns, while Paul decided there and then that if this was only the beginning, they were going to gain by their home education. That their uncle knew his subject there could be no doubting, and, rather to the surprise of the Listers, Hugh proved a worthy opponent, giving quick, decisive answers that were quite as much to the point as Paul's longer, fuller statements.

"I like this," Joanna said happily later, when her mother

interrupted the class to point out that Sarah was sound asleep on the hearthrug.

"Someone seems to have been bored, anyway," Paul observed, brushing back a lock of hair that had fallen over his face during a heated discussion. "Yes, I've enjoyed it, too, Uncle."

Mr. Eldon looked pleased, and more content than they had yet seen him in the evenings, as he leaned back in his chair.

"If you go on like this you'll all be making great headway," he observed.

"I've never found history so interesting before," Louise said, picking up her sewing again. "What do we do now?"

"Have supper," her uncle said promptly, though smiling at the unconscious compliment in her question. "We've done enough for one evening."

When the boys were undressing that night Paul looked round at his cousin.

"Have you really been working at home ever since you came here?"

"Yes," Hugh said briefly, and then added: "Uncle's very good—you'll find he's as good as any schoolmaster—and better than most."

"I thought that to-night," Paul nodded.

"What's Aunt Ruth like?" Hugh asked abruptly, and Paul gave a little chuckle.

"Wait and see."

They worked out of doors the next day as usual, though Sarah, to her great disgust, was made to settle down in a shady spot in the afternoon to start her easier lessons, but in the evening they gathered in the snuggery where they could have the books about them, and Mrs. Lister, to the surprise and horror of her nephew, addressed them without any warning in fluent French.

"Oh, do look at Hugh's face!" Joanna exclaimed, bursting into a fit of laughter.

"I'm sorry," Hugh stammered. "I wasn't expecting——"

Mr. Eldon, who had again joined their group instead of wandering restlessly about the house, gave a chuckle.

"Your French should improve by leaps and bounds, Hugh."

"It's far too fast for me," Hugh said, with a despairing gesture.

"It often is for me," Joanna said. "I've never been keen on languages—and I *hate* irregular verbs and idioms."

To Hugh's surprise, Louise, scarcely faltering at all, answered her mother in French, and as Paul joined in, though not so fluently, Joanna treated her cousin to a laughing grimace.

"We're definitely at the bottom of the class in this," she murmured. "Louise is better because she was friendly with a French girl who was in her form at school, and she and Yvonne usually spoke French."

Hugh was greatly relieved when Mrs. Lister handed them over to her brother for Latin, for in this he and Paul were definitely ahead of the girls.

"Joanna is much better in subjects where she can use her imagination," Mrs. Lister remarked with a smile as her middle daughter floundered helplessly in ablative absolutes.

"And French is the only subject I can shine at all in," Louise added ruefully, almost as much at sea as Joanna in Latin.

Although it seemed strange at first, they soon got used to doing their outdoor work during the day and their lessons in the evening or when the weather was too bad to work out of doors, and it soon became a familiar sight to see the group sitting listening with deep interest while Mr. Eldon or Mrs. Lister expounded, or the four heads bent over exercise books. The snuggery was now devoted entirely to study, and frequently one or more of the students, with an hour to spare, would retire there to work quietly during the day, and all four elder ones felt they were making astonishing headway, even Hugh, used as he was to this mode of studying, finding the presence of his cousins a welcome spur. There was soon keen competition between the boys, and Paul found his cousin a a foeman worthy of his steel.

"He's good," he remarked one day to Louise and Joanna in some surprise. "When I first saw him I thought he was going to be a real country bumpkin, but he's awfully good."

"You can say what you like," Joanna remarked. "I like him."

"No doubt that knowledge would ease his mind a lot," Paul said lazily. "As a matter of fact, I find he improves tremendously on acquaintance."

"I wish he wouldn't be so secretive, though," Louise complained, wrinkling her nose thoughtfully, fortunately unconscious of a splash of distemper on it. "There's that room of his upstairs. He's never once unlocked it so that we can keep it clean. Mummy asked him about it once, and he just said he dusted it himself. He didn't attempt to explain why he wouldn't let us in."

"He's obviously got a body hidden in there," Joanna said ghoulishly, and the discussion ended in a laugh.

CHAPTER EIGHT

A PARTNERSHIP IS FORMED

AT LAST the dining-room was finished, and to the amusement of the rest of the family, and particularly Annie and Joe, they all found neatly worded invitations on their plates at the breakfast table.

> Mrs. and Miss Lister request the
> pleasure of the company of
> . . . .
> at the opening of the Dining-Room
> at 6 p.m. prompt (!!!!!!) to-night.
> Dress optional
> (but shoes must
> NOT be muddy!)

"That last bit is Louise's!" Joanna exclaimed.

"As a matter of fact it was Mummy," Louise said composedly. "She spent ages sponging the carpet. And you know you do forget to wipe your feet half the time."

"Life's too short to think of everything!" Joanna said equably.

"I'm sorry to have to give away what part of the menu is to be," Mrs. Lister said, "but I'm wondering if we could have one of Joanna's chickens?"

"Oh, no!" Joanna exclaimed tragically.

"You're no good on a farm if you feel like that," Joe guffawed.

"I should feel an absolute murderer," Joanna declared,

and her uncle smiled across at her horror-stricken face.

"I'm afraid we must sacrifice one, Joanna. Hugh, will you see to it after breakfast?"

Hugh nodded, and glanced across wickedly at Joanna.

"Remember our bargain. If I kill it, you must pluck and draw it."

"Oh!" There was a general shout of laughter at Joanna's expression. "Oh, no! I couldn't!"

"I thought you never went back on your word?" Hugh exclaimed, and Joanna gave a wail of woe as he got up.

"Don't let me hear or see you do it!" she begged.

"If you stay here you won't," Hugh said as he went out. Mrs. Lister, used to country life, laughed.

"Cheer up, Joanna! If you're going to look after the poultry you must get used to this kind of thing."

"Paul! I'll swop my chickens for your horses," Joanna exclaimed. "They won't want to kill and eat Shamus and Jessamy."

"I hope not," Paul agreed. "But I'm not swopping. You took the poultry on of your own accord."

There was a general pushing back of chairs, but no one had gone when Hugh walked in carrying a feathered body, and Joanna cowered back in a chair with a horrified wail as he brandished it before her.

"You—you murderer! Go away. Take it away!"

"Come on," Hugh said cheerfully. "You've got to learn to pluck and draw them some time, so you might as well start now."

"Let me do it," Annie offered.

"No, Joanna's got to. Come on!" Hugh said inexorably, and with a resigned sigh Joanna rose, looking slightly green. She nearly had a relapse when she actually recognised the body, but Hugh refused to let her go back on her word, and proceeded to initiate her into the mysteries of this branch of poultry keeping.

At last the horrible task was completed, and only then did her stern taskmaster allow Joanna to escape.

"Now you'll know how to do it another time," he said cheerfully, and Joanna glowered.

"You must have the mind of a medieval torturer! I believe you've really enjoyed making me do it," she declared as he went to get on with his neglected work.

Some time later, as he was returning to the house, followed by Sarah, Hugh suddenly heard Louise calling: "Paul! Paul!" at the top of her voice, in an urgent way very different from her usual quiet manner, and almost instinctively he broke into a run, just as Paul came racing from the stables. The two boys reached the back door almost together, while Sarah panted excitedly in their rear.

"What's the matter?" demanded Hugh, as Louise hurried to meet them.

"Joanna—cut herself," Louise gasped, and the boys followed her into the kitchen, where Joanna, with a very white face, was regarding a nasty jagged cut across the palm of her hand.

Hugh's eyes glanced from a broken tumbler on the floor back to the cut. "Any glass in it?" he demanded.

"Doesn't look like it," Paul said, peering at the cut in anything but his usual indolent manner. "Got some water and bandages, Louise?"

"Oh, I feel so——" Joanna's voice faded away, and both boys grabbed at her and forced her head down between her knees, while Louise brought a bowl of water and drew a clean, unfolded handkerchief from her pocket.

"I don't know where there are any bandages," she said.

"In the left-hand drawer of the dresser," Hugh said, as Joanna gave a grunt of returning consciousness. "Thanks," he added, as Louise returned with some rolls of bandage.

Paul had already started to bathe the cut, and then between them the boys bandaged up the hand, while Joanna leaned back in her chair feeling curiously sick, and Louise carefully picked up the broken glass.

"What happened?" asked Paul, securing the bandage.

"She tripped over the cat, dropped the tumbler and fell on it," Louise said, while Hugh eyed Joanna dubiously, glad to see some colour beginning to return to her face.

She smiled up faintly at the two boys.

"Very useful having two of you keen on tying people up," she murmured.

"Oh, I'm going to be a doctor," Hugh said in a matter-of-fact tone, and all the Listers stared.

"What!" Joanna gasped, almost forgetting her faintness.

"So am I," Paul said. "That's why Louise called me."

"Well!" Hugh suddenly began to grin as if at some secret joke. "I'd not the faintest idea——"

"I never thought of mentioning it," Paul said.

"Does Uncle know?" Hugh demanded.

"Not unless Mother's told him. He's never asked me what I intended to do. Why?"

"Oh, I just wondered."

"I think that's the queerest coincidence," Joanna declared, beginning to recover a little.

"I don't know," Louise said thoughtfully. "Grandfather was a doctor, so I expect it's in the family. It's rather nice, because now you'll be able to work together."

The two boys looked at each other, and Hugh grinned again.

"It all depends. Do we set up in opposition to each other, or do we go into partnership?"

Paul glanced at Joanna's neatly bandaged hand.

"As there's such a limited number of patients, I think we'd better go into partnership. After all, we worked quite well together on this case."

Hugh smiled and held out his hand. "Partners, then!" he exclaimed, and they solemnly shook hands. Then Hugh glanced at Joanna. "Feeling fairly fit again?" he asked. "Fit enough to come upstairs?"

"I think so. Why?" asked Joanna curiously. The horrible feeling of nausea that had made her feel so faint was rapidly passing off.

"I want to introduce Paul to our surgery," Hugh said. "Come on!"

They accompanied him curiously, and Annie, who was busy making beds, popped her head out of the boys' room to see what all the noise was about. At the top of the house Hugh stopped, drew a key from his pocket, and opened the mysterious, locked door.

"There you are!" he exclaimed, throwing it open. "I wouldn't have made such a secret of it if I'd known. Your guess wasn't so far wrong, Joanna, was it?"

Horrified exclamations came from the girls, and Paul gave an ejaculation of excitement, for inside the room, against the far wall and facing the door, stood a skeleton!

"Wherever did you get it?" demanded Paul, advancing to examine it enviously.

"Uncle Bob—Sir Robert Temple—gave it to me."

"You are lucky, knowing him so well," Paul said enviously.

"You'll probably meet him some time. He often comes here for a week-end," Hugh said. "When he found out I wanted to follow in his footsteps—I'm very keen to be a surgeon—he gave it to me. And he gave me these books, too," he added, crossing to a couple of bookshelves filled to overflowing with textbooks.

His cousins looked round curiously. The room boasted two chairs, an ordinary upright one, and an old-fashioned wooden arm-chair which stood near the small, empty fireplace, a small table in the middle of the room, and a larger one against a wall, on which stood a small spirit lamp, a number of bottles and jars partly filled with mysterious powders and liquids, and a few pieces of simple chemical apparatus. These Paul examined with deep interest.

"I've collected that a bit at a time," Hugh said. "And I've given Uncle my word to be frightfully careful." He grinned. "I've no desire myself to blow the place up."

The girls, who were not interested in such scientific details, were concentrating on the skeleton.

"And to think we've been sleeping up here with that just outside our door!" Joanna exclaimed. "Hugh, why didn't you tell us?"

"I thought you mightn't like the idea of having it so near your bedroom," Hugh said. "But if Paul is to know there doesn't seem to be much point in not telling you." He glanced a little doubtfully at Sarah, but, far from being afraid, that young lady was examining the skeleton with wide, inquiring eyes.

"Do I look like that inside?" she demanded.

"More or less—a bit smaller, of course," Hugh said, and Sarah gave a sigh of relief.

"I'm glad I'm covered," she declared in a tone of considerable satisfaction. "Hugh, if I ever cut myself, will you tie me up?"

"As often as you like," Hugh promised very rashly.

"Here, you can't go pinching my patients like that. 'Tisn't professional etiquette," Paul protested.

"I'm not pinching them if we're partners," Hugh returned, sitting down at the smaller table in a most professional manner. "You know, if we're going to do things properly, we ought to keep a record of all our cases, and what treatment we give."

"So that you can tell the Coroner afterwards, I suppose," Joanna said, with a lamentable lack of faith in her medical advisers, as she sank down in the arm chair. "This is great fun. We must do a notice for your door. Now what shall we call you? I know! Drs. Dilly and Dally——"

"Sheer slander!" Paul protested. "You can't say either of us dillied or dallied when Louise called."

"It seemed ages," Joanna admitted, eyeing her bandage through which a stain of crimson was still creeping. "There seemed such an awful lot of blood."

"I wonder if we ought to get old Davies from the village to have a look at it," Hugh said, a trifle dubiously. "You didn't cut an artery or anything, fortunately, but it was a nasty cut all the same."

"Oh, it will be all right," Joanna said optimistically. "I'm always half-killing myself. Mummy says she's sure I do it to give Paul practice."

"I'm glad to hear it—I mean that you're always knocking yourself about," Hugh said. "I've not been able to get much practice with only Uncle and Joe."

"You will now," Louise said. "Sarah's pretty bad, too."

Hugh looked round sharply as he was reminded of his shadow's existence, and he and Paul spoke together.

"Leave those alone!"

"I was only looking," Sarah said plaintively as she turned away from the row of fascinating jars.

"Well don't," Paul said authoritatively. "You're not to touch *anything* in here, Sarah."

"I will if Hugh says I can," Sarah declared, retreating to her unwilling guardian, but he let her down badly.

"Sorry, Sarah. You mustn't touch any of those. Promise you won't——"

"But I want to hel——"

"You'll only help by not touching," Hugh said firmly. "Promise or you won't be allowed in here again."

Sarah's plaintive expression deepened, but Hugh was adamant.

"All right," she said reluctantly. "But why can't I if Louise and Joanna can?"

"But they're not going to touch them, either," Paul said hastily.

"I wouldn't go near them for anything," Joanna declared. She had never been fond of chemistry.

"Neither would I," Louise agreed.

Paul looked dubiously at Joanna's hand.

"I think you'd better keep it up in a sling," he decreed. "If I know you you'll be going and trying to clean out the pigsties or something with it. Have you anything we could use for a sling, Hugh?"

"I've got a scarf," Louise offered, as Hugh rather doubtfully opened a drawer neatly stocked with lint, bandages and other medical equipment.

"I say! You've got everything," Paul exclaimed approvingly, as Louise slipped across to her room for the scarf.

"I keep some downstairs so that I can get at them quickly, and the rest up here," Hugh said.

"And Uncle lets you deal with all the casualties?"

Joanna asked, as Paul took the scarf from Louise and improvised a sling out of it.

"Yes, he says it's all practice for me," Hugh said, shutting the drawer again. "Well, let's go down, or they'll be thinking we're all lost." He shepherded them out, and carefully locked the door again. "I've got another key somewhere, Paul. I'll dig it out and let you have it."

Paul gave him an appreciative glance as they followed the girls downstairs.

"You're being very sporting, sharing with me."

Hugh gave the pleasant smile that altered his face so completely. "It will be much more fun working together—and we can probably help each other a lot."

"Wherever have you all been?" asked Mrs. Lister, as they clattered into the kitchen, and then added resignedly: "Oh, Joanna, what have you been doing now?"

"While you were out getting the vegetables I dropped a glass and fell on it," Joanna said cheerfully, as if that were quite a common occurrence. "So Drs. Dilly and Dally gave me first aid."

"Who?" asked Mr. Eldon.

"The boys," Louise explained. "Uncle, did you know they both want to be doctors?"

"Both?" their uncle repeated, looking at Paul curiously. "No, I didn't. I've meant several times to ask Paul what his ideas for the future were, but——"

"They're going to be partners," Sarah said. "An' Hugh's been showing us his lovely skeleton——"

Her dutiful children broke into delighted laughter at Mrs. Lister's expression.

"Not *Hugh's* skeleton," Joanna chuckled. "But one he's got in his mysterious locked room. You see, I was quite right, Mummy."

Mrs. Lister stared at her nephew, who had laughed as much as anyone at her bewildered expression.

"A skeleton! Wherever did you get that?"

"Bob Temple gave it to him," Mr. Eldon said.

"Do you still see him now you live here?" Mrs. Lister asked curiously.

"He often drops in for a day or two when he feels he needs a change and can get away," Mr. Eldon said. "He never gives us any warning—he just arrives, and we fit him in somewhere."

"I'd like to see him again," Mrs. Lister said. "It must be years since we met."

"You probably will," her brother assured her. "As he hasn't been just lately he's liable to turn up any day." He laughed. "Do you remember when you pushed him in the brook because he would tease you?"

"He used to pick me up and dump me in a bramble bush whenever I annoyed him too much," Mrs. Lister said reminiscently. "Has he altered much?"

"Not at all," Mr. Eldon said promptly, and the younger ones shouted with delighted laughter at the idea of the famous surgeon dumping Mrs. Lister in a bramble bush.

As the laugh died down Mr. Eldon turned to Joanna.

"But how is your hand? Is it bad?"

"It's still bleeding a bit," Joanna said carelessly, "but it will be all right."

Her uncle glanced at his nephews.

"I did wonder if we ought to ask old Davies to come along," Hugh said.

"He's over at Fontroy Royal," Joe interpolated unexpectedly, having just returned from the village. "I saw him go."

"Well, if it doesn't stop bleeding soon I'll try and get

in touch with him," Mr. Eldon said. "I know the boys will have done their best, but it may need a couple of stitches."

"Oh, it will be all right," Joanna said easily.

After lunch they scattered, and while Mrs. Lister and Louise put the finishing touches to the dining-room, and set to work on the unusually good dinner they had planned, the two boys disappeared into the stables together, whence came fragments of medical knowledge as they compared notes.

Sarah would have followed them, but Joanna, finding herself badly handicapped, called on her for assistance, and for once Sarah actually found herself in demand and pattered round happily in Joanna's wake.

It was quite late in the afternoon when they finished, and, forgetting all about Sarah, who wandered off on her own devices, Joanna strolled off to look for the boys. The sound of voices took her to the paddock, where Paul, mounted on Jessamy, was practising trotting, while Hugh, seated on the gate, shouted instructions.

"Where's Sarah?" he asked, as Joanna joined him and watched Paul critically.

"I don't know. I've lost her," Joanna said absently. "Paul, let me try."

"You can't with your arm in a sling," Paul said quickly, as he rode up to them, looking distinctly heated.

"I can take it out," Joanna retorted, suiting the action to the word. "I——"

She broke off as Sarah's voice came to them, raised half in triumph and half in fright.

"Hugh, come an' tie me up. I've got a lovely cut——"

Hugh had swung himself over the gate and was off before Paul could scramble off Jessamy, and Joanna, with a sigh of resignation, set off after him, while Paul brought up the rear. As they ran, Sarah, her face a study of mixed emotions, came to meet them with blood streaming down her bare arm.

"I did it," she shrieked. "I didn't think I could, but I did! I only meant to make a little cut, but it's ever so big. You said you wanted practice, Hugh, an'——"

She broke off with a gasp of mingled surprise and fear as a car which had, unnoticed by them all, been coming slowly down the rutty lane, pulled up beside her and the driver jumped out and swung her up in his arms.

"Bring my bag, Hugh," he ordered, and bore her, despite her protests, into the house, while the others followed, Hugh clutching the bag he had pulled out of the car, and Paul and Joanna wondering who the stranger could be, though they strongly suspected that their uncle had fulfilled his threat and sent for Dr. Davies.

"I don't want you, I want Hugh," Sarah protested as the stranger sat her down on a chair in the empty kitchen and proceeded to examine her arm with a practised eye. "I did it because Hugh said he wanted practice."

Hugh groaned. "You little idiot! You didn't do it on purpose?" he exclaimed ungratefully.

"Yes, I did," Sarah proclaimed proudly. She tried to pull her arm away from the stranger. "I don't want you to do it—I want Hugh to."

"Hugh can't do this," the stranger declared, though his blue eyes were beginning to twinkle suspiciously. "But he can bandage you up after I've done the rest. My bag, Hugh—and some water——"

Hugh brought the bag forward, while Paul got a bowl of water, and then they and Joanna watched with deep interest as the newcomer dealt expeditiously with the gash.

"There!" he said. "Now you can carry on if that will appease her, Hugh." He surveyed Sarah with amused eyes. "Just how did you manage to do it?"

"On the scythe," Sarah said proudly, watching complacently as Hugh bound up her arm. "Can I have my arm in a sling, too, like Joanna?"

The stranger turned to survey Joanna in perplexity as she furtively and somewhat guiltily slid her arm back into its sling at this reminder.

"Just what is this? A suicide club, or is Hugh paying you so much to allow yourselves to be practised on?"

"Mine was an accident," Joanna said hastily. "But Sarah's so horribly literal. Just because Hugh said he was glad to have some practice——"

"She *will* try to be helpful," Paul sighed. "You've no idea how wearing it is."

The stranger's amusement deepened.

"It must be, if this is a fair example."

"We'll have to lock up the scythe now, too," Paul went on. "Thank heaven she doesn't think she needs to give me practice."

"I will if you like," Sarah offered cheerfully, gazing proudly at her arm. "Hugh, I want a sling."

"We'll have to see if Louise has another scarf," Paul said resignedly, and the stranger, trying to hide a smile at Sarah's autocratic tone, looked at him curiously.

"Do I gather you're another recruit for the medical profession?"

"I hope to be," Paul said. "I did enjoy watching you at work."

A curious light—probably of amusement—shone in the stranger's eyes, and Hugh grinned as if at some great joke.

"I wish you'd have a look at Joanna's hand," he said.

"Paul and I did our best with it, but I'm not too happy about it. It's a horribly jagged cut."

Joanna backed hastily. "No, it's all right. I'm sure it is. I told Uncle he needn't send for you——"

The stranger stared, and Hugh suddenly began to chuckle.

"This isn't Dr. Davies," he exclaimed. "He's at least eighty——"

"Not a day more than sixty-five," the stranger said, and Joanna stared at him, for he himself could not be more than forty—indeed, he looked less—with his slim, vigorous figure, fair hair, and curiously boyish grin.

"Then—then who are you?" she exclaimed, a sudden suspicion dawning on both her and Paul.

"This is Uncle Bob—Sir Robert Temple," Hugh chuckled. "No wonder you enjoyed watching him at work, Paul!"

Paul crimsoned, and Sir Robert laughed.

"I appreciated the compliment. Come along, Joanna! No arguing! Let me see what their work's like." Joanna reluctantly capitulated, and let him remove the bandage. "Yes, that will be all right," he announced. "But don't try to use that hand."

"This sling's an awful nuisance," Joanna grumbled.

"But highly necessary with Johnny," Paul declared, beginning to recover a little. "She'll probably try to clean out the hen houses to-morrow."

"I shan't," Joanna said calmly. "Sarah and I did them this afternoon."

"Which no doubt accounts for the bandage," Sir Robert said gravely, taking a fresh one. "I wondered what you could have been doing with it—only my guess was that you'd been sweeping the chimneys."

F.D.

B

Joanna laughed up at him. "It is pretty filthy, isn't it? But I didn't dare let Sarah do them on her own. Goodness knows what would have happened!"

Sir Robert laughed delightedly, while his eyes sought Hugh, wondering what effect his cousins had on him; and he was pleased to see that Hugh laughed back.

"You don't know Sarah yet," he said warningly.

"I'm beginning to think I do," Sir Robert said. "Oh, here's John! Can you put me up for a day or two?"

"Of course," Mr. Eldon said, obviously quite used to this question, and not at all surprised at the sight of his visitor. "I was telling Ruth only to-day that you were liable to turn up at any moment." Then his eyes fell on Sarah, who was leaning back in her chair with a delightful sense of importance. "What's been happening now?"

Everyone explained at once, the heroine of the occasion as loudly as anyone, and her uncle, used though he now was to her, stared incredulously.

"You actually cut your arm on the scythe on purpose!" he exclaimed despairingly, wondering whether it would be easier to lock up all the farm implements, or to keep his youngest niece herself under lock and key.

"It's Johnny's fault for letting her out of her sight," Paul remarked.

"I like that!" Joanna exclaimed. "How can I guess what she'll think of next!"

"Well, I shouldn't think anyone would have expected that," Sir Robert said soothingly, and then swung round as Mrs. Lister came in. "Ruth! I see your children resemble you very closely."

Mrs. Lister smiled as she held out her hands.

"Bob, how are you? You haven't altered a bit! What have the children been doing now? I suppose it's Joanna or Sarah," she added resignedly, and then caught sight of her youngest daughter. "What *has* she been doing?"

"I want a sling like Joanna's," Sarah said firmly. "Hugh——"

Hugh turned in desperation as Louise came in and stood hesitating near the door, obviously wondering who the stranger was.

"For the love of mike, have you got another scarf, Louise?" he demanded. "Sarah, if ever you do anything like this again—we'll just leave you to bleed. Do you understand?"

Sarah, seeing Louise go for the scarf, beamed seraphically.

"Yes, Hugh—but you did get practice bandaging me, didn't you? An' I'll keep getting it nice and dirty so that you'll have to keep on doing it over again."

Sir Robert watched in obvious amusement as Hugh obediently fixed her up with the required sling. He had wondered very much how the taciturn, self-contained boy would mix with a family of cousins, but he had never dreamed of seeing him the resigned slave of an autocratic young lady of ten, who, despite her imperiousness, was prepared to go to such lengths solely for his benefit.

This operation completed, Joanna went off to feed her poultry and Hugh to do the milking, and it took the united efforts of her mother, Paul and Sir Robert to stop Sarah following her cousin, and instead to deposit her in an armchair in the sitting-room, with Woggles for company, and strict instructions to rest quietly for a while after all the excitement. Then Paul, suddenly remembering that Jessamy had not been unsaddled, went off to see to him, while Louise turned to her uncle in perplexity as she began to collect dishes on a tray.

"What happened?" she asked, and then nodded when her uncle explained. "I half expected something like that. She was far too interested in Joanna's hand, and in Hugh's room upstairs. I hope she never has a chance to get at those chemicals up there."

"Another one for the medical profession?" Sir Robert asked with interest, and Louise laughed.

"Oh no, but she follows Hugh round like a dog, and insists on meddling in everything that concerns him," she explained.

"That should please Hugh!" Sir Robert said dryly, but Louise shook her head as she picked up her tray.

"As a matter of fact, he's astonishingly patient with her," she admitted a trifle wistfully.

She always felt that if her cousin could be so patient with Sarah, he might have forgiven her unfortunate words a little more readily, for though he was now always quite polite to her, she was convinced that underneath he had neither forgotten nor forgiven. Sir Robert did not miss the faint note of wistfulness, and silently resolved to discover what it was all about.

"Let me take that tray," he said, suiting the action to the word. "Where do you want it?"

"In the dining-room—but you mustn't go in——" Louise was beginning, and then stopped again as she remembered that she did not even know the identity of the visitor. "I—at least—we——"

"Ruth and Louise have been doing up the dining-room," Mr. Eldon said, "and no one has been allowed to see it yet. But the official opening takes place to-night, so you've just arrived at the right moment, Bob."

Louise stared at the youthful-looking stranger holding the tray.

"Are you—Sir Robert Temple?" she hazarded, suddenly remembering the conversation at lunch-time.

"I am. And you must be Louise. I've heard about you all in Hugh's letters," Sir Robert returned, and Louise eyed him uncertainly, wondering what her cousin had said about her.

"How's Hugh getting on with you all?" Sir Robert went on, noticing her doubt.

"Oh, quite well," Louise said cautiously. "And now he and Paul have found they both want to be doctors, I expect they'll get on better still."

"I'm glad to hear they've decided to collaborate," Mr. Eldon said, looking pleased.

"Obviously Hugh doesn't dislike Sarah," Sir Robert observed with considerable amusement.

"It wouldn't matter if he did," Sarah's mother said with laudable but unmaternal frankness. "If she's decided in his favour, that's all there is to it."

"Sarah, as you can tell, bears a strong resemblance to her mother at the same age," Mr. Eldon said gravely.

"So I've noticed," Sir Robert agreed. He had known the Eldons all his life, being, in fact, the son of the farmer whose land they had haunted as children.

Mrs. Lister suddenly laughed.

"Bob, do go and put that tray down somewhere," she exclaimed. "You can't stand holding it all evening."

Both men laughed, and Sir Robert obediently deposited the tray on the dining-room table.

CHAPTER NINE

PAUL ON TRIAL

WHEN THE company gathered in the sitting-room, Mr. Eldon looked round proudly. Louise was a picture in pale blue, Joanna looked almost pretty in a glowing pink, and Sarah was a dainty elf in pale green. The two boys, too, had changed in honour of the occasion, and altogether a general air of smartness pervaded the assembly.

"Well, a family of this size is a change after just two of you," Sir Robert remarked, just as Joe, also dressed up in his Sunday best, appeared at the door to request their presence in the dining-room.

That gloomy chamber was completely transformed. Instead of dark tapestry wallpaper, cream walls showed up the dark woodwork. Odd pieces of silver and brass, well polished, were scattered about, great vases of tawny and yellow dahlias made vivid splashes of colour here and there, the Listers' books filled the shelves of the alcove, and, instead of the usual lamp, the table was illuminated by candles set in a pair of antique silver candlesticks and the quaint china one the girls had so much admired in the sitting-room. Rain was blowing up out of doors, so the long curtains were drawn already over the creeper-framed window, and in the light of the candles and the leaping flames of the log fire Mrs. Lister looked in a perfect setting as she sat at the table, her green silk dress shimmering in the ever-changing light.

Even the boys exclaimed at the picture, and Sir Robert

looked round appreciatively as Annie, thoroughly enjoying herself, came bustling in with the chicken.

"Typically Ruth!" he exclaimed.

"And Louise," Mrs. Lister added, with a smile at her eldest daughter. "She's done a lot of the work."

"I envy you, John," Sir Robert declared.

"I'm wondering why on earth I didn't insist on them all coming long before," Mr. Eldon declared, gazing round. "It's a miracle, the way they've transformed this room. I should have given it up as hopeless."

"I told you it had possibilities," Mrs. Lister said triumphantly. "And so has the rest of the house. Louise and I have all sorts of ideas for it."

"You can get on with the house when the bad weather comes," her brother said. "At present I want more help out of doors. There are the last of the plums to be picked, and then the pears and apples——"

"Can I have some of the fruit?" Mrs. Lister asked. "You seem to have large stocks of jars, and I'd like to bottle some fruit and make some jam for the winter."

"Take all you want," Mr. Eldon said. "I know we're going to be a large family to feed, so make sure you keep plenty."

Louise began to look interested. She liked making preserves.

"That sounds nice. And perhaps later, when the blackberries are ripe, we could make some bramble jelly," she suggested.

"There's a crab-apple tree simply covered with fruit," Joanna said. "Crab-apple and blackberry together——"

"Won't you all come and live with me?" Sir Robert asked. "You're making my mouth water. My housekeeper never goes to all this trouble for me."

"We'll give you some when it's made," Joanna promised. "Louise loves making jams and things, and they're always delicious."

"If you're not careful, John, I shall be adopting Louise," Sir Robert said, and she smiled a little shyly at him.

"I'm not really such a good cook. It's just that Johnny happens to like jam."

"We *all* like jam," Sarah said gravely, making good headway with her meal despite her injured arm.

"It's a pity Sarah won't be able to help to pick the plums, isn't it?" Paul remarked to the table at large, and his youngest sister flashed him a look of deep suspicion.

"What do you mean?"

"You'll need two hands for that," Paul said. "If you hadn't gone and hacked yourself about like that——"

"I can do it with one hand," Sarah asserted, though looking round uneasily. "Can't I, Hugh? And anyway, if I can't, Joanna can't."

"You'll both have to sit about indoors until the cuts have healed—won't they, Sir Robert?" Paul said, turning to appeal to the surgeon with deep gravity.

"Paul, stop teasing," his mother said, while Sarah gazed at Sir Robert in dismay. Then she turned to her usual Court of Appeal.

"I can go out and help pick, can't I, Hugh? If *you* say I can——"

The entire table dissolved into a shriek of delighted laughter at the idea of Hugh's opinion counting for more than Sir Robert's.

"Do leave her alone, Paul," Hugh said resignedly. "Yes, you'll be able to help, though not as much as if you could use both hands. It was a silly thing to do."

"All right, I won't do it again," Sarah promised

thoughtfully. "It wasn't a very nice feeling, anyway."

"I shouldn't think it was," her uncle agreed gravely.

Sarah's face lit up as she gazed at her cousin in sudden inspiration.

"But I'll tell you what, Hugh! Do you like bumps and bruises?"

"On you or me? Not particularly in either case."

"To tie up, of course," Sarah declared, her face falling at his palpable lack of enthusiasm. "Because I could get some of those quite easily."

"I don't want to tie you up at all," Hugh declared, while the others watched his harassed face with great enjoyment. "Look here, Sarah, if you keep knocking yourself about you can't be half as much help to me."

Sarah considered this as she masticated a mouthful of tart. Then she reluctantly nodded.

"No, I s'pose not," she agreed. Then her face lit up again. "But I'm always getting them without trying, so that's all right, isn't it? You'll tie me up then, won't you?"

"*And* gag you, if this goes on much longer," Paul said. "And no one will blame him."

"Ruth all over again!" Sir Robert murmured reminiscently, no doubt thinking of the bramble bushes, and Mrs. Lister laughed.

"Bob, I will not have you undermining my authority— if any—by disclosing all the misdeeds of my past." She pushed back her chair. "Have you all finished? Then let's clear away, and——"

"No, you go and sit down and rest," Sir Robert ordered. "This is where I start working. Now let's get this organised properly. Joanna and Sarah are no use, so they can go and keep you company, but the boys and Louise can come and help me. If I wash up, Louise and Hugh can wipe, while Paul can put everything else away."

"What about me?" asked Mr. Eldon meekly.

"You can all run away and leave it to us," Sir Robert said firmly.

"Annie and I must see to your room now dinner's safely over," Mrs. Lister said. "Will you be quite comfortable in that dressing-room off John's room?"

"Perfectly," Sir Robert said easily. "I thought I'd probably have to go upstairs with the skeleton now the house is so full."

"You couldn't *sleep* in there with it, could you?" Louise asked with a shudder. "I don't really even like to think it's on the same floor as us."

"I could sleep anywhere if I was tired enough," Sir Robert said.

"I *like* the skeleton," Sarah observed. "It's Hugh's."

"I thought it belonged to the partnership now," Joanna laughed. "Sir Robert, did you know I've christened them Drs. Dilly and Dally?"

"Perfect!" Sir Robert exclaimed delightedly, while those eminent medicos looked highly confused and glared at the cheerful Joanna. "I've never heard anything better. But I wish you wouldn't keep Sir Robert-ing me. Can't you all adopt me as an honorary uncle as Hugh has done?"

"Of course," Joanna agreed promptly. "I thought when I said it how horribly stiff it sounded—especially as you used to dump Mummy in bramble bushes."

"I used to——" Sir Robert broke off and subjected Mr. Eldon and Mrs. Lister to a severe glare. "Just who has been talking?"

"Then it's really true?" Joanna demanded gleefully, and Sir Robert looked suitably guilty.

"I'm afraid so—but only under strong provocation, I assure you," he added, and then hastily changed the subject. "But come along, or we shan't be finished before bedtime."

He swept Louise and Hugh off before him in a manner that brooked no denial, and as the others followed, Paul gazed blankly at the table.

"You might tell me where everything goes, Johnny," he begged. "I haven't the faintest idea."

"Fancy Sir Robert Temple doing the washing-up!" Joanna exclaimed delightedly, as she helped him to clear the table. "But I do like him, don't you? It would be a pleasure to be operated on by him!"

"Hugh was telling me all about him this afternoon," Paul said. "He thinks an awful lot of him."

"I think Sir Robert is very fond of Hugh, too," Joanna agreed. "I suppose we should try to get used to saying Uncle Bob, but somehow it seems positively presumptuous, doesn't it?"

"From what Hugh was telling me, although legally he's Uncle's ward, Uncle and Sir Robert have always behaved as if they're his joint guardians. Fancy having Sir Robert Temple as one of your guardians, and living in the same house," Paul said enviously, so carried away by the thought of his cousin's luck that he carefully put away some used knives and forks.

"Paul! Do think what you're doing!" Joanna exclaimed, pouncing on him in exasperaton and firmly removing the cutlery from the sideboard drawer. She wrinkled her brows thoughtfully. "I wonder what made Uncle come and live out here in the wilds? It obviously wasn't because he'd quarrelled with Sir—with Uncle Bob."

"Especially as he was doing awfully well at the Bar,"

Paul added. "It does seem rather eccentric when you think about it."

Out in the kitchen Sir Robert was washing up in a capable manner that surprised Louise, and he laughed as he caught her watching him.

"You see, I was brought up properly in my youth, and I always take my share of any work that's going when I come here. It's a nice change—almost as good as camping out. So you're the domesticated member of the family?" he added, curious to find out why Hugh's accounts of her had been so lukewarm compared with what he had said about the others.

"I suppose I am," Louise agreed. "At least, I'm not awfully keen on the humdrum work, but I love making things look nice."

"I know how you feel," Sir Robert nodded understandingly. "You're like me. You like to take an artistic pleasure in your work. Now Hugh's weakness is thoroughness."

Hugh, who had been wondering at Sir Robert's unexpected interest in Louise, started, and nearly dropped a plate at suddenly finding himself the subject under discussion.

"Yes, I suppose it is," he agreed shortly.

"It definitely is. Whatever you do, you have to do thoroughly, whether it's working or playing."

"Joanna's rather like that," Louise said thoughtfully, surprised to find how easy it was to talk to the visitor. It did not occur to her that it was part of Sir Robert's work to persuade people to talk to him freely. Then she looked round rather apprehensively as Paul and Joanna came into the kitchen. "Where's Sarah?" she asked uneasily, and Paul grinned.

"Probably collecting some bruises for Hugh's benefit. I can't help feeling hurt. She wouldn't even prick her finger to help me, and yet she's known me all her life."

"That's why," Joanna said promptly.

"I wish she felt the same about me," Hugh groaned. "I feel somehow as if that cut was my fault."

"Rubbish!" Joanna retorted. "Nobody can be responsible for any ideas Sarah gets in her head."

"I shouldn't have left the scythe about," Hugh said gloomily.

"If you hadn't done, she'd have got at it all the same once she'd made up her mind to it," Paul said reassuringly. "Or if she couldn't get that she'd have used the carving knife. I suppose we should really be glad she didn't try to cut her throat."

As they all laughed Mrs. Lister came into the kitchen and looked round. "Where's Sarah?" she asked.

"Hasn't she been with you?" Louise returned.

"No. I thought she was probably with Hugh."

"She's up to something," Joanna said with conviction as her uncle, too, joined them.

"I suppose she isn't in the sitting-room?" Sir Robert suggested, drying his hands.

"Not when everyone's out here," Paul said, but he was wrong. When they entered the sitting-room they found that young lady seated in an armchair in chilly dignity, with Woggles at her feet.

"Why didn't you come to help us?" asked Sir Robert, looking down at the small figure in much amusement.

"Because I wasn't wanted," Sarah returned with a dignity marred rather by the pathetic droop of her mouth. "You said I couldn't help, an' you wouldn't let Hugh do my cut when I'd done it specially for him, an'——"

Mrs. Lister turned a despairing eye to the visitor, who, however, seeing now how the land lay, ignored his obvious unpopularity and, picking Sarah up bodily, sat down in her place and deposited her on his knee.

"Listen, Sarah. That cut was too bad for Hugh to deal with——"

"He an' Paul did Joanna's," Sarah protested, unconsciously revealing where the trouble really lay. "And hers looked nastier than mine."

"Yes, I know, but it wasn't really. Hers was all jagged and the flesh was all torn, but your cut went much deeper, and if I hadn't dealt with it quickly you'd have lost more blood than you could really spare, and that would have been very serious."

Sarah's gloom lifted a little as she gazed up appraisingly into his face.

"Is my cut really much worse than Joanna's?" she asked, a faint touch of pride in her tone.

"Much more serious," Sir Robert answered with becoming gravity. "Joanna wouldn't have lost half as much blood as you would have done."

"But Joanna nearly fainted," Sarah protested, still not too willing to be convinced. "An' I didn't. I don't know how to," she added somewhat regretfully, and Joanna hastily smothered a giggle.

"I expect it was the shock of the fall that affected Joanna," Sir Robert said, wondering what objection Sarah would think up next. "Or perhaps she faints more easily than you do. But your cut was definitely more serious than hers."

Sarah nodded, a touch of importance in her air.

"Then it wasn't just that you wouldn't let Hugh do it?"

"Good gracious, no!" Sir Robert returned. "When

anyone is very badly hurt their ordinary doctor calls in a specialist to deal with it, and that's what Hugh did with you. He knew it was too difficult for him, so he left it to me."

"Was it too difficult for Paul, too?" Sarah asked, still a trifle suspiciously, and Mr. Eldon gave a peculiar choke that might have been a hastily smothered laugh, while Louise turned away hastily to hide her face. Sir Robert however, preserved his gravity admirably.

"Definitely. He couldn't have done it, either," he answered, and Sarah cogitated for a moment, while the others found it more difficult every minute to hide their amusement.

"But you called Hugh to help with the washing-up, an' Louise went to help him instead of me," she protested, and Sir Robert bit his lip, while Hugh ran a despairing hand through his hair. At times Sarah was completely beyond him.

"I told both my patients to go and rest, but whereas you were good and did as I told you, Joanna disobeyed my strict orders," Sir Robert said, and at long last Sarah was satisfied.

"I didn't think of that," she said complacently, and, wriggling off his knee, sat down beside Woggles on the hearthrug with a satisfied air.

"What a handful!" Sir Robert laughed later that evening when all but he and Mr. Eldon had gone to bed.

"Sarah's a character, isn't she?" Mr. Eldon agreed. "Of course, she follows Hugh like a pet dog, so one could understand her attitude to a certain extent, but her jealousy because Joanna was treated by the boys and she wasn't, was rather amusing."

"I don't seem to have much of a reputation at Long

Barrow," Sir Robert said, sounding quite pleased about it. Then he grew serious. "Why doesn't Hugh like Louise as much as the others?" he went on unexpectedly, and Mr. Eldon stared at him for a moment.

"I hadn't realised it showed quite so plainly. I think probably because of something he overheard just after they came," and Mr. Eldon told the story of Louise's unfortunate remark.

"So that's it," Sir Robert commented. "Knowing Hugh, I don't think he'll forget it very easily."

"No!" and Mr. Eldon sighed. "It's a pity. I'm fond of them all, and I wanted them all to be good friends. I'm glad the two boys have found something in common."

"You couldn't get two more unalike," Sir Robert remarked musingly. "So far as force of character is concerned, Joanna is more like Hugh's sister."

"I think I've got a particularly soft spot for Joanna," her uncle confessed, "though I wouldn't let the others know for anything. I hate favouritism."

"I like Louise," Sir Robert said thoughtfully. "Sarah's very amusing, of course, but she's rather a spoilt young woman——"

"The youngest often is," Mr. Eldon interjected. "But I refuse to have you criticising my family——"

"*My* family! I like the pride in that possessive pronoun! Ruth won't be able to call her children her own soon. And you don't want to make Hugh jealous, John."

"I shan't. Hugh knows he's really mine. After what that boy's done for me I'd be a pretty rotten specimen if I ever let anyone take his place. When I think that he could have stayed on with you—and how much help that would have been to him—and that instead he chose—and insisted on coming—to bury himself here with me—

but I've made up my mind. If Ruth decides to stay with me, he's going back to London to start studying seriously the moment he's old enough, whatever I do. I suppose he and Paul will go together now. I hope so, anyway, though I haven't had a chance to talk to Ruth about it yet." He yawned and stood up. "I don't know about you, but I'm tired. We keep early hours here."

"All right, there's no need to be offensive about it," Sir Robert retorted. "But I do *not* intend to rise at five-thirty to-morrow."

"I'll wager you won't stay in bed much after six," Mr. Eldon returned. "It's not the old days when Hugh and I got up and went straight out of doors. You'll have the girls galloping and calling all over the house, and the entire family trying to get Paul out of bed."

"He has my sympathy," Sir Robert declared. "All right, I'm coming."

When he wandered out of his room the following morning, much earlier—as Mr. Eldon had prophesied—than he had intended, he found the house a hive of activity. Annie was cooking breakfast, Mrs. Lister making the tea, Louise was setting the table, Paul came in with an armload of firewood, Joanna was feeding the poultry, and Hugh was busy at the well, superintended by Sarah and Woggles.

Although it had rained hard during the night, it had stopped now, and the sun was shining brilliantly on a rain-washed world.

"It's glorious!" Joanna exclaimed, coming in. "And I'm so hungry."

"How's your hand?" asked Sir Robert.

"Oh, all right, thanks," she replied easily, and then chuckled. "What you said to Sarah was most effective. When Paul asked how her arm was, she said: 'You must ask my specialist!' She's frightfully proud about it. But you should just see her bandage! Mine's pretty grubby, but she's been nursing our babiest pig, and although it's perfectly sweet, it really *is* a pig!"

"Hugh can keep putting a fresh one on top," Sir Robert said, strolling to the door. "That will keep them both amused."

After breakfast Mr. Eldon swept them all off to the orchard armed with baskets and ladders, and they spent a hilarious morning there stripping the plum trees of their purple fruit.

"I feel that so far I know less about Paul then any of them," Sir Robert remarked reflectively to Mr. Eldon as they strolled across the orchard together. "Is it all pose, or is he really as careless and indolent as he appears?"

"As far as his brain is concerned, he's brilliant," Mr. Eldon said promptly. "And I think he'll go far in whatever profession he takes up. He seems to have no difficulty whatever in grasping any subject, however obscure. As far as physical effort or practical responsibility are concerned, however, he's only just becoming aware that they exist."

"Assisted by you, I gather," Sir Robert said, looking amused. "Ruth has been telling me the story of the firewood that wasn't. I like a mother who has sense of humour enough to appreciate the deficiencies and backslidings of her children."

"Yes, I'm doing my best to wake him up," Mr. Eldon agreed. "Unfortunately Joanna has been awfully bad for him until now."

"Joanna?" Sir Robert looked across speculatively to where she was standing under a tree shouting instructions to Hugh.

"Yes, she's so ready to accept responsibility that Paul has been quite content to let her. However, I'm hoping that Hugh will wake him up a bit."

"I should have thought from what you say that he'd be inclined to sit back and let Hugh shoulder all the responsibility."

"No, I don't think so," Mr. Eldon disagreed. "You see, there is a certain amount of rivalry underneath."

In the afternoon Mrs. Lister and Louise set to work making jam and bottling some of the fruit, which Annie selected carefully, and Joanna helped as well as she could with her one hand. Sarah probably would not have joined them, but to her great disgust Sir Robert took the two boys out for a walk across the windswept downs, while Mr. Eldon rode to the village and so, finding herself deserted, she joined the party in the kitchen and proceeded to get in everyone's way.

"If you don't stop Sarah eating plums soon she'll be sprouting shoots," Joanna declared, as she once again caught Sarah's sound hand in the basket of fruit she was examining. "Don't you think she ought to do some lessons, Mummy? She hasn't done any for two days now."

"Neither have you," Sarah retorted, determined to fight for her liberty. "An' I'm not going to do lessons when no one else is. I wish Hugh would come back. I don't think I like Uncle Bob."

Up on the downs Sir Robert and the boys were enjoying striding along in the face of a brisk wind.

"This is good!" Sir Robert exclaimed, gazing across line after line of downs. "I always wonder, when I'm here, why I didn't stick to farming like most of my ancestors."

"There is something very satisfying about it," Hugh said, "but then, I always do enjoy a good hard tussle with anything."

"I'm afraid I can't say the same," Paul said, with a fleeting grin at himself. "Uncle will tell you I'm bone lazy," he added, turning to Sir Robert.

"I haven't noticed it," the latter remarked, refraining from committing himself on what their uncle had or had not said. "I admit you haven't got Hugh's bulldog technique, but I should imagine that if ever you did take anything really seriously——"

"Most people would tell you I never do," Paul said, and Sir Robert looked at him questioningly.

"But what do you say yourself?"

Paul grinned. "Oh, I'm serious enough about some things. F'rinstance, I've never had the slightest doubt about what I intend to be—only it never seems to me much use talking about things until they're a *fait accompli*— but that doesn't make me any the less determined." For a moment his expression of determination left no doubt as to his being Joanna's brother; then it faded. "Which makes it the more surprising that I'm talking to you about it now."

"I don't think so," Sir Robert said. "After all, we all three have the same interest."

Tea was ready when they reached Long Barrow, and they were quite ready for it.

"This jam's extraordinarily good," Sir Robert declared, helping himself liberally.

"It would be better if it was quite cold," Joanna said critically. "Being still slightly warm doesn't improve it."

"I refuse to agree. It's perfect," Sir Robert exclaimed,

and Louise went quite pink with pleasure, for she had been responsible for the jam.

"I think we'll do some work to-night," Mr. Eldon remarked when the meal was over.

"Not when we've a visitor," Joanna protested.

"We don't count Bob as a visitor. He's one of the family," her uncle declared. "Besides, he can lecture to you to-night and give your mother and me a rest."

"What on?" demanded Joanna. "If it's going to be skeletons and corpuscles and all those awful, long words Paul revels in, I shall go on strike. My brain just couldn't cope with them."

"Don't worry, I'm here for a holiday," Sir Robert said hastily, rather to the regret of the boys. "I shall just sit back and listen."

"Nobody will dare to say anything before such a distinguished audience," Joanna said demurely.

"It would take more than that to stop you talking," Paul said, and Louise laughed.

"I don't believe Joanna's ever been shy or afraid of anyone in her life," she declared, a trifle enviously.

"Are you?" asked her uncle.

"Often," Louise said frankly, and Hugh eyed her in some surprise. She always looked so quietly sure of herself that he had never thought of her as being shy.

When they had all settled down, there was a moment's pause.

"What's the subject to-night?" asked Sir Robert with interest. "And are you all at the same stage?"

"It depends on the subject," Paul said. "We are in history, geography and English; Hugh and I are ahead of the girls in Latin——"

"Well ahead," Joanna declared with a groan.

"Louise leaves us all standing in French," Paul went on, and Sir Robert flashed a quick glance at that young lady, who looked quite embarrassed.

"I've had more opportunities than the others," she murmured quickly, almost as if she felt she ought to make some excuse.

"And what is Joanna ahead in?" queried the visitor, smiling at her cheerful face.

"Nothing," Joanna declared, apparently quite pleased and content with this state of affairs. "Anyway, don't forget I'm younger than the others."

"No one would think it, to hear her order us about," Hugh remarked with a teasing glance at her, and Joanna laughed.

"If I didn't we'd never get anywhere half the time. What are we starting on to-night, Uncle?"

"*Richard II*," her uncle said, and Louise picked up a much-used volume of Shakespeare.

"The trouble is that we always all want to read the same parts," she remarked.

"Except for the fact that Joanna won't read Richard if she can help it," Paul said lazily.

"I've no time for him, either in the play or in history," Joanna said severely in her most forthright tone. "I like a man who knows his own mind, and isn't a silly, petty tyrant. Give me Bolingbroke! Now he was a man!"

Her elders all laughed at her trenchant tone.

"I mean it," she insisted. "And Hamlet's just as feeble. If I'd been Hamlet I'd have killed the uncle in the first act——"

"But then there wouldn't have been any play," Paul pointed out.

"Hm! There is that to consider, I suppose," Joanna

conceded. "But I do like books and plays about people who know their own minds——"

"But if they always did, half the books and plays couldn't be written," Sir Robert objected, enjoying himself vastly.

"And a good thing, too," Joanna said firmly.

"What a blessing for the family that women got the vote before Joanna's time," Paul remarked. "I know she'd have been a suffragette, and it would have been so embarrassing for the rest of the family to have her chaining herself to railings in Downing Street——"

"I should have thought it might have been a relief," Louise laughed. "At least we'd have had some peace while she was harrying the Premier."

"Well, there is that way of looking at it," Paul agreed.

"We seem to be wandering from the point," Mrs. Lister said, and Louise opened the volume.

Sir Robert listened with interest as they read, and with even more interest when they discussed the scenes afterwards, even Sarah putting in her comments. If Louise's contribution was merely that of any average schoolgirl of her age, Joanna's was original in the extreme, and while of the boys, Hugh's was extremely matter of fact and to the point, Paul, as his uncle had said earlier, betrayed unmistakable brilliance in his grasp of the subject.

The discussion finished, Mr. Eldon demanded essays that had been written during the past two or three days, but a howl of protest arose.

"Wrong order!" Joanna proclaimed. "With a visitor here, you can't expect us to read our poor efforts after he's been listening to Shakespeare."

"Read them?" Sir Robert queried.

"Yes. Uncle always makes us read them aloud," Paul

said with a grimace. "He says it makes us used to the sound of our own voices. Personally, I feel it's highly unnecessary in Johnny's case, but——"

"You're all right," Louise said, "but I never was much good at essays, and mine always sound far, far worse read aloud than when they're being written."

"Unmitigated drivel," Joanna agreed. "No!" she howled, as everyone laughed. "I don't mean Louise's, I mean that's how I feel about mine."

"What's the subject?" asked Sir Robert, with a quick glance at their uncle, who was lying back lazily in his chair with Sarah on his knee.

"The Brontës," Mr. Eldon answered, smiling slightly as he caught his friend's glance. "And we always start with the youngest and work up. Now, Sarah!"

"And does Sarah know much about the Brontës?" asked Sir Robert in some surprise, as Louise passed Sarah a much dog-eared exercise book.

"Yes. There were three of them and they wrote books and died," Sarah said triumphantly, not a whit abashed by the general merriment with which her information was received.

"Somehow one feels the same fate should overtake certain other authors," Sir Robert said appreciatively, "only not necessarily *after* writing."

"Go on, Sarah!" Mr. Eldon said encouragingly, preserving his gravity with a strong effort, and thus encouraged, Sarah read through two pages of large, laborious writing which contained little more information than she had already given them.

Joanna followed with an essay that, although written in a crude, schoolgirl style, was original enough in its matter, and not a little amusing in parts. Louise followed (out of turn, but she had refused to be the last) with a perfectly normal, average effort, and Hugh in his turn read a well-thought-out piece of work which met with an approving smile from both his aunt and uncle. Then Paul read carelessly an essay that made Sir Robert glance sharply at Mr. Eldon, who gave him a triumphant nod.

The reading finished, Mr. Eldon proceeded to criticise and award marks, thereby displaying his magnificent memory, for he did not need to glance at one essay to refresh his recollection of it, but Sir Robert said nothing on the subject until he and his friend were alone that night.

"Was that essay Paul's unaided work?" he demanded.

"It was," Mr. Eldon nodded. "I can vouch for that because I sat and watched him write it. Do you believe me now?"

"And he's the same in everything—not just English?"

"Every subject. He just doesn't need to make any effort at all. French is probably his weakest subject—he isn't particularly interested in languages—but he's better than average even in that."

Sir Robert nodded thoughtfully.

"In any case I'd like to do my best for Ruth's boy—but now that I know this—I'll do all I can for both him and Hugh. So don't kill him with overwork—I mean physical, not mental work."

Mr. Eldon laughed as he pictured the imperturbable Paul.

"Don't worry. He'll see I don't do that."

CHAPTER TEN

HUGH'S MEETING

Sir Robert's visit had meant the postponement of the next meeting of the Society, and as Hugh did not mention it during the next few days his cousins were beginning to wonder if he had forgotten it was his turn to play host, or even if he was deliberately ignoring the fact, when Sarah, full of a delightful sense of importance, came round and summoned them all to a meeting by the pond. Hugh was already there when they arrived, and plunged into his subject without any preliminaries.

"I've got an idea for our next meeting, but I can't do it without your help," he declared, rather to their surprise. "Particularly Louise's," he added, a little uncomfortably.

"I'll do anything I can," Louise said willingly, feeling that his singling her out was a good sign.

"Don't commit yourself until you know," Paul said warningly. "He might want you to finance it."

"He wouldn't get much," Louise laughed. "I believe I have about sevenpence-halfpenny in hand at the moment."

"What do you want us to do?" demanded Sarah, turning curiously to her cousin.

"Well, I've spoken to Uncle, and he agrees that it would be a good idea to have a Harvest Home——"

"Oh! What fun!" Joanna exclaimed, without waiting for him to finish.

"My idea was that we should only eat our own home-grown produce——"

"So that's where I come in?" Louise laughed. "Chief cook?"

"Yes, I wondered if we could prepare the whole thing, and let Aunt Ruth and Annie just be guests——"

"Annie won't like that," Joanna declared.

"We must assert our authority," Paul said gravely.

"It all depends on what you want to eat," Louise said doubtfully, turning to Hugh.

"Uncle says we can have a goose, and then there'll be vegetables, and I suppose you could make fruit tarts or something like that?" Hugh asked. He had evidently put in quite a lot of thought on the subject.

"I don't know about the goose," Louise said dubiously, "but if Joanna will help me, I could manage all the rest."

"And just what are you boys going to do towards the entertainment?" asked Joanna suspiciously.

"We'll take on the job of decorating the place," Hugh said. "Should we hold it in the kitchen or the barn?"

"In the barn," Joanna said promptly. "We'll be using the kitchen."

"How many will we have to prepare for?" Louise asked apprehensively.

"Uncle, Aunt Ruth, Annie and Joe, and five of us. Oh! I wonder if we could get George——"

"Who's George?" demanded Sarah.

"Joe's friend. He's got an old fiddle, and he can play anything on it."

"This sounds great fun," Joanna said enthusiastically. "I'm really looking forward to it. When shall we have it?"

"I thought the day after to-morrow," Hugh said. "Paul, would you like to ride to the village with me to ask George if he can come?"

"I can't," Paul said reluctantly, with a grimace. "I got

behind with the logs while Uncle Bob was here, so I must try to get some done."

"Joanna?"

"Give me ten minutes to change," Joanna said eagerly, and within that time she ran downstairs clad in a new pair of jodhpurs of which she was so proud that Paul declared he believed she even wore them in bed.

Louise watched them go rather wistfully, and then went slowly into the house. Her mother was in the sitting-room marking their French exercises, and she looked round with a smile which held a trace of anxiety.

"What's the matter? You look very depressed."

"I was just wishing I wasn't too scared to ride," Louise said dolefully. "I do get tired of never being able to get far away from here unless Uncle takes me in the car."

Mrs. Lister's forehead creased in a frown. She had been thinking for some time that it was not good for Louise to be so shut away without any means of escape. The other three were all making such good progress in their riding lessons that their uncle now permitted Paul and Joanna to go out alone, while Sarah often went with Hugh, so that they were all more or less independent.

"It is a pity," she agreed. "Don't you think you could make an effort?"

"No!" Louise gave a little shudder. "It isn't that I don't like horses, but the only time I got on one I felt so far from the ground and so horribly insecure."

Mrs. Lister said no more, for she knew that Louise had a bad fear of falling, but she thought a lot during the rest of the afternoon and evening, and the following morning set off on a private exploring expedition round the farm buildings, with the result that when Hugh came bolting into the barn, looking for Paul, he found his aunt meditatively regarding a trap that had been standing there since long before Long Barrow came into Mr. Eldon's hands.

"Is there anything organically wrong with this, or is it just that no one ever uses it?" she asked in her quick, impulsive way as she swung round to face him.

"So far as I know, it's all right," Hugh said. "Why?"

"Because I want it," his aunt said briskly. "If I could drive that I could go into the village whenever I felt like it, instead of having to drag your uncle away from his work to take me in the car."

"It is a pity you can't drive the car," Hugh agreed, surveying the trap doubtfully. He was afraid it would take a lot of cleaning to make it usable again.

"It is, but I've never wanted to learn," Mrs. Lister confessed. "What about the horses? Oh, there's John! John, come here!"

Her brother came, accompanied by Joanna, and surveyed his excited sister whimsically.

"What bright idea have you got now?" he demanded.

"This!" Mrs. Lister exclaimed, indicating the trap. "Could I drive either of the horses in it if it was cleaned up a bit?"

A smile of approval crossed Mr. Eldon's face. "A splendid idea! You'd be quite independent of me then. Yes, I believe Uncle James used to drive Jessamy in it."

"But can you drive?" inquired Joanna in some surprise.

"Of course I can," her mother declared. "And ride, for that matter—though I haven't been on a horse for years."

"Don't you ever tell us anything?" Joanna asked severely. "Fancy hushing all that up!"

"I just didn't think of mentioning it," her mother laughed. "Who'll help me to spring-clean it?"

"Leave it to us," Hugh said quickly. "We'll clean it."

"Yes, we'll do it," Joanna agreed. "I'll go and find the others."

"And I'll look out the harness," Mr. Eldon said, always willing to do anything to make life pleasant for his sister.

Joanna soon returned with Paul and Louise, and followed by Sarah.

"We'll want plenty of water," Hugh said, surveying the trap critically. "And we'll need polish for the brasswork. Come and help me with the water, Paul."

Louise at first surveyed the old trap with horror, but as it improved in appearance she began to think vaguely that it might have possibilities, although it never once entered her head that her mother was having it cleaned entirely for her benefit.

They spent a merry but damp morning on the trap, which certainly looked a completely different vehicle by the time they had finished work on it.

"I wish Mummy could try it at once," Joanna said, but her uncle, who had been called to admire the result of their labours, shook his head.

"No, Joe and I must overhaul it first."

There was great excitement when, later, the trap was finally pronounced fit for the road, and the entire family assembled to see Mrs. Lister take her place in it and gather up the reins in a highly professional manner.

"Are you sure you're all right?" Hugh asked, rather anxiously. His aunt always looked so young and small that he found it difficult to take her seriously.

"She may be out of practice now, but I can remember the time when she'd drive anything," Mr. Eldon said, chuckling reminiscently. "She and Bob used to scare the lives out of people——"

"Now John! You're undermining my authority," Mrs. Lister said warningly. "You can stand away."

Mr. Eldon, who had been standing at Jessamy's head, stepped back, and off went the trap, leaving no doubts whatever as to Mrs. Lister's capabilities as a driver as she steered neatly through the gateway and up the lane. Then she stopped and looked back.

"Louise, you want to come into the village with me, don't you?" she called.

"Can't we all come?" Joanna asked breathlessly, as the entire pack ran up the lane to join her.

"I've got some work to do," Paul said, somewhat mysteriously.

"So have I," Hugh said. "But all the girls could go."

In an astonishingly short time the trap was bowling down the road along the top of the downs at a spanking trot that the girls found most fascinating.

"It's nearly as much fun as riding," Joanna said.

"I believe I'd like to be able to drive," Louise said thoughtfully, watching the calmly confident way in which her mother handled reins and whip, and Mrs. Lister was delighted to find that there was no need for the suggestion to come from her.

"I'll teach you," she said promptly. "Then you'll be able to go to the village as often as you want."

"I was thinking that," Louise confessed. "And somehow it doesn't look half as frightening as riding."

They had now reached a long, level stretch of road, and Mrs. Lister pulled Jessamy up.

"You can have your first lesson at once," she remarked, and while Joanna and Sarah watched enviously, Louise, not a little apprehensively, actually found herself in charge of the reins. Fortunately Jessamy behaved well, and as, to her mother's relief, nothing occurred to shake her nerve in any way, they returned home with Louise waxing enthusiastic about the new equipage.

The following afternoon the two elder girls took over the kitchen, while the two boys, assisted by Sarah, who had been sworn to secrecy, continued with the metamorphosis of the barn, which Paul had started in the morning while Hugh, having killed a goose, was preparing it for cooking—a usurpation of her work at which Joanna did not raise a single protest when she discovered what he had been doing. The stuffing caused the girls some anxiety, but once the goose was safely in the oven they were able to give their attention to the vegetables and tarts.

Out in the barn, the boys were proceeding with the decorations. Their mysterious work the previous afternoon had been the manufacture of a number of turnip lanterns with which they proposed to illuminate the barn; Paul made intricate patterns with carrots and tufts of hay flanking two or three huge marrows; while Hugh disposed other vegetables about with careless abandon.

"I can't help thinking it looks rather like a church at Harvest Festival," Paul said, stepping back.

"Not with those lanterns," said his uncle's voice behind him as Mr. Eldon stood in the doorway surveying the effect. "I'm glad it's likely to be a warm evening. I'm rather surprised you aren't holding it in the kitchen."

"The girls are working there, and there's more room here for after supper," Hugh explained.

With the lanterns lit, the barn really looked very festive when the company collected. Sir Robert, hearing about it in some mysterious way (it was strongly suspected that Mr. Eldon had rung him up) stole a few more hours from his patients and turned up at the last minute, claiming that as he had helped to gather in the plum crop he had a right to be present. To the relief of the girls their cookery turned out very successfully, and George the Fiddler, as Joanna had christened him, arrived in good time, and enlivened the company with snatches of tunes between the courses, thereby easing the rather long waits as everything had to be brought out from the house.

When everyone had eaten his or her fill and the table had been pushed back, Sir Robert, who was in high spirits and had insisted on making a most amusing speech, jumped up and, without waiting for his hosts, demanded *Sir Roger de Coverley* to start the ball rolling. George, nothing loath, struck up that irresistible air at once, and Sir Robert led Mrs. Lister forward. As the boys looked at each other in dismay, Mr. Eldon caught hold of Louise and ran her on to the floor, and Joanna eyed her brother and cousin severely.

"One of you must ask Annie," she said firmly.

"But I don't know it," Hugh protested cravenly.

"You'll soon learn," Joanna said inexorably. "Go on, Paul! I know you hate dancing, but you've got to do your duty. I'll teach Hugh. Sarah, go and ask Joe to dance."

Joe, wearing his broadest beam, willingly led Sarah on to the floor, and as Joanna dragged her reluctant cousin after her, Paul gallantly led Annie out.

Once the dance started in earnest the fun grew so infectious that even the two boys forgot to feel awkward and embarrassed, and bounced and hopped as gaily as anyone, while Sarah pranced up and down without ceasing.

"She reminds me of Mr. Pickwick," Joanna muttered breathlessly to Hugh as they joined hands and the others ducked underneath the arch, and he grinned back as he recognised the reference.

"I feel more like old Mrs. Wardle," he gasped. "How long does this go on?"

At last the music stopped, and the dancers dispersed.

"What now?" demanded the insatiable Sarah, while her exhausted elders gladly sat down to recover.

"As soon as he's got his breath back Joe's going to give us a song," Paul said, and their faithful henchman grinned sheepishly, but did not refuse, having already been approached by the Masters of Ceremonies.

"Look! It's a real harvest moon," Louise said from the door, and several of the others joined her to watch the great yellow orb just rising from behind the downs.

"It's a lovely evening," Mrs. Lister said appreciatively. "But I think Joe's ready now."

Looking larger than ever, and infinitely more sheepish, Joe entertained them in a strangely mellow baritone with an old Wiltshire song that brought loud applause.

"Now we'll have musical chairs, if George will play for us," Paul announced. "And don't be too rough."

Everyone but Paul, who was running it, entered for this, and the fun waxed fast and furious when only Sir Robert, Joanna and Hugh were left in. George entered into the fun and the music went on and on until the three thought he was never going to stop.

"Look here!" Hugh protested. "We can't go on for ev——" Even while he was speaking the music stopped abruptly, and although he made a dive for a chair, he was too late.

"Johnny's always in last," Sarah exclaimed, dancing with excitement. "Ooh! Johnny!"

Amid a roar of delighted laughter the music stopped

again, the last two dived for the chair, and Joanna slid gracefully to the floor, leaving Sir Robert in possession.

One game followed another, and the time fled unnoticed until Mr. Eldon, glancing at his watch, exclaimed in astonishment that it was after eleven.

"We can't break up just yet," exclaimed Paul, who had been officiating as M.C. by himself during the absence of Hugh. "They're just—oh, here they are!" he added in relief as Louise entered with a tray of sandwiches and cakes, while Hugh followed bearing two large jugs of steaming coffee.

Sir Robert watched with approval, and then turned to Mrs. Lister, who also looked pleased to see them apparently working together quite amicably.

"I hope he's getting over it gradually," she said. "I told Louise the only way to make him forget it was to keep on behaving as if she certainly didn't think it now."

"Mummy! A sandwich?" Louise asked, coming up to them, her face bright with enjoyment, and certainly showing no signs of boredom. "Hasn't it been fun?"

"It certainly has," Sir Robert said, helping himself. "It's been well worth having to rise with the lark tomorrow to drive back to Town. Thank you, Hugh," as he was handed a cup of coffee. "I wouldn't have missed this for anything."

"Bless you, you should have let me do this," Annie protested, as she was provided with coffee.

"I say, couldn't we finish with *Sir Roger*?" Hugh asked, when everyone had been served, and he grinned as the girls laughed. "Well, it's not like ordinary dancing," he said in excuse. "I enjoyed it."

"You look as if you did," Joanna laughed.

"I'll dance with you this time," Sarah said with imperious condescension, bolting a piece of cake in order to say it before anyone else could, and then having to be patted on the back by Paul as she choked. "Come on," she added eagerly, as soon as she had recovered.

This time Annie was led out by Mr. Eldon, Mrs. Lister danced with the beaming Joe, looking like a sprite beside a giant, and Sir Robert pulled Joanna on to the floor, while Louise and Paul followed more decorously. Determinedly forgetting that he was a famous surgeon, Sir Robert flung dignity to the winds and, ably aided and abetted by Joanna, turned the dance into a complete romp, while George, entering into the fun, played faster and faster, until it finally ended in the collapse of all but two couples, Sir Robert and Joanna, and Hugh and Sarah, who stuck it out gamely until George gave in.

"You idiots!" Louise laughed helplessly. "Fancy trying to do *Sir Roger* with only four of you."

"It certainly doesn't give you much rest," Sir Robert declared, mopping his face. "Is this really the end of the revels?"

"I think it will have to be," Mrs. Lister declared. "As it is, I'm sure Sarah's too excited to go to sleep."

"Never mind, we don't often have an evening like this," remarked her brother, who had enjoyed himself as much as anyone.

"It's been our best evening yet," Joanna declared, and as the others agreed a pleased light shone in Hugh's eyes. When Joanna had first suggested these meetings he had never dreamed for a moment that they would get so much enjoyment out of them.

CHAPTER ELEVEN

SARAH ENTERTAINS

LEARNING TO drive proved to be the beginning of a new interest for Louise, and one that got her out in the fresh air far more. She also had the satisfaction of knowing that she was being taught properly, for even her inexperienced eyes could tell that her mother drove extremely well, and Louise could never bear to do anything if she could not do it correctly.

Mrs. Lister entered into this new interest with equal keenness, and every day they took the trap out for an hour or two in the afternoons, sometimes with one or both of the other girls as passengers, and explored in every direction until, as she became familiar with the country beyond the downs that hemmed in Long Barrow, Louise began to lose the feeling of being trapped and imprisoned that had been growing stronger as the others went out riding more and more frequently, and her spirits increased in cheerfulness as her proficiency in driving grew. It was not long before her mother allowed her to go by herself, and then she felt really independent.

While these driving lessons were going on, the boys settled down to work together in earnest. Doctors Dilly and Dally now had an established practice up in the surgery, and it was surprising how frequently the rest of the family—to say nothing of Annie and Joe, who enjoyed the fun immensely and had a truly astonishing number of minor mishaps—found it necessary to consult them. Indeed, the two doctors began to suspect the existence of a conspiracy and several times taxed their patients with it; without success, however.

Sarah, in particular, was so delighted with the idea that she nearly lived in the surgery, and bade fair to become a perfect valetudinarian, while Joanna was forever arriving claiming to have the most astonishing diseases, from housemaid's knee to water on the brain (in this case both doctors heartily agreed with her), or even, on occasion, impossible-sounding diseases she had made up herself. She would enter the surgery, sit down comfortably, reel off a list of impossible symptoms with a gravity and volubility that left the medical practitioners breathless, and finally dissolve into shrieks of laughter as they strove to stem the tide of words. They tried to retaliate by prescribing the most unpleasant treatments they could devise, but as she never took their advice they were invariably left at a decided disadvantage.

"What's going on here?" Joanna opened the surgery door one day and popped her head in curiously, for as she ran upstairs she had been met by a chorus of loud and frantic barks and roars of laughter.

Mrs. Lister was sitting in a chair with her head well back, with Hugh standing beside her, while Paul vainly chased a frantic Woggles round the room.

"Aunt Ruth has got something in her eye, and every time I touch her Woggles nearly goes mad," Hugh explained, and gave a sigh of relief as, with a quick movement, Joanna fielded the dog and swung it up under her arm. "Do put her out for a minute. I'll never do this while she's here." Joanna accordingly ejected Woggles, and then watched with interest as Hugh investigated, it being his turn to deal with a case. "It's one of your eyelashes," he exclaimed. "I think I can get it. There!"

Mrs. Lister blinked as he stepped back triumphantly.

"Thank you," she said gratefully.

"Has anyone seen Sarah?" queried Joanna, remembering why she had come now the excitement was over. "It's her turn to run the meeting to-night, but neither Louise nor I have heard if she's got any plan."

"She has thought of something," Hugh said, "though she hasn't told me what—just dropped all sorts of mysterious hints," he added.

"I suppose she isn't by any chance in your bedroom?" queried Paul. "I've noticed some peculiar bumps and bangs going on there. As a matter of fact, until you came bouncing upstairs I thought it was probably you."

"I'll have a look," Joanna crossed the landing and flung open the bedroom door, disclosing Sarah, an expression of determination on her small face, tugging at the foot of the double bed.

"Whatever are you trying to do?" asked Mrs. Lister, as she and the boys came to look over Joanna's shoulder.

"Move it back here," Sarah said.

"You'll hurt yourself," Paul said. "Where do you want it?"

"But why?" asked Joanna, as the boys moved the bed according to Sarah's directions.

"For to-night," Sarah said mysteriously, and refused to tell them any more.

The four older ones looked at her expectantly when tea was over, and swelling visibly, as Paul said, with importance, she beckoned them mysteriously to the stairs.

"Up in our bedroom to-night," she announced. "Uncle, can we have a lamp up there, please?"

"Of course." Mr. Eldon said willingly. "Hugh, will you get one from the snuggery?"

Up in the bedroom Sarah turned and surveyed the other four. "Sit down," she ordered, indicating the beds. "Now to-night we're going to have a concert. There are lots of things in the closet to dress up in, an' each one has to do something in turn."

Hugh looked appalled, but the others laughed.

"We might have known!" Louise exclaimed. "Sarah loves any excuse for dressing up."

"You needn't talk! We're all as bad as each other," Joanna said.

"But I haven't any party tricks," Hugh protested, staring at Sarah in horror. "I don't mind acting audience, but I can't act or sing or anything."

"*Everyone's* got to do something," the Mistress of Ceremonies said firmly. "Joanna's an' Louise's an' your evenings went off well. You're not going to spoil mine."

This was an appeal that could not be ignored, and Hugh sank down on a bed a prey to a bad attack of stage-fright.

"I've got an idea," Joanna murmured in his ear, "if you can't think of anything yourself."

"Just what?" demanded Hugh, eyeing her suspiciously, but Sarah demanded silence.

"I'll begin if you like," she offered kindly, and disappeared forthwith into the closet armed with a large torch she had abstracted from Paul's room.

"I didn't say she could have that, but I suppose it's safer than a candle in there," he said resignedly, while they all made themselves comfortable on the double bed.

In a remarkably short space of time Sarah returned in a dress of the eighteen seventies, much too long for her, and with a large Edwardian hat balanced precariously on her small head. The effect was so ludicrous that the entire audience collapsed, and the boys rolled helplessly on the bed, while Joanna and Louise, seeing the entertainer's offended expression, tried to prod them into a due sense of decorum. When order had finally been restored, Sarah broke into song, and treated them to *Lily of Laguna*, sung with much expression and in a surprisingly sweet and clear voice. Hugh sat up and stared in surprise, and Joanna gave a little nod.

"Sarah and Louise both sing like birds," she declared.

"So does Johnny—like a crow," Paul added.

"*Shurrup!*" the singer exclaimed, pausing for a moment in her song to direct a withering glance at the offenders.

"She got that idea from one of those Edwardian show films," Louise murmured under cover of the applause.

"Now!" Sarah said, "who's next?"

"Come on!" Joanna jumped up from the bed and pulled the two boys up as well. "We'll do a charade."

"Oh, goody!" Sarah exclaimed, so proud of her borrowed plumes that she did not stop to change before climbing on the bed beside Louise. "Hurry up."

The three actors retired into the closet, from which explosive chuckles came until the door opened and the boys emerged, both clad in voluminous skirts and bonnets, although whereas Hugh, looking highly self-conscious, was evidently a staid matron, Paul, in delicate pink, made a positively ravishing girl with his fair skin and hair, while his coy looks made Louise laugh till she cried, and she went off into another paroxysm when Joanna entered, clad in a pepper and salt Victorian suit, much too large for her, and an old-fashioned bowler. While "Mamma" discreetly looked the other way, Joanna proceeded to go down on her knees and propose to the fair charmer. As Hugh was only now discovering, all his cousins had a decided flair for burlesque, and Paul's coy simpers made his "mamma" double up in helpless laughter and nearly spoil the scene.

"I can't help it," Hugh gasped painfully, when the other actors protested. "You can't see yourselves!"

"Do go on," Joanna urged. "I'm getting cramp in my knees. Can I or can I not wed your daughter?"

Forewarned now, Hugh was more successful in preserving his gravity in the next scene, perhaps because he and Joanna were supposed to be two giggling pupils in a young ladies' seminary run by Paul; while the last scene, three ladies drinking tea and talking gossip left the two on the bed in a puzzled silence until Louise's face suddenly cleared.

"*Candid!*" she exclaimed, and her guess was acclaimed by the actors.

"You now!" Sarah announced, and Louise obediently disappeared into the closet, reappearing shortly after dressed, to her cousin's astonishment, as a rakish Edwardian cockney. It had certainly never occurred to him that his neat, dainty cousin could ever cheerfully make such a sight of herself. With a bedraggled feather boa tossed round her neck, and a large hat set at a rakish angle, she came forward without any sign of shyness and beamed at the two gentlemen.

"Me first song, ducks, is dedicated to two well-known perfessional gentlemen," she announced, and to the delight of Joanna broke into "We Dillied and Dallied", while the boys laughed helplessly. Her song was greeted with roars of applause, the boys drumming on the floor with their heels, until Annie, who had come up to her room next door for something, peeped in to see whatever was happening.

"Come in and sit down," Joanna said hospitably.

Annie settled herself on the single bed near the door as Louise, discarding the boa, straightening her hat, and picking up a parasol, gave them *Daddy Wouldn't Buy Me a Bow-wow*, and everyone joined in the chorus the second time, Annie as loudly as anyone.

"Now something straight," Joanna urged. Perhaps because she could not sing a note herself, she was very proud of her sister's voice.

"All right! Only you must give me a minute to change," Louise declared, betraying that she, too, enjoyed dressing up. "Paul, you do something while I'm out."

Paul, who was still attired in his voluminous skirts, cogitated for a moment, slid off the bed, and then pulled Joanna aside and whispered something.

"All right!" she agreed with a chuckle, and, having pulled up a couple of chairs, they proceeded to give the famous quarrel between Sairey Gamp and Betsey Prig from *Martin Chuzzlewit*, a favourite with both of them. There was, of course, a considerable amount of gagging, but not for a moment did they lose the atmosphere, and Hugh and Annie rocked helplessly with laughter, while the closet door was seen to open slightly so that Louise could follow their performance while she changed.

This scene ended, Louise appeared again, clad in a pale blue dress of the eighteen thirties and proceeded to sing *Alice Blue Gown* in a voice that was only now really given a chance to do its best.

Hugh gazed at her with a new respect.

"I'd no idea you could sing like that," he said frankly. "Oughtn't you to have your voice trained?"

To his surprise Louise looked positively embarrassed, and shot a swift glance at Joanna, who gave the questioner a quick, silencing frown.

"Perhaps I shall—some day," Louise said awkwardly.

"You ought to have invited your mother and uncle to see this," Annie said, gazing at them all admiringly.

The light that always betokened some fresh idea shone in Joanna's eyes.

"Let's!" she exclaimed. "Not now. But let's give it all over again and invite Mummy and Uncle and Annie and Joe."

"No!" Hugh said firmly. "I don't mind making a fool of myself with just us here——"

"But they'd love it," Sarah wailed, unable to bear the thought of missing such a wonderful opportunity for dressing up.

"What? Hugh making a fool of himself?" Paul inquired.

"He isn't making a fool of himself—not any more than the rest of us, anyway," Joanna conceded.

"I believe they would enjoy it," Louise said. "After all, it is quiet here for them as well—and you must admit we've had some good laughs to-night."

Hugh capitulated abruptly.

"Yes, I hadn't looked at if from their point of view. All right, I'm game! But couldn't you let me stage manage or something? I'd be much happier."

"We must arrange a proper programme," Joanna said, getting down to business without loss of time. "And then rehearse——"

"I think we're funnier unrehearsed," Paul objected.

"No doubt, but we ought to have some semblance of order," Louise said.

"While you talk it over, I'll go and make you some cocoa and something to eat," Annie offered.

"You angel!" Joanna declared, breaking off the discussion to give her a hug. "But don't tell anyone about this yet, will you?"

"Not a word," Annie promised, probably deriving more pleasure from the plan even than they were.

Over sandwiches, cakes and cocoa the programme was thoroughly discussed and finally settled, and the rest of the evening developed into a rehearsal, with everyone frankly criticising everyone else, and no one agreeing with any one other person. Despite these drawbacks, however, considerable progress was made, and a few days later the performance was given before a delighted audience who laughed till they cried.

"I've never enjoyed any show in Town as much as this," Mr. Eldon gasped, wiping his eyes after a spirited dance by Sarah, who had insisted on wearing one of the long dresses for it, with the result that she measured her length on the floor no fewer than five times.

"She wanted Hugh to be her partner in a *pas de deux*," Joanna said, leaning over her mother's shoulder. "You should have seen his face!"

Louise's voice aroused general admiration, while Sairey Gamp and Betsey Prig received so much applause that they had to give the whole scene over again.

Sir Robert received several and varied, but all highly coloured, accounts of the performance, for he now received letters from most of the family, and he laughed over them nearly as much as if he had been present, and wrote back at once demanding a repeat performance at Christmas, when he would be at Long Barrow.

Sarah was delighted with the success of her evening and its sequel, and Paul, the only one who had not yet prepared an evening's programme for the Society, racked his brains for something that would rival the other efforts.

For several days he was unusually taciturn, and the others, guessing the cause of his preoccupation, watched him curiously until one day his face cleared, and he disappeared from sight into the snuggery, firmly locking the door, to the annoyance of Louise and Joanna, who had wanted to retire there to struggle with a Latin unseen.

"Go up to the surgery," Hugh suggested, hearing their complaints. "I shan't be going up there because Uncle wants me to help him outside. But be careful to lock the door when you come down. I don't want Sarah to get in there by herself."

At first Louise had found it difficult to behave as if nothing was wrong in the face of his obvious hostility, but she had persevered, and Hugh, finding at their meetings that she was nearly as much fun as Joanna, though in not quite so riotous a fashion, and that she had never since those first days shown the faintest sign of looking down on him, was gradually coming round, although he still could not quite forget her stupid words.

Louise herself, with the interest of looking forward to each meeting and wondering what form it was to take, was looking quite different from the forlorn damsel who had gazed round at the isolated Long Barrow in such dismay.

"In the snuggery to-night," Paul announced on the evening of their next meeting, and they crowded in curiously. "Now, if you will kindly seat yourselves," he went on gravely, taking up a commanding position on the hearthrug, "we'll start with a quiz."

"Oh! We might have guessed he'd choose something to make us use our brains," Louise said ruefully.

"Any prizes?" demanded Joanna suspiciously.

"Yes. Presented by Uncle," and Paul indicated a basket

of fruit on the table. "For the one who loses least points
during the evening. After the quiz we'll have a spelling
bee, and then——" The remainder of his speech was lost
in groans from his audience.

"Don't we work hard enough?" Joanna demanded.

"Ask me easy ones," Sarah begged.

"I've endeavoured to suit the questions to your mental
capabilities," Paul announced gravely, and Joanna leaned
back comfortably in her chair.

"That puts me out altogether. Thank you, Paul!"

Despite their groans and complaints, however, they
really enjoyed themselves, and loud and tumultuous
applause greeted the announcement at the end that
Joanna, of all people, had won the prize.

"It's a fluke!" she declared, as Paul gracefully presented
it to her, although as a matter of fact, having a quick
brain and a retentive memory, and being a keen reader,
her general knowledge was very good—a fact of which her
family were quite aware.

"This evening has been as much fun as any," Louise
said, as Joanna handed the basket round, and they all
refreshed themselves with her prize. "Even if we have
had to work hard."

"What happens next time?" asked Hugh, surprised
to find how eager he was for their meetings to continue.

"Start all over again with Johnny," Paul said, while
the two elder girls exchanged a swift smile of congrat-
ulations at Hugh's unconscious admission of his interest
in the future of the Society, and Sarah beamed happily.

"Mine spread over two evenings, and no one else's
did," she announced proudly.

CHAPTER TWELVE

JOANNA PLAYS EAVESDROPPER

LOUISE RAN out of the house, laughing as she pulled on her gloves, just as Sir Robert got out of his car.

"A happy Christmas Eve to you!" he exclaimed, thinking how much happier she looked than the first time he had seen her. "Where are you off to?" he went on, as the boys and Sarah came bursting out to greet him.

"I'm just going to the village," Louise answered, while the boys fell upon his luggage and bore it into the house.

"Shall I run you there?" he asked, half turning back to the car, and Louise laughed again—suddenly looking very like Joanna at her most mischievous.

"No, thanks! But if you hadn't only just arrived I'd have offered to drive you there," she declared, as Joe led Jessamy and the trap into view.

"I'll accept your invitation all the same," Sir Robert said promptly. "Sarah, tell your uncle and mother that Louise has kidnapped me and borne me off in her magic chariot, and that I'll see them later."

"But the boys will be furious if I do take you," Louise demurred. "They've been watching for you all day."

"They'll see enough of me while I'm here," Sir Robert said, calmly handing her up into the trap, and getting in after her.

Louise picked up the reins and they set off, Sir Robert calmly waving to his perplexed host, who had just come round from the stables, and to the two infuriated boys, who stood glaring after the retreating vehicle. It was a

dull, grey afternoon with the sun setting in a red ball
behind some leafless trees, and a crisp touch of frost in
the air that made their faces tingle as they bowled merrily
along to the brisk clip-clop of Jessamy's hoofs.

"We went out yesterday and got masses of holly," Louise said, keeping a firm hand on Jessamy, for the keen air
was apparently going to his head and making him feel a
little above himself. "I drove Jessamy, and Paul and
Hugh took it in turns to ride Shamus. We went miles,
and had great fun. Hugh knew all the best spots."

Sir Robert quite enjoyed himself in the little village
shop, trying to identify the mingled odours, while Louise
gave her order. Then they stacked her purchases in the
trap and set off for home along the fast darkening road.

"I'm glad I came with you," he said, as they climbed
slowly uphill under a dark archway of trees. "It's much
too dark and lonely for you to be out alone."

"I don't mind so much driving, but I'd be terrified
walking," Louise confessed. "I'd meant to set out earlier,
but got delayed." She chuckled. "Well, I wasn't really,
but I just had to stay and watch. Joanna was so funny.
Hugh went out and killed a couple of chickens, and then
he made her help him to pluck and draw them, and you
know how she hates doing it." She gave a little shudder
herself. "I can't help feeling Hugh should be awfully
good at dissecting."

"He's certainly got very steady nerves," Sir Robert
agreed.

It was almost dark when they reached their destination,
and Sir Robert looked round guiltily as they made their
way into the lamplit kitchen after handing over the trap
to Joe.

"I hope I'm forgiven for disappearing like that, but if

you will allow the young ladies of the family to wander round the countryside in the dark alone——"

"I was so relieved when I heard you'd gone with her," Mrs. Lister exclaimed, as they deposited their parcels on the table. "I sent Paul out to go with her, but you'd just gone, so he would have been too late in any case."

"She shouldn't have stayed to laugh at me," observed Joanna darkly.

"I believe Hugh's been keeping you to your word?" Sir Robert said, turning to her in amusement.

"Yes, the beast!" Joanna said, and Hugh laughed.

"You brought it on yourself."

"I said I'd help," Sarah remarked gravely from a corner where she was sampling a surreptitious mince pie.

"We've got to *eat* the chickens," Joanna pointed out.

"Poor Sarah!" Sir Robert laughed. "I see you're still not appreciated properly yet."

Hugh grinned across at his small cousin, who beamed back at him adoringly.

"You don't do so badly, do you, Sarah?"

"No, I help Hugh a lot," Sarah declared, and Louise looked at her suspiciously.

"Just what have you got there? Sarah, it's not one of the mince pies!"

"I thought you'd like someone to try them," Sarah said in a deprecating tone as she retired cautiously behind Hugh, and Louise sighed.

"Mummy, I can see we'll have to lock the larder door."

"We certainly shall," Mrs. Lister agreed. "John, what have you got?" she added accusingly, and Mr. Eldon eyed her guiltily as he hastily swallowed something.

"Well, Sarah and I thought they looked so tempting——"

"I'm glad we're going to be fed well," Sir Robert remarked, creating a diversion.

"You'll need to be," Mr. Eldon said darkly. "They've saved all sorts of jobs for you to do to-night."

"Just what?" demanded his guest, looking alarmed.

"Helping us to put up the holly," Joanna said, dancing round excitedly. "I think this Christmas is going to be great fun, there's such a crowd of us."

It was certainly a very merry group that gathered round the table for tea, and Sir Robert glanced in amusement at Hugh, as, seated between Joanna and Sarah, he carried on a cheerful argument with the former as to the best way of decorating the house. It was hard to realise that he was the same boy. The slightly sulky expression appeared very seldom now, and the teasing smile with which he was regarding Joanna made his face look quite attractive.

As soon as tea was over Sir Robert was called upon by first one and then another to help with all sorts of things, some highly secret, like the Christmas tree prepared ostensibly for Sarah's benefit. At the cost of many pricked and scratched hands holly and mistletoe were distributed round the house, and it was late in the evening before everything was ready and the family settled down for a few minutes' rest after supper.

Hugh found the change from the previous Christmas Eve very great. Then he and his uncle and Sir Robert had been alone, and he was wondering vaguely whether he could really have enjoyed it as much as he had thought he did, when Louise, who had been out into the kitchen, came in humming a carol, and immediately Joanna and Sarah joined in. Louise had not even realised that she was singing, and she broke off in surprise for a moment; then with a laugh she went on, her voice and Sarah's

more than balancing Joanna's cheerful disregard of all
the rules of music. Mrs. Lister, who, like her eldest and
youngest daughters, had a very clear, pleasant voice,
also joined in, and in a moment or two the whole party
were rendering *The First Nowell* with great expression
and enjoyment, even Hugh, to his own astonishment,
bearing his part with dogged persistence. From one
carol they went on to another, led by Sarah, who started
a fresh one the moment the previous one was finished, in
the belief—correct, as it happened—that while they were
singing her bedtime would be forgotten.

"I enjoyed that," Sir Robert ejaculated when throats
were sore and their repertoire was exhausted. "Ruth,
some of your family sing like birds."

"It depends what bird where Johnny's concerned,"
Paul remarked.

"It's too much to expect to be beautiful *and* have a
wonderful voice," Joanna simpered, apparently not at all
hurt by this brotherly comment.

"As a matter of fact I don't believe Johnny is quite as
gawky as she was," Paul observed.

"She's certainly filled out," Mr. Eldon said, surveying
his niece gravely.

"Anyway, what about Paul?" demanded Joanna. "He
used to be like a lath, but now you can actually see him
when he stands sideways."

As Paul grinned lazily, his mother and uncle both
studied him with approving eyes. He certainly was
looking both sturdier and browner after the autumn spent
in the open air and much hard physical exercise.

"He's stronger, too," Sarah said unexpectedly from her
seat on the hearthrug at her uncle's feet. "The other day
he an' Hugh had a wrestling match, an' Hugh couldn't

get him down as easily as he could when we first came."

Both boys sat up abruptly at this unexpected speech, Paul flushing uncomfortably, and Hugh directing a frown at the small gossip.

"Just how do you know anything about that?" he demanded, perhaps rather unwisely.

"I watched you," Sarah said guilelessly. "Just after we came. You told Paul if he didn't do the logs Uncle would be angry, an' Paul told you to mind your own business—an' then you started fighting, an' you got Paul on the ground an'——"

"Sarah! Do be quiet!" Both boys were scarlet before Louise had presence of mind enough to interrupt, and Hugh gave her a grateful glance.

"But he did an'——"

"You weren't supposed to see that," Louise said desperately, feeling sorry for both boys.

"But what were you fighting about recently?" asked Joanna, allowing her curiosity to override her tact. "Paul does his work now——" she was going on naïvely when Louise interrupted reproachfully.

"Joanna!"

"We weren't really fighting," Hugh said desperately, seeing that Paul, perhaps for the first time in their acquaintance, was really tongue-tied. "It was only a friendly bout."

Paul recovered himself with an effort. "We'd been talking about that first one, and I challenged Hugh to see if I could stand up to him now that I'm in better condition." He eyed his youngest sister disapprovingly. "I can't help feeling Sarah has far too much time on her hands. If she had a few more lessons to do——"

"No!" A wail of woe arose from Sarah. "Mummy, I'm

not going to do more lessons." She glared at her brother. "I wish Hugh had sat on you again an'——"

"I'm sure it's long after her bedtime," Louise said desperately, and Joanna rose firmly to her feet.

"Come on, Sarah. Say good night and——"

Sarah embraced her uncle's leg fervently. "No! Mummy said I could stay up to-night. I can, can't I, Uncle?"

Sir Robert leaned back in his chair and gave way to his laughter. "Ruth! I wish I could adopt them all! Will you make them over to me?"

Mrs. Lister laughed as she leaned down to ruffle Sarah's curls. "You want the whole of my kingdom. Sarah dear, I do think it's time you went to bed. After all, the sooner you're asleep, the sooner to-morrow will be here."

Sarah rose reluctantly. "All right. But I'm not going to bed early to-morrow night—nor the next night——" she paused and eyed her mother speculatively "nor——"

"and so on *ad infinitum!*" Joanna laughed, gripping Sarah's hand and firmly removing her.

When Hugh slid out of bed the following morning, Paul rolled over and groaned, ruffling his already tousled hair.

"I'll get the water while you do the milking," he offered, and as he quietly followed his cousin downstairs he grinned wryly to himself as he suddenly saw the humorous side of starting a Christmas Day in this manner. Certainly a year ago he would never have dreamed that now, before six o'clock, he would not only be up, but going out to get water from a well!

By the time they came in, Joe had got the fire burning well, and when the rest of the family came down, roused by an impatient Sarah, who wandered from room to room singing *Christians Awake* at the top of her voice as a slight hint, the kitchen was looking cheerful with the fire blazing away, a kettle boiling, and the lamplight showing a bunch of mistletoe suspended from a rafter.

"Merry Christmas!" Joanna exclaimed, bursting in with even more energy than usual. "I meant to come down earlier, but I didn't wake until Sarah sat on my tummy."

"Well, you just wouldn't wake up," Sarah said, casting an anxious eye round the kitchen in search of the presents.

"Breakfast before anything else," Mrs. Lister said briskly, and Sarah's face fell. Her mother, however, was adamant. She knew from past experience that if presents came first, her youngest daughter, at any rate, would not eat anything. The moment the meal was over, however, Sarah was no longer to be denied.

"Where are they?" she demanded, looking round. "Joanna made me give all mine to her last night."

"Try the sitting-room," Mr. Eldon said, opening the door into the hall, and Sarah shot through almost too swiftly to be seen.

Inside the sitting-room she stopped dead, gazing breathlessly at the tree that rose nearly to the ceiling. It had been smuggled in by her uncle and Joe late one night after she was safely in bed and kept under lock and key in the snuggery until the previous evening, when Sir Robert had taken his valuable life in his hands balancing on top of a stepladder to fasten on the topmost decorations.

"I haven't spent a family Christmas like this since soon after I left school," he declared, as the presents were handed round by the two elder girls. "Sarah, this cake of soap will be most useful," he added, unwrapping a a parcel that had just been handed to him.

"Well, you take so long washing your hands that you must use an awful lot of soap," remarked that observant young lady, who had insisted on doing all her shopping herself, with no advice from anyone, when Mr. Eldon ran them all into Shaftesbury for that purpose, although Hugh had afterwards been the enforced recipient of endless confidences regarding it.

Sir Robert stared at her, and then laughed.

"Do I? Force of habit, I suppose. I hadn't realised it."

"You just go on an' on an' on," Sarah remarked. "I think it's a waste of time myself. I just wash once, an' I'm quite clean."

"Or so we fondly think," Paul murmured *sotto voce* to Louise.

At last all the presents were opened, and Mrs. Lister swept the younger ones off into the kitchen to help, only Joanna, who had slipped into the snuggery for a moment to see that everything was there for their evening performance, remaining. She glanced round critically, and, satisfied, had just turned to the door, which was slightly ajar, when she realised that her uncle and Sir Robert were still in the sitting-room, and obviously thought themselves alone.

"And Ruth still has no idea?" Sir Robert was asking.

"Not the slightest," Mr. Eldon returned.

"I never thought you'd manage it."

"I couldn't have done it if hadn't been for Hugh. He's saved the situation again and again," Mr. Eldon said, and then went on warmly: "I shan't forget what he's done. At first, of course, he helped because he knew I wanted him to, but now—he's very fond of Ruth, and he doesn't want her to be upset."

"Personally, I think you underestimate Ruth," Sir Robert said thoughtfully. "Although she's so small and impulsive, there's a lot of character and good sense behind her impetuous manner."

"Oh, I know—but why should she be worried—I hope unnecessarily?"

Joanna looked round wildly. They were in the middle of their conversation before she realised what they were saying, and, while she could not bear the thought of continuing to listen unseen, she hated the idea of bursting out upon them and letting them know they had been overheard. Her eye fell on the window, and with a sigh of relief she crossed to it, softly opened the casement, and climbed out, while the two men went on talking, quite unconscious of the fact that she had been an unwilling eavesdropper.

Joanna's brow was furrowed in deep thought as she made her way round the house, shivering in the cold wind, and wondering what the secret was that her mother must not know. Evidently Hugh knew all about it, whatever it was. She had a strong suspicion that it must have some connection with her uncle's sudden and unexpected retirement into the country, but what it could be she could not guess. For a moment she toyed with the thought that perhaps he had in some way transgressed the law, but, vivid as her imagination was, she just could not envisage him as a criminal hiding from the police; nor could she picture Hugh, with his blunt honesty, mixed up any nefarious doings.

Unconsciously shaking her head she made her way in by the back door, and her mother stared in surprise at her sudden appearance.

"Joanna, where have you been? And without a coat, too! You are silly! You'd better make yourself a hot drink at once. And sit by the fire until you're quite warm."

Hugh grinned as he passed her with an armful of logs.

"Trying to get pneumonia?" he inquired. "That would be practice for us."

Joanna turned and stared after him curiously. He certainly didn't look as if he had anything on his conscience. Quite unconsciously she shook her head again, and Paul chuckled.

"Look at her, sitting nodding away like an old owl! Johnny, wake up! It's Christmas!"

Joanna pulled herself together as her mother turned to look at her anxiously.

"I was only thinking—I wish it had snowed," she said hastily. "Christmas doesn't seem complete without."

"I'm afraid we can't arrange that for you," Paul said. "But no doubt we'll get some before the winter's out."

"Johnny!" Louise looked into the room. "You might come and help me to make the beds. Where have you been? I've been looking everywhere for you."

Joanna sighed as she got up. She had never known her family so curious before. "I—I just——"

"I'll help," Sarah said, and for once her offer was warmly received by at least one of her sisters as Joanna leapt at the opportunity to change the subject.

"Come on, then! We'll soon be done with three of us helping. Louise, I do love that pretty scarf Uncle Bob gave you."

As she intended, Louise's mind was immediately diverted to a subject of much greater interest to her, and by the time they came downstairs again Joanna found to her relief that all interest in her movements had died away.

CHAPTER THIRTEEN

A DISASTER

Mr. Eldon strolled into the barn one day in mid-January and eyed the two boys speculatively.

"Where are the girls?" he asked.

"Sarah's doing lessons—officially," Paul said with a grin, for that small and unwilling student never attempted to concentrate unless someone was actually standing over her.

"And Louise has driven Joanna into the village," Hugh added.

"What's the matter with Joanna lately?" Mr. Eldon asked unexpectedly.

"Is there anything?" asked Paul in surprise.

"Yes. She seems to have spells of being unusually quiet and thoughtful——"

"Then you should be thankful for small mercies," Paul said promptly.

"And I've found her watching me in the strangest fashion——" Mr. Eldon broke off as his other nephew's face changed. "What is it Hugh?"

"She's been watching me, too," Hugh said. "What is the matter with her, Paul?"

"I haven't the slightest idea." Paul shrugged his shoulders. "I hadn't even noticed she was different."

"She is," Mr. Eldon said. "She's been very much quieter——" He broke off as the sound of hoofs and wheels on the cobbles proclaimed the return of the two girls in the trap. "The very people I want," he exclaimed, hurrying to help them out, while Joe took charge of Jessamy. "Come into the barn for a few minutes."

The girls followed him in with mystified faces, and the boys looked equally perplexed as their uncle leaned against the shafts of a cart and surveyed them critically.

"I've got to go up to Town for a few days," he said abruptly, and Joanna, quite unconscious of the fact that her uncle was watching her, shot a quick glance at Hugh, whose eyes showed a sudden flash of comprehension. She had not been able to forget the portion of conversation she had overheard between her uncle and Sir Robert, though she had not mentioned it to anyone. Puzzle as she might, however, she had not been able to discover any likely explanation for it, though Hugh's momentary expression now made her suspect that there was some connection between the secret, whatever it was, and this impending visit to London.

"Going up to Town?" Paul repeated.

"Yes, and your mother wants to go with me. I believe she wants to do some shopping. But the point is, can you four carry on on your own? Joe will be here to help with the outdoor work, but unfortunately Annie has just been asked to go and nurse old Mrs. Lacey in the village—Dr. Davies rang up a few minutes ago to say the old lady's been taken ill and is all alone. Now can you girls run the house? The chief responsibility will fall on you, Louise, though I'm sure Joanna will help."

"Of course I will," Joanna said readily, but Louise looked rather startled at the proposition. She never accepted responsibility as readily as Joanna.

"Well—I suppose we can manage," she said, not too confidently.

"If you'll undertake to take charge of the housekeeping I'm sure you'll be all right," her uncle said encouragingly.

"And I know I can trust you boys to work together out of doors. Hugh has a very good idea of what needs to be done, and——"

"We'll get on all right," Paul said quickly. "I don't say I'd always accept Hugh's ruling in everything, but where farmwork is concerned I'm quite ready to give him best."

Mr. Eldon's face cleared, while Hugh grinned, quite unmoved by this doubtful compliment.

"He's thinking of that Latin unseen you set us," he remarked. "We put in an hour over it last night, and scarcely agreed on one line."

"I thought unseens were supposed to be done on your own," Joanna said severely.

"Not that one," Hugh declared. "You try it yourself, and you'll soon agree."

"No, thanks," Joanna returned hastily. "I've no desire ever to catch you up in Latin. Caesar's quite difficult enough for me."

"We seem to be wandering from the point," Louise said. "When are you going, Uncle?"

"The day after to-morrow. Oh, and talking of lessons, someone will have to take over Sarah's education while we're away."

Four blank faces gazed at Mr. Eldon, each waiting for someone else to offer. The education of Sarah was a task that had to be undertaken in the face of the stiffest opposition.

"Paul's the brainiest, so he's the obvious one," Hugh said basely.

"No good at all. You're the one with most influence over her," Paul returned swiftly. "She'd listen to you."

"I'll be too busy out of doors," Hugh retorted, his eyes turning to the two girls. "It seems to me it's a woman's job——"

"My hands will be quite full with the housekeeping," Louise declared.

"And I, being the youngest, am behind you all in learning," Joanna said with most unusual modesty. "Only the best is good enough for Sarah, so——"

"No!" Paul said flatly, as she looked at the boys, while Hugh shook his head firmly.

"I already have her pretty well from the time she gets up till the time she goes to bed——"

Mr. Eldon began to laugh.

"Poor Sarah! If she only knew——"

"She'd be most relieved, and hope we'd never agree," Joanna said. "Listen! I've got an idea! Let's each teach her a different subject; then no one will have to bear the brunt of it. Louise can take her for French—and sewing; Paul can teach her English and history; and Hugh, geography and maths——"

"And Joanna?" demanded Hugh suspiciously, and Joanna laughed at the accusing silence around her.

"Oh, I'll surpervise generally, and——" She dodged hastily as Paul descended on her. "No, I'll play fair. If you'll teach English grammar, I'll take her for reading and dictation, and——"

Paul looked relieved. The idea of listening patiently while Sarah read aloud did not appeal to him.

"All right! And you can supervise when she's learning any poetry. But perhaps, on the whole, I'd better take on the grammar, as you will split infinitives on the slightest provocation——"

"We'll all see she does her share," Louise declared. "But

I do think it's a good idea to share the lessons out."

"We'll be able to find out who should take up teaching as their vocation," Joanna declared. "Uncle, when you and Mummy come back, you'll have to decide in which subject she's made most progress—I say, that would be fun! Let's have a competition."

"Poor Sarah!" Paul ejaculated. "Four of us, all trying to force her on——"

"And trying to put her off in everyone else's subjects," Hugh said with a chuckle. "Though I believe we'd be worn out first."

"It will be an interesting experiment," Mr. Eldon remarked, as he turned to go, but he was not referring merely to Sarah's education.

Mrs. Lister did not go away without some trepidation at the thought of leaving the young ones alone—though she was reassured by the thought that Joe would be on the premises—and on the evening before her departure she went out to the barn where Hugh was doing the milking, alone for once, as Sarah was indoors supervising—un-asked—her mother's packing. He looked round with a smile as she came in. Although too undemonstrative to show his feelings much, he had been steadily growing fonder of his aunt.

"Hugh!" she exclaimed in her usual impulsive fashion. "I want to talk to you! Do you really think you'll all be all right while we're away?"

Hugh looked round at her with his usual steady gaze.

"I don't see why not. Louise is a good cook, so we shouldn't starve, and Joe and I know what needs doing out of doors—and Paul and Joanna are both a good help—now," he added, almost to himself, and Mrs. Lister laughed.

"Yes, I believe Paul really enjoys a little manual labour now, though naturally he'd never admit it," she agreed. "Of course, the trouble with Joanna is to restrain her. Hugh, don't let her do too much, will you?"

Hugh looked at her queerly, and did not reply for a moment. Then he asked quietly: "Why are you asking me, and not Paul?"

Mrs. Lister looked back at him steadily.

"Because I know you both. Paul would do his best if I asked him, but he isn't as used to responsibility as you are—and he isn't as forceful. If Joanna wouldn't listen to him he'd just shrug his shoulders, give it up as a bad job, and go back to his books or whatever he was doing."

Hugh suddenly laughed.

"And what do you expect me to do? Pick her up and lock her up somewhere until you're home again?"

"No, of course not! Though it mightn't be a bad idea," Mrs. Lister said in a reflective tone, while her eyes twinkled mischievously. "No, but I think you'd have more influence over her than Paul, and could probably persuade her to see reason——"

"In other words, talk her down," Hugh said with a chuckle. "Well, I've never tried, but if necessary I'll do my best."

"And Sarah," Mrs. Lister added. "I've never been away from her before, and I'll feel much happier if you'll promise to look after her."

"I'll do my best," Hugh said again. "And I'm pretty sure I can handle Sarah." He frowned as he stood up suddenly and added: "As long as you don't ask me to try to interfere with Louise."

Mrs. Lister looked at him anxiously in the dim light.

"I thought you'd got over that, and were quite friendly now?"

Hugh kicked the side of the barn moodily.

"I suppose I should have got over it—but underneath a thing like that goes on rankling for a long time. You see, no one had ever looked at me like that before. Louise is pretty, and she's jolly and friendly, but I can't lose the feeling that underneath she might still be—despising me," he muttered. It was always very difficult for him to put into words anything that really mattered to him, but now somehow he felt he was cornered and it all had to come out. "You see, Louise came here, all dressed up, and turning up her nose at the place we lived in, and the work we were doing. It was obvious that she looked down on us—well, if not on Uncle, on me—because some of the work was dirty, and I couldn't help getting in a mess doing it. Personally I don't see it's any good doing any work unless you're willing to do it all—and do it thoroughly. I daresay, if I'd asked, Uncle would have let me choose the clean, easy jobs, and let Joe do the others—but he wouldn't have thought half as much of me—and I shouldn't have thought anything of myself. Besides, I specially asked when we first came if I could take charge of the animals——"

Mrs. Lister had seated herself on his stool and was listening intently as Hugh, standing with his back to her, made his confession in a shamefaced mutter. Nevertheless, it did him good, after being bottled up for so long.

"When Uncle came here I needn't have come," he went on bitterly. "Uncle Bob wanted me to stay with him and remain at school, but I chose to come with Uncle and do all I could to help—he didn't ask me to—and then Louise came and looked down on me. If she'd come when we lived in Town she wouldn't have looked at me like that——" His voice died away, as if he felt his feelings were too childish to be given expression, but it was obvious to his aunt that he had been very deeply hurt.

"When we first came here Louise was a silly child who needed a good slapping," she said unexpectedly, "but never, since the first day or two, has she looked down on you. Her sense of values has altered a lot since she has been here. I'm convinced she realises, like the rest of us, that, even if you haven't been much used to companions of your own age, you are none the worse for being more sensible than most boys—and girls—of your age, and that you do whatever happens to be your work at the moment in the most thorough and trustworthy way, and that when you are grown-up you will be doing work of great importance in the world while she will be just a cipher—of no real value to the world at large. Don't you see, Hugh, that the way you work here is a foretaste of what your chosen profession is going to mean to you when you are grown-up. We've all seen and realised it, and we all respect you for it. *All* of us! Not just John and Bob and me! Why do you think Sarah follows you as she does, and appeals to your judgment in everything? Because she trusts and has complete confidence in you. Why do you think Paul, who has never worried about anyone's opinion in his life, is glad to study with you, and willingly defers to you on all the work here? Because he recognises what you're worth! And you've been making yourself miserable because you thought a silly girl sneered at your old, muddy clothes! If my family haven't yet learned to look beyond clothes, I give them up. You've got Louise all wrong, Hugh. She loves beauty, and she loves orderliness, but that doesn't mean to say she can't see the greater things beyond them. And I know she thinks as much of you now as the others do."

Hugh had turned now and was surveying his aunt with an incredulous face in which his eyes were shining with a new confidence, while the last feeling of bitterness vanished.

"I—I didn't know—anyone had been thinking so much about me——"

"You're not the only one who thinks," his aunt laughed, holding out her hands for him to pull her up. "And now you must finish the milking. And Hugh—don't go worrying again over what people aren't thinking at all!"

She was gone, leaving the boy with a warm clasp of the hands that meant more to him than she could ever know. Deeply though he cared for his uncle and Sir Robert, Mrs. Lister represented something he had never known since the death of his mother, and he had found to his surprise that he had been able to talk to her as he could never have talked to either of the men.

His pleasant reverie was broken by the appearance of Sarah, who had been removed forcibly from the scene of the packing after it was discovered that she had carefully packed a pair of shoes in her mother's favourite hat. She was looking very doleful, and Hugh grinned at her consolingly.

"Cheer up! They'll only be away a few days," he remarked.

"Mummy's never gone away without me before," Sarah sniffed dismally.

"But she couldn't take us all, and you wouldn't want to leave the rest of us in the lurch when we'll be needing so much help, would you?" Hugh asked cunningly, and Sarah's woebegone face brightened.

Early next morning their uncle and Mrs. Lister set off, the latter full of dire imaginings of all sorts of incredible mishaps that might overtake them in her absence, and Mr. Eldon quietly confident that nothing untoward could or would happen. He proposed to leave the car at the village where they were to get the train, and retrieve it on his return, so for transport at Long Barrow they would either have to ride or drive Jessamy in the trap for the next few days.

It was a bleak, grey day, and Louise gave a shiver as the car disappeared from sight over the top of the down, and they turned away from the gate where they had been waving frantically.

"Oh dear! Doesn't the house seem empty without Mummy," she moaned as they went indoors. "I always hate it even if she's only away for a day. Somehow the whole centre of the family seems to have gone."

"Then it's up to you to fill her place," Joanna remarked bracingly, after a glance at her sister's forlorn countenance.

"I never could," Louise said despondently. "However much I tried, I should be hopelessly inadequate."

"You never know what you can do till you try," Joanna said sagely. "Oh dear! I suppose I'd better go and make the beds. How I do hate housework!"

The boys worked hard out of doors all morning, trying to share with Joe the work usually done by their uncle, and all three were very hungry by the time they went indoors for dinner, half wondering if the absence of both Mrs. Lister and Annie had affected the catering department very badly. To their relief, however, they found a warm, spotless kitchen and immaculate table, and if Louise looked a trifle more heated and ruffled than usual as she served out a hot, appetising stew, no one complained. She was plainly nervous as she sat in her mother's place, and she eyed the others apprehensively as they began their dinner. Although she normally did quite a lot of the cooking, it had seemed a very different matter doing it entirely on her own, without even her mother's supervision. There were no complaints, however, and she gradually gained confidence as the plates began to empty, and second helpings were demanded on all sides.

It seemed very strange that evening on their own.

"I suppose we ought to do some work," Paul said, as they gathered round the fire in the snuggery. "Come on, Sarah! Lessons! You've got off scot free all day as we've all been so busy."

"I'm not going to do lessons," Sarah exclaimed in an outraged tone. "Not while Mummy's away."

"Oh yes, you are!" Paul said cheerfully. "Lots of them!"

"I'm not!" wailed the spoilt baby, gazing round in dismay and seeing only adamantine faces.

"Of course you are!" Joanna said briskly. "We're all going to."

Sarah's mouth drooped in an obstinate manner her family knew of old.

"You must," Louise urged. "Mummy and Uncle want you to."

Sarah turned in despair to her last Court of Appeal.

"Hugh!" she exclaimed appealingly.

"No good, Sarah! We promised Uncle not to let you slack," Hugh said. "Look here," he added desperately, as signs of an approaching storm manifested themselves, "we thought perhaps we'd make it into a competition, and see who can teach you most. Don't you think that would be fun?"

Sarah paused to consider whether there might not be a catch of some kind in this proposal—as indeed there was—but failing to see it, slowly nodded, perhaps because she recognised the inevitable.

"I s'pose so," she said dismally.

"You start," Paul muttered, nudging Hugh. "She'll take it best from you."

Hugh nodded, and took a large atlas from one of the bookshelves.

"Come and sit on the arm of my chair so that you can see, and we'll start on geography," he remarked, and Sarah, suddenly deciding that there might be fun in it somewhere after all, obeyed.

The others listened critically for a few minutes as Hugh began to expound, and then settled down to work of their own; Louise and Joanna, with many groans on the part of the latter, on the task of translating a long descriptive paragraph into French, and Paul on a Latin unseen.

All went smoothly for the next few days, and then a letter came from Mrs. Lister to say that she and their uncle were staying a day or two longer, but the news did not cause them as much dismay as it might have done, for so far everything had gone so well that they were feeling generally pleased with themselves, and considered themselves quite capable of holding their fort indefinitely.

The weather had suddenly turned much colder, with a keen wind carrying a faint flurry of snow now and again, and they all felt they wanted to keep moving briskly whether indoors or out. In the house Joanna made the

beds at a lightning speed, while Louise stoked up the
kitchen fire, determined that the outside workers should
have a warm room in which to thaw, and then proceeded
to make cups of scalding hot cocoa for everyone before
setting to work to prepare the dinner.

"I shouldn't be surprised if it snows heavily," Joe remarked as he pushed his chair back after dinner. "I must
try to do something with my window. It stuck last night,
and I had to leave it wide open. I don't want that again
to-night if we have snow."

"Want any help?" asked Hugh.

"No, you get on with your own work," Joe said. "I
can manage it."

He went off to his room over the stables, and Paul
returned to the logs he was sawing, while Hugh, who was
working beyond the paddock, also hurried off.

"I must go and see if there are any eggs," Joanna said,
a short time later, pulling on an old coat and some even
older gloves. "Grr! It's cold!"

She ran out of the house, and then stopped dead as
she came in sight of the stables, to watch in dumb horror
as the ladder on which Joe was perched up at his window
begin to slither on the cobblestones. She tried to shout a
warning, but no sound would come, and then, just as
she managed to give a strangled gasp, the ladder and Joe
came down with a crash. It was not a great height to
fall, but he was a heavy man and the cobbles not the
softest ground to land on. For a moment Joanna felt
sure he must be dead, then to her relief he stirred and
tried feebly to disentangle himself from the ladder, which
was lying across him.

"What was that?" came Louise's startled voice from the
back door, and as Joanna, beginning to recover her wits,

moved forward, Louise ran past her, flung the ladder aside, and helped Joe into a sitting position.

" 'Tis my arm," he gasped, as Louise knelt beside him, supporting him, and she turned to Joanna.

"Get the boys, while I help him into the kitchen. Fly!"

Joanna flew. Calling to Paul, whose saw had drowned the noise of the fall, she set off to find Hugh, and they both came tearing back in time to see Louise and Paul between them helping Joe into the house.

"The cobbles were probably slippery after last night's frost," Louise said, tenderly rolling back Joe's shirt sleeve. "It's fractured, isn't it?"

There could be no doubt of that.

"And not a simple one," Paul said gloomily. This was an utter disaster to happen in their uncle's absence.

"Joanna, ring up Dr. Davies," Hugh said. "And ask him to come as soon as he possibly can."

Joanna rushed to the telephone, and while the others did what they could for Joe, they listened anxiously to what she was saying.

"Oh dear!" she exclaimed. "Then you can't come just yet? Yes, it looks in a horrible mess. Can we get him to you? Well, I suppose we could use the trap. All right, we will," She put down the receiver and hurried back to the group round the fire. "Something's wrong with his car. They're working on it now, but it won't be ready for an hour or two, and he says the sooner the arm's set the better, so he wants to know if you can make Joe as comfortable as possible and take him in the trap."

Joe set his lips.

"I—you just patch me up, Master Hugh, and I can get there——"

"Idiot!" Hugh grunted, as his eyes met Paul's. "It's the

only thing we can do. Look here, Joe, we'll probably hurt you, but we can't leave your arm like that. We'll be as gentle as we can. Louise, can you get lots of blankets, while I get some splints and bandages from upstairs?"

Louise hurried away without a word, and when she staggered downstairs with her arms full she found the boys dealing with the injured limb as well as they could, while Joe continued to protest, rather faintly, at the trouble he was giving.

"Where's Johnny?" asked Louise quietly.

"She went outside," Paul said, without looking up.

Hearing a sudden clatter of hoofs, Louise ran into the hall, caught down a coat from a hook, and then ran out to the stables in time to see Joanna leading Jessamy to the barn where the trap was kept.

"I'm no good at that kind of thing," she said, nodding towards the house. "It makes me feel sick. So I thought I'd try to get Jessamy harnessed ready."

The girls had only once or twice helped with the harnessing, but with some trouble they managed it, and while Joanna led the pony round to the door Louise ran into the house again, pulled a scarf from a drawer and tied it round her head, and then got out her warmest gloves. By this time the boys had fixed up the injured arm as well as they could, and were wrapping Joe up warmly for the drive.

"You can't come in this weather," Hugh said, suddenly noticing Louise's preparations.

"Of course I can," she returned in an unusually decisive tone. "Besides, the roads are bound to be slippery, and I'm more used to driving than you are."

Hugh was forced to agree with this. Although he had tried driving once or twice, he much preferred riding, and he could not deny that Louise had had far more experience, while Paul had never even troubled to try.

"All right," he agreed, and turned to Paul, who was still concentrating on their patient. "What do we do about going?"

Louise glanced nervously at Joe, who was looking very exhausted.

"Hadn't you better both come? If he should faint or anything—he's so big——"

"I was thinking of Joanna and Sarah," Hugh said, remembering his promise to his aunt. "It's such an isolated spot to leave them here alone."

"We'll be all right," Joanna said flatly from the door. "We'll have Sam and Woggles, and if anything went wrong on the road Louise would need you both."

Paul nodded as he glanced anxiously at Joe, who was leaning back in his chair looking very white.

"Yes, I think we'd both better go if Johnny doesn't mind."

"And it will be dark when you're coming back," Joanna said. "Louise, do drive carefully. It's snowing harder now."

"I'll be very careful," Louise promised. "One accident is quite enough while Uncle and Mummy are away."

"Lock all the doors after we've gone," Hugh ordered, turning to Joanna as he struggled into his coat, and for once she was unexpectedly docile.

"Yes, I will."

She and Sarah followed them to the door, and helped to hoist Joe into the trap, where he was nearly smothered in blankets. Hugh sat beside him, Paul sprang in last, and Louise picked up the reins and turned Jessamy in the gate. She drove carefully up the rutty lane, trying not to jog Joe more than she could help, but once she reached the level road up on the down she put Jessamy into a trot and they bowled along smoothly, while the fine snow stung their cheeks and the wind made their faces tingle.

Back at Long Barrow Joanna closed and locked the back door and then lit the lamp in the kitchen. It was not dark yet, but the lamplight seemed to make the place look more cheerful and less deserted. She was not normally nervous, but she had never known the house so empty, and suddenly she realised for the first time just how isolated it was. The thought of the telephone was a great comfort, although common sense told her that if any prowling tramp or gipsy did arrive to frighten them, even the telephone could not summon help quickly. Her greatest comfort was the sight of Sam's powerful body sharing the hearthrug with Woggles. Surely two dogs should prove a good protection. Fortunately it had not occurred to Sarah to be nervous, and she was sitting in the rocking-chair by the fire, already settling down to a battered volume of *Alice*.

To fill in the time Joanna set the table in the kitchen ready for tea. This done, she tidied round a little, and then realised with a start of horror that there were the poultry and animals to feed, and, if the others did not get back in time, the milking to be done. She had never before milked more than one or two cows at a time, but she was thankful now that her insatiable desire to try her hand at everything had made her insist on learning how to do it.

The afternoon grew darker, and there was still no sign of the trap or its passengers. Joanna watched the clock anxiously, but the hands crept on inexorably.

"It's no good, I'll have to feed the chickens and animals,

and start the milking," she said, jumping up. "Will you be all right here, or would you rather come with me?"

For the first time Sarah seemed to become aware of their isolated state.

"I'll come with you," she said promptly.

"All right!" In her heart of hearts, Joanna was not sorry to have the company even of her small sister. "And we'll take the dogs—only you'll have to hold Wogs while I'm feeding the chickens."

This done, and the poultry safely shut up for the night, they fed the animals, and then Joanna settled down to start the milking. All the time she was listening anxiously for the trap, but it did not come, and they were still alone when the last cow was milked.

"Hugh didn't want to teach me, but he'll be glad I insisted now," Joanna observed in a tone of satisfaction as they thankfully returned to the warmth and light of the house. It seemed to be snowing harder than ever, and the ground was already completely covered with a white carpet. "I wish they'd come," she added, frowning anxiously as she moved a boiling kettle back a little and glanced at the clock again. "I'm so glad both the boys are with Louise." Although she did not say so, she was terrified by the thought of the long, steep hill that led down to the village. If Jessamy had slipped there and fallen——

At long last came the sound of hoofs, and both girls flew to the back door as the trap drew up outside.

"Are you all right?" Hugh's voice demanded, as they peered out into the darkness.

"Yes, are you?" asked Joanna.

"Yes, only I think Louise's hands must be completely numb by now."

"Pretty well," Louise agreed, as the boys helped her out.

"Go in by the fire while we see to Jessamy," Hugh ordered, following her into the kitchen with an armful of tangled blankets, while Paul brought up the rear similarly burdened.

"How's Joe?" demanded Joanna.

"He's gone to Shaftesbury Hospital," Louise said. "That's why we've been so long. We waited until the ambulance came for him."

"He'll be all right," Paul said, "only his arm's in rather a mess." He reluctantly turned away from the fire. "Let's go and see to Jessamy at once. He deserves his supper."

Hugh gave a sudden start. "I've got the milking to do, too!"

"No, you haven't," Joanna said, and her cousin gave her a grateful glance.

"Have you done it? Bless you!"

By the time the boys came in again Joanna had made the tea, and Louise's fingers were beginning to return painfully to life.

"Snowing worse than ever," Paul reported, pausing in the back kitchen to shake off his white covering.

"It's going to be a regular blizzard," Hugh said, looking rather worried.

"What fun!" Joanna exclaimed.

"I'm not so sure," Hugh said, frowning.

"All the stock's safely under cover, isn't it?" Paul asked.

"And we're cosy enough," Joanna added, looking round the kitchen contentedly as she began to pour out. It seemed a very different place now that the others were back.

"I must admit I'm glad to be home," Louise said, sipping her hot tea appreciatively. "The last part of the drive I scarcely knew whether I had hold of the reins or not. And I was so glad Jessamy knew the lane down here, because it looked so different in the snow and the darkness, and I was terrified of getting into a ditch and the trap overturning."

Joanna positively paled at the thought.

"Whatever should we have done if that had happened?"

"Well, it didn't," Paul said coolly. "And Louise drove awfully well."

"Extraordinarily well," Hugh said unexpectedly, helping himself to toast. "I know these roads much better than she does, but I should have hated to have been driving."

The whole table paused to stare at this totally unexpected admission, and Louise went crimson.

"In fact both Louise and Joanna are heroines," Paul summed up, making a hearty tea.

"Why me?" demanded Joanna in surprise, and Paul grinned at her accusingly.

"Admit it, Johnny! You were in a blue funk about being left here," he said, and Joanna stared at him.

"How did you know—I mean, what makes you think that?" she amended hastily, and her brother laughed.

"The meek way you agreed to lock the doors when Hugh suggested it. If you hadn't been in a funk you'd have nearly murdered him for daring to suggest such a thing."

"All right!" Joanna laughed. "I was! I'd never realised how lonely this place is till then. But there was nothing brave in being scared."

Hugh looked across at her approvingly.

"No, but there was in telling us both to go with Louise."

CHAPTER FOURTEEN

A NEW EXPERIENCE

The following morning the girls were sleepily thinking of getting up, and dreading facing the frosty atmosphere, when they heard someone running upstairs and the door of their room flew open violently, displaying Paul in a state of most unwonted excitement.

"Disaster number two!" he proclaimed, and the girls woke up abruptly.

"What is it?" demanded Louise apprehensively.

"We're snowed up!" Paul announced.

"Snowed up!" Louise repeated dazedly.

"What fun!" Joanna ejaculated.

"Does that mean Mummy can't come back?" Sarah demanded in dismay.

"Not at present," Paul said cheerfully, as the other two girls looked concerned. "The blizzard's still raging, and doesn't show any sign of stopping."

He ran downstairs again, and the girls quickly dressed, excitedly discussing this new development. In the kitchen they found Paul struggling with the fire, while outside Hugh was endeavouring to dig a path through the drifts to the well.

"We've hardly any water," Paul said, giving a sigh of relief as the fire began to blaze up.

"Is the well frozen?" asked Louise in alarm.

"We hope not. Hugh says wells very seldom freeze. But the difficulty is getting to it," Paul said. "A lot of the snow's drifted down here from the higher ground. Will you look after the fire now while I go and help him? There was enough water indoors to fill the kettle, so you can make some tea."

He hurried out, and, seizing a second spade from the back kitchen went to join in the battle with the drifts.

"If you'll do the breakfast, I'll go and help as well," Joanna said as she seized the coal shovel, eager to get out in the snow. "How is it the spades were in the house, instead of one of the outhouses?" she asked, as she joined the boys and set to work with a will.

"I had a feeling this might happen, and brought them in last night," Hugh said, working like a beaver. "It didn't happen last year, but I believe that whenever there's heavy snow this valley gets cut off." He gave a grunt of satisfaction as he reached the well, which fortunately was not far from the house, and under cover. "Will you see to getting water, Johnny, while we go on clearing a path to the animals and poultry? Some of these drifts are horribly deep."

"Yes, carry on," Joanna agreed. "I'll come and help as soon as I've seen to this." She staggered to the house with two or three bucketfuls, losing a considerable amount on each journey, and then set off after the boys, who were digging their way through to the barn where the cows were.

"At least we'll have milk," Hugh said, when he finally came into the kitchen for breakfast, and Louise looked at him in startled dismay.

"You don't mean—we might be cut off long enough to run short of food?" she faltered.

"No, not quite that," Hugh said hastily. "But it might be quite a while before anyone can get through." He frowned as they sat down at the table. "Last night I was wondering if we ought to go to the village while the roads were clear, but we were cold and tired, and I hoped the snow might not be too bad—but now I'm sorry——"

"I'm not," Joanna said emphatically. "This is going to be much more fun. And besides, we couldn't have left the animals——"

"I know. I'd have come back," Hugh said simply, and a general howl of wrath arose.

"Oh, would you?" Joanna exclaimed indignantly. "If you can stand it, we can!"

"I'd have come back if you had," Sarah declared.

"And do you think I'd have let you return on your own?" Paul inquired in his usual lazy tone, though his expression belied it.

"No, I didn't," Hugh said pacifically. "But I feel we should have got the girls out of this——"

"Rubbish!" Joanna snorted. "I'm enjoying every minute of it."

"And what kind of meals would you have had?" Louise inquired, and then gave a start. "Oh, meals! I wonder how we're off for food?"

"Not too badly," Hugh said. "Uncle knew there was a chance that this might happen some time during the winter, so he got in good stocks. We've plenty of potatoes and other vegetables stored away—if only we can get at them——"

"And Mummy's put lots of eggs down," Joanna said.

"And if necessary we can kill a few of the chickens—or even one of the pigs," Hugh said thoughtfully, but there was a howl of protest.

"I couldn't touch it," Joanna wailed.

"You would if you were hungry enough," Hugh said.

"Who'd kill it?" asked Paul practically, and Hugh grinned.

"I don't know. I've certainly never tried. Of course, if Joe were here we'd be all right. But if we were really short we'd have to do something." His eyes wandered round the kitchen and fell on his uncle's gun, which, as it was always kept unloaded, stood in one corner of the room. "I think I could probably shoot it if I had to."

Joanna eyed her cousin with loathing. "There are times when I think you're revolting," she declared with quiet conviction, but Hugh was quite unmoved.

"Even if I were doing it to save you from starving?" he inquired.

"Hugh!" Louise spoke with sudden decision. "Just how long may we be snowed up here?"

Hugh hesitated.

"You might as well tell us," Louise said. "I'd rather know the worst at once and be prepared for it."

"Weeks," Hugh said reluctantly. "Of course, that doesn't happen often, but it has been known if a really bad cold spell sets in. You see, apart from the drifts, the hills leading up to the main road on the downs become impassable if it freezes badly."

Louise went white, while even Joanna looked slightly sobered.

"Then Uncle and Mummy may not be able to get back here for a long time?" Louise faltered, and Sarah's face puckered up suspiciously as Hugh nodded.

"Uncle was wondering if he ought to risk going, but he had rather an important appointment, and the weather wasn't too bad then. It's changed very suddenly."

A sob from Sarah drew their attention to her.

"It's going to be fun," Joanna announced hastily.

"You see if it isn't, Sarah! I'm looking forward to it."

"I'm not," Louise said frankly. "Hugh, if what you say is true, we'd better work out clearly just what food we have."

"Bread's the worst difficulty," Hugh said candidly. "But we've got a fair amount of flour, and if you can't go on making bread, you'll have to make scones or something like that."

Joanna suddenly began to laugh.

"Cheer up, Louise! It may start to thaw in a few hours. Anyway, I refuse to start worrying until I've got to." She jumped up. "And now I must get through to my chickens. Now the cows are all right, will you help me, Hugh? And we must see to the pigs, too."

"I must try to get round to the logs," Paul said. "We must keep a decent fire going this weather."

Louise looked round doubtfully.

"I think perhaps we'd better just keep the kitchen fire going while the weather's so bad."

"I was going to suggest that," Hugh agreed, and Joanna laughed.

"It's almost like living in a state of siege, isn't it?"

"Anyway, the phone's still all right," Hugh said, as the telephone bell rang. "I was half afraid the wires might be down." The others listened curiously as he answered it. "It's the Vicar," he murmured, covering the mouthpiece for a moment, and then took his hand away again. "No, I'm sure it's no use your trying—especially while this blizzard lasts. And even if they got here, I doubt if the girls could manage the journey back. Sarah definitely couldn't. Paul and I couldn't leave because of the animals, and I think the girls would rather stay with us—even if you could get them to the village. Yes, I think we've got quite a good supply of food—if everything else fails, we can live on potatoes and milk! And the animals are all right for two or three weeks. Yes, it is rather a blow coming right on top of Joe's accident, but we'll be all right. Thanks awfully for ringing up. Yes, I'll ring you at once if anything goes wrong." He replaced the receiver and turned to his listening cousins. "He and the doctor were worried as they knew Joe wasn't here, and they wanted to know if they should organise a party from the village to try to get through to us and evacuate us to semi-civilisation." He grinned suddenly. "As a matter of fact, if this blizzard goes on much longer the village will be cut off, too."

"I'm glad you refused," Louise said. "We couldn't go and leave you here, with no hot meals or anything."

"I assure you we shouldn't starve," Paul remarked.

"Yes, but you'd never bother to prepare proper meals," Louise objected.

"As a matter of fact I don't believe the Vicar thought there was very much chance," Hugh said. "But come on! We must get on and feed the pigs and poultry. I managed to get to the stables after I'd seen to the cows, so the horses are all right."

While the two boys and Joanna, almost lost in the whirling, flying cloud of snow, fought the drifts until backs and arms ached intolerably, Louise muffled Sarah up in a coat and sent her to make the beds, while she herself, with a very sober face, took a careful inventory of their stocks of food, and tried to work out how long they would last if used with the greatest care. To her relief she found that her uncle had indeed done his best to prepare for this possible contingency, and that if she were very careful they would be safe for a few weeks, even if on a very monotonous diet.

At lunch-time the three outdoor workers came in and sank wearily into chairs, Joanna in particular looking completely exhausted.

"I like snow in moderation," she gasped, "but there can be too much of a good thing."

Hugh sat up and looked at her anxiously as he suddenly remembered his promise to his aunt which he had forgotten completely in the battle with the snow. Paul, on the other hand, looked across at her with a grin.

"Good old Johnny! Always rides every hobby horse too hard! You should have come in for a rest when I told you."

"Rubbish!" Joanna retorted with a flash of her usual spirit. "I can keep going as long as you two can."

Paul sat up and regarded her with unusual firmness.

"That's just what you can't do. And you're not going to try it again. You young idiot! What are we to do if you knock yourself up? We can't get a doctor here at present, and if you think we want you ill on our hands, you're mistaken. Next time you'll do as you're told, or we'll jolly well carry you in."

Hugh stared at Paul in amazement, for it was the first time he had seen his cousin even attempt to assert any authority, and Joanna for once was completely silenced.

After a hot meal all three felt better.

"Though I suppose if the blizzard keeps on we'll have it all to do again to-morrow," Paul remarked philosophically as he sat back with a sigh of repletion.

"I'm coming out to help this afternoon," Sarah remarked.

"You're not," Paul said, almost automatically.

"We've done all we're going to do to-day," Hugh added. "We all need a rest."

"Well, I shall help to-morrow," Sarah announced.

When the meal had been cleared away and everything was tidy, Paul looked round lazily.

"I suppose Sarah ought to do some work. Come on, brat, get your exercise book and let me see your latest effort at composition. Then we'll do some history."

"No," Sarah protested. "I'm not doing lessons when it's snowing."

"Why not?" asked Hugh, coming into the kitchen with an armful of books. "I'm going to, and Joanna is."

Louise looked round with a smile at the figure in the rocking-chair. There was certainly a book on Joanna's knee, but her eyes were closed, and her steady breathing suggested that she was sleeping rather than meditating on her studies. Hugh glanced round, too, and grinned as he sat down at the table and spread his books out.

"My mistake!"

Sarah looked round desperately, but there was no escape, so she reluctantly fetched her exercise book and sat down beside her brother, while Louise tried to work out menus that would provide nourishing and satisfying meals while using the least possible amount of food.

They were just finishing their tea when the telephone rang again, and Joanna, who answered it, gave a cry of delight as she heard her uncle's voice.

"Yes, we're quite all right," she assured him, "but it's no use you and Mummy coming back, because we're snowed up, and you couldn't get here. Yes, honestly, we are. We've had a blizzard raging since yesterday evening. The Vicar rang up earlier to know if men from the village should try to get through to us, but Hugh said 'No!' After all, some of us would have to stay here to feed the animals. Of course, the boys said they'd stay, but Louise and I said we wouldn't leave them, even if we could get away, and—what was that?"

"What about Joe?" her uncle repeated, managing to get a word in at last. "Why, couldn't he have stayed?"

Joanna gave a slight gasp of dismay as she realised she had let the cat out of the bag.

"Oh! Well—as a matter of fact he's in Shaftesbury Hospital," she said reluctantly.

"*What?*" her uncle gasped, and Joanna proceeded to explain, while the others gathered round her. "He's getting on all right," she finished. "We rang up to inquire this morning. And we're all right," she went on hastily. "We've got plenty of food, and we've made paths to the stables and barn and the poultry and pigs. Ooh! And wasn't it back-aching work!"

Her uncle gave a chuckle, and then grew serious.

"But something must be done——"

"Nothing can be done," Joanna said cheerfully.

"I don't believe you want to be rescued!" her uncle exclaimed accusingly, and she chuckled.

"I don't! I think it's rather fun. Louise is looking a bit worried over the catering—she's afraid if the snow lasts long enough we may have to live on potatoes and milk—but there's nothing to do out of doors once the animals are fed, and we're making Sarah do her lessons——"

"Beasts!" Sarah exclaimed dispassionately.

Hugh reached out and took the receiver from Joanna.

"We really are all right, Uncle, so there's no point in your rushing back. Besides, by the time you got here the village would probably be cut off, so you wouldn't even be able to get as near as that. I promise we'll send word the moment there's the faintest chance of your getting through, so don't drag Aunt Ruth on a beastly cold journey all for nothing. And Louise is feeding us awfully well, so you needn't worry about that." He paused while his uncle delivered a scathing denunciation of himself for ever leaving them alone at Long Barrow in the winter, and then asked eagerly: "Have you had the verdict yet?" As his cousins stared at this unexpected question, Hugh's face lit up. "Honestly? As favourable as that? Have you told Aunt Ruth now? I feel like standing on my head. I've been longing to ring up, but I wouldn't in case the news wasn't good. Yes, we'll look after the girls. I don't care how long we're cut off here now. Besides, if you can't come back, you and Aunt Ruth and Uncle Bob will be able to celebrate!"

At long last he put down the receiver, and turned to face a circle of inquisitive faces.

"And now, perhaps, you'll be good enough to explain what all this is about," Paul remarked.

"Yes, what are they to celebrate?" asked Louise.

"I've known all along there was some kind of secret," Joanna said darkly.

Hugh's eyes were glowing with excitement as he looked round at them.

"Well, it's rather a long story. Come and sit down and I'll explain."

"Is it something to do with why Uncle came to live here?" Joanna asked, as they settled round the fire.

"Yes. A few months before we came to live here Uncle was in a bad car smash——"

"But we never heard a word of it," Louise protested, while the others stared.

"I know. He wouldn't let us tell your mother because he didn't want her worried. Well, he got over his other injuries quite well—and so he should have done with

Uncle Bob looking after him—but unfortunately he got a crack on the head that was rather more serious." Hugh frowned as if the memory was not a very pleasant one. "It was ghastly, because at first they were afraid he'd go blind."

"What?" Joanna gasped in horror, but Paul gave a thoughtful nod as if not as surprised as his sisters.

"They operated, and it seemed quite successful, but he was told that for at least eighteen months—probably more—he mustn't do anything to strain his eyes—read, write, or anything at all."

His cousins were beginning to see daylight now.

"So that's why he never used books when he was lecturing to us, and why he never seemed to read and was so restless," Louise said.

"And made us read our essays aloud—making us used to the sound of our own voices, indeed!" Joanna exclaimed indignantly.

"As soon as he was fit enough to travel he decided to come here where he could occupy his time out of doors, and wouldn't be tempted to use his eyes as he would be if he stayed in Town," Hugh went on. "It was a good idea because it gave him an interest. I don't know what would have happened to him if he'd stayed in London with nothing to occupy him. Of course, he wanted you all to come here, but he didn't want your mother to find out about the accident and that he didn't know yet whether his sight was safe. The letters he wrote to Aunt Ruth are the only ones he's written since the accident—he had to write those himself because your mother knows his writing. Uncle Bob has a power of attorney to deal with all business matters, and as far as other correspondence is concerned, Uncle's had to rely on me. It's been awfully awkward sometimes, doing it without your finding out, but Joe's let us use his room over the stable—oh yes, he knew!—I did most of my secretarial work up there as it was the only place in the house where you wouldn't see what I was doing—though I've had a job to shake Sarah off sometimes," he added, smiling at his faithful follower, whose eyes were like saucers. "And Joanna caught us once. I don't know what she thought we were up to."

"Well!" Joanna gasped. "I just couldn't guess. But this explains everything." She suddenly eyed her brother accusingly. "You don't seem particularly surprised."

"I don't think I am," Paul said thoughtfully.

"Why not?" asked Hugh curiously.

"Well, I happened to notice that amongst your books upstairs those dealing with eyes have obviously been studied over and over again—and parts underlined. Yet you've never said you were particularly interested in that subject, so it looked as if you'd been thinking of some special case. And although Uncle used to be an awful bookworm we never see him reading now—and there had to be some reason for his giving up his work and coming here. So I couldn't help putting two and two together—and after that I watched him more, and noticed that he avoided looking at anything closely."

Joanna gazed at her brother in astonishment.

"Well! And I always thought you were unobservant!" she exclaimed in a tone that made everyone laugh.

"Only when it's easier to be," Paul said lazily.

"And is Uncle really going to be all right?" Louise asked, and Hugh nodded.

"Yes. When Uncle Bob was here at Christmas he arranged for Uncle to go up to Town for an examination." He grinned suddenly. "I think Uncle was a bit taken aback when your mother decided it would be a good opportunity for her to go and do some shopping. You see, if he wasn't cured he didn't want her to discover what he was really going for."

"It must have been awkward," Paul agreed.

"I do think Uncle might have told us," Joanna remarked in an aggrieved tone.

"Much better not," Paul said. "Any of us might have let it out to Mother. And she would have worried if she'd known."

"And Uncle can use his eyes as much as he likes now?" Louise asked.

"I wouldn't say that." Hugh said. "He'll have to go slowly at first, I expect, but gradually he'll be able to get back to work again." He glanced at Joanna curiously. "I thought somehow you had a good idea of what was wrong."

"I knew there was something," Joanna admitted, "but I couldn't make out what." She hesitated for a moment, and then told them of her involuntary eavesdropping at Christmas. "I couldn't help puzzling over it afterwards, but I couldn't make head or tail of it."

"So that's why he complained that you'd been watching him," Hugh exclaimed.

Paul looked at his cousin curiously.

"It was rather hard on you being dragged away from school to live out here in the wilds——"

"I wasn't dragged away," Hugh said quickly. "Uncle wanted me to stay on at school, but I couldn't let him come here alone when he'd had to give up his work and all his other interests. I'd got my matric, and knew I shouldn't have any difficulty in getting to a university later, so I said I'd go on working on my own, and they both promised they'd help me all they could. And once I got here and we started work trying to pull the place together, I got really interested."

"Like me," Joanna said, leaning forward with her chin cupped in her hands and her face full of attention. "I always get interested in anything I do."

"But you haven't any particular goal you're working for," Paul said. "I think you gave up a lot, Hugh."

Hugh jumped up abruptly, looking uncomfortable.

"I can never repay all Uncle has done for me. If he hadn't given me a home I'd have had to go to my mother's brother and his wife, and I *loathe* them. They'd have made me go in an office the moment I was sixteen. They would never have agreed to my going to a university. Even if I'd managed to win my way through they'd never have let me do it. So now you can see why I had to work—at whatever I happened to be doing at the moment," he went on. "I owe Uncle so much, I've just got to do my best, both here, and at my real work."

"I do now," Joanna said eagerly. "And I know in future I'll do all I can to help you."

"I always do," Sarah observed in a self-righteous tone.

"Unfortunately for you," Joanna murmured to her cousin, who laughed.

"Though you oughtn't to overdo it," Louise ventured.

"No fear of that," Hugh said quickly. "I'm as strong as a horse."

Paul said nothing, but he was thinking a lot—chiefly of the way his own family had always taken it for granted that he must concentrate on his studies and be spared any extraneous worries. He suddenly felt a kind of regret that he had not had the opportunity of living with his uncle, despite his sometimes Spartan ideas, and Sir

Robert, rather than with his mother and—despite their sometimes outspoken remarks—self-denying sisters. Perhaps, if he had, he would have faced up to things as Hugh did. Then he suddenly pictured his mother and felt he was being bitterly ungrateful. It wasn't her fault that he was so indolent where everything but studying was concerned. He should have thought things out for himself— as he felt Hugh would have done in his place.

"It looks as if we've both got to do well, whatever happens," he said at last. "You'll feel you must because Uncle's giving you the chance, and I've got to because I know it's all Mother can do to send me to a university."

"You both will," Louise said with quiet conviction. "There's no doubt of that."

"It won't be my fault if I don't," Hugh said grimly.

"Nor mine," Paul said, with, for him, most unusual determination.

The two elder girls did not pass any comment, but their eyes met, and an agreement was entered into tacitly between them.

"We must try to help them more," Joanna said later as they did the washing-up, while the boys saw that everything was safe outside. "They did make me wish I had some goal to work for. But unfortunately there isn't money enough for either of us to do anything exciting," she went on, looking regretfully at her sister. "Of course, by the time Sarah is old enough to leave school Paul should have qualified, so we may be able to afford to do something for her."

"She'll have to work harder then she's doing at present," Louise remarked, looking thoughtful. She had a secret ambition of her own, as Joanna well knew, but they had long ago agreed that Paul must come first.

"I don't know whether it's worse to have a talent and not be able to use it, like you, or to be like me, with nothing," Joanna sighed.

As she turned to spread out the tea-towel to dry, the door burst open and Doctors Dilly and Dally, covered with snow, appeared on the threshold, shaking themselves and laughing. With an exclamation of dismay Louise came out of her vain dreams of standing on a concert platform thrilling a great audience with her voice, and ran to drive them out into the back kitchen to get rid of their powdering of snow.

"Joanna, pass me their slippers. They'll make a terrible mess of the floor if they come in in those boots," she sighed, and the boys meekly changed before entering.

Sarah, who was supposed to have been struggling with a French exercise while they were out, looked round at them with a seraphic smile.

"Louise an' Johnny are going to help you," she announced, "an' I am, too. An' then, when I leave school, you can help me, because Johnny says there may be money again by then. It's a pity there won't be any for them, isn't it?"

The boys looked at each other and then at the two elder girls, who were glaring at the small prattler.

"We only meant with the work here so that you can spend more time studying," Louise said hastily.

"Oh, we're not overworked," Paul said quickly. "As a matter of fact we'd only get stale if we stuck at it too long without a change of some sort."

Hugh did not say anything, but he was frowning as he got out his books, and Paul, too, looked up once or twice at his sisters with a thoughtful air as if his mind were not entirely on his work.

CHAPTER FIFTEEN

PAUL WAKES UP

"Paul!" Hugh, who had been poring over a textbook on physics in the surgery, swung round suddenly, and Paul, who had been conducting some experiment with the chemicals, nearly dropped a test-tube at his cousin's abrupt exclamation.

"I wish you wouldn't be quite so violently unexpected," he complained, not without reason. "What's the matter?"

"I've been thinking."

"Well, there's nothing particularly surprising in that, is there?" Paul inquired, obviously still with half his mind on his experiment.

"I've been thinking about the girls," Hugh said, pushing his book aside.

Paul put the test-tube down with great care, and came across to the fire.

"What about them?" he asked, rather as if his own mind had been running on the same theme.

Several days had passed since the blizzard, and although there had been several fine but dull spells, there had been more snow, and as yet there was no sign of a thaw to open up the way to the outside world. Indeed, they were more isolated than ever, for the telephone wires were now down, and they had no means at all of communicating with their neighbours. Apart from feeding the animals and poultry there was little that could be done out of doors, and so, at the instigation of the elder girls, the boys were putting in most of their time studying.

Hugh hesitated at Paul's question, and looked rather uncomfortable. "Well—I hope you won't think I'm interfering, but—what are the girls intending to do? After all, Louise had left school before you came here, hadn't she? And Joanna is fifteen——"

"I've never heard them say." Paul shook his head. "As a matter of fact I've been thinking about it, too. They made me feel such a selfish beast the other day——"

"Louise has got an unusually good voice," Hugh said thoughtfully, and Paul looked at him quickly and a little uncomfortably.

"I know. I'd never really thought about it until Sarah blurted out about there only being money enough to give me a start. I've been feeling a—an absolute rotter ever since, I can tell you. And then for the girls to decide to try to help us——"

"Yes, I haven't been able to get that out of my head," Hugh said, reflecting yet again how he had misjudged Louise.

"What I can't understand is why Louise has never said anything about having her voice trained," Paul said in annoyance directed more against himself than his sister.

"She wouldn't," Hugh said abruptly.

"Why not?" demanded Paul.

"Because all your family worry about is how you get on," Hugh said bluntly.

"Yes—I wish they didn't," Paul said moodily. "They've made me beastly selfish between them." He regarded his cousin dubiously. "I wonder what Joanna wants to do?"

"I've no idea," Hugh said.

"Neither have I. As a matter of fact I doubt if she has any particular ambition," Paul said thoughtfully. "She's one of those people who are so vitally interested in what they're doing that they live completely in the present." He glanced out of the window and grinned. "If you'll come and look you'll see exactly what I mean."

Hugh laughed as he gazed down at the snow-clad scene. Joanna and Sarah were toiling up the lane with an ancient toboggan they had found in a barn, while the two dogs raced round them barking, and as the boys watched the girls seated themselves on it and set off down the hill to the accompaniment of squeals of apprehensive excitement from Sarah, while Joanna's flushed cheeks and sparkling eyes proclaimed her enjoyment.

"You're probably right," Hugh agreed, and then, as his cousin seemed disinclined for further discussion, turned back to his book. Paul strolled back to his neglected experiment, pondered over it for a moment, and then wandered downstairs to the kitchen, where Louise was sitting rocking lazily before the fire. She looked round with a smile at the sight of him.

"Tired of work? Come and be lazy with me."

Paul accepted the invitation and sank down in the chair opposite to her, stretching out his long legs to the fire.

"Hugh and I have been talking," he observed.

"Oh? What about?" asked Louise.

"You and Joanna—you particularly," Paul said, a trifle accusingly.

"What about us?" asked Louise in surprise.

"We're wondering what you want to do now you've left school."

"Nothing," Louise suppressed a sigh. "What can I do?"

"Sing," Paul said bluntly, and this time the sigh refused to be suppressed.

"Some day, perhaps, I may be able to have some

lessons," she said, a little wistfully, and Paul glared at the unoffending fire.

"If it weren't for me——"

"No!" Louise would not let him finish. "I can sing to amuse myself, but you'd be miserable if you were anything but a doctor."

Paul got up and paced up and down restlessly.

"I can't tell you what a selfish beast I feel. I'd never even thought about you having any ambitions until Sarah gave it away the other day."

"I could murder her!" Louise said with unusual vehemence.

"I'm going to talk to Mother about it, anyway," Paul said, looking obstinate.

"You mustn't! It will only worry her, and you know we can't afford to do any more——"

"I shall do something," Paul declared obstinately. "Hugh would, in my place——"

"Nothing can be done at the moment," Louise said with conviction. "Perhaps when you've qualified——"

"I'm not waiting till then," Paul said, privately deciding to discuss the subject with his uncle, and, seeing that it was useless to argue further, Louise changed the subject.

"Have you heard Joanna and Sarah? They've been screaming like a couple of seagulls." She smiled. "Johnny's excuse is that she's keeping Sarah away from Hugh and giving him a chance to get on with his work."

"We have been singularly free from interruption," Paul agreed.

"But I'm sure they've been out long enough," Louise went on, a little anxiously. "They must be absolutely soaked to the skin, and it's one of those bitingly piercing winds."

"I'll go and tell them," Paul offered, getting up with unusual alacrity.

He found Sarah endeavouring to pull Joanna, helpless with laughter, out of a snowdrift, and, lending a strong hand, he hauled the latter to terra firma.

"You'd better come in and change," he remarked, "Or we'll have you both down with pneumonia."

Both girls stared at such unexpected solicitude.

"What's come over you?" inquired Joanna. "You aren't sickening for anything, are you?"

"I'm not wet, an' Hugh didn't say I'd got to come in," Sarah said cheerfully, pulling on her soaking wet glove.

"Woggles has had enough," Paul said, as that wise animal made for the house.

"I'm not coming. I'm enjoying myself," Sarah said firmly.

"Yes, we're all right," Joanna said cheerfully, turning to salvage their toboggan.

Paul shivered in the icy wind, and then looked down at Sarah, whose mouth was assuming its most obstinate expression.

"It's nearly time for tea, so you might as well come in now," he urged. "You've certainly been out long enough."

"No!" Sarah said flatly. "I'm—Oh!" She broke off with a gasp of indignation as she was suddenly swept off her feet and her brother set off for the house with her tucked helplessly under his arm.

Joanna stared after them in astonishment. In her heart of hearts she knew Sarah was very wet and should go in and change, but Paul's arbitrary methods put her in her most obstinate mood, and so she began to drag her toboggan up the hill again, even though she knew there would be no further fun in it alone.

In the kitchen Louise and Hugh, who had just come downstairs, stared as Paul set his squealing captive on her feet again.

"I thought you were killing one of the pigs," Hugh observed.

"No, you don't," Paul said, grabbing Sarah's arm as she turned and made for the back door. "Louise, she's absolutely soaking."

Louise gave an exclamation of dismay as she examined Sarah's state more closely.

"Come on! Off with your coat and stockings at once," she ordered. "And your frock," she added. "Paul, you might go up and get her dressing-gown. Joanna ought to be ashamed of herself, letting her get in this state."

"She's just as nice an' wet," Sarah said defiantly.

"Where is Joanna?" asked Hugh.

"Outside still. She'll probably stay out till it's dark now as I interfered," Paul said going in search of the dressing-gown, and Louise and Hugh looked at each other.

"No one will be able to do anything with her if she's really got her back up," Louise sighed, as she pulled Sarah's damp dress over her head. "And goodness knows what kind of state she'll be in by the time she comes in!"

Without another word Hugh went into the back kitchen, pulled off his shoes and got into rubber boots, and then, pulling on a coat as he went, tramped out into the bitter east wind. Joanna had just sailed down the hill as he came in sight, and, guessing why he had come, she jumped up hastily, seized her toboggan, and started up the hill again. Rather to her surprise Hugh did not call out or follow her, but calmly waited at the foot of the slide. Having toiled to the top, Joanna hesitated, but the wind was even more piercing there, and realising that she could not stay there indefinitely, and suspecting that even if she did her cousin would still wait for her, she seated herself on the toboggan and hurtled down with an air of bravado that did not hide her uneasiness.

As frequently happened, she came to grief at the bottom, and as she floundered in the soft snow a hand gripped hers and she was hauled unceremoniously to her feet, to find Hugh holding the rope of the toboggan in his other hand.

"And now come in," he said shortly.

"I'll come when I want to," Joanna retorted, uncomfortably aware of the fact that her strength was no match for her cousin's.

"Don't be an idiot," Hugh said patiently. "You must be soaked through. Sarah was."

"I'm all right."

For a moment they stood facing each other, and then Hugh grinned into her defiant face.

"You'll either come in on your own two feet or I'll carry you. Which way will you choose?"

Joanna made a sudden effort to pull herself free, but her cousin's fingers closed round her wrist until they hurt.

"All right!" he said coolly, dropping the rope. "If you won't be reasonable——"

As he caught hold of her, fully expecting to meet with strong resistance, Joanna suddenly doubled up in helpless laughter.

"Oh, dear! Would you really have carried me?" she gasped.

"I still shall if you don't come sensibly," Hugh declared. "Honestly, Johnny, you ought to have more sense! What on earth should we do if either you or Sarah got a chill? It's all very well our joking and playing being doctors, and doing odd bits of first aid, but we shouldn't know how to deal with a real illness—and we couldn't even ring up Dr. Davies and get instructions from him."

The defiant amusement died out of Joanna's face.

"All right, I'll come," she agreed, trying to suppress a shiver. "I probably should have done in any case if Paul hadn't been so unexpectedly high-handed with Sarah."

Hugh looked at her shrewdly as he picked up the cord of the toboggan again and began to walk towards the house.

"You should be glad he was," he remarked.

"Why?" demanded Joanna, secretly relieved to be going in.

"Because it shows he is thinking about you girls," Hugh said, and she looked round at him quickly.

"You mean——" She frowned. "Hugh, these last few days he has seemed more awake, somehow. Why?"

"I shouldn't ask," Hugh advised her. "I'd just accept it—and welcome it. After all, as your only brother, he should think about you all sometimes."

"Oh, I know he should but he never has done," Joanna said casually.

"I think he's going to now," Hugh remarked, and laughed as Joanna made a grimace.

"I don't know that I'm keen. If he's going to start throwing his weight about as he did this afternoon——"

"You won't be able to have everything your own way any more," Hugh finished wickedly for her as they reached the house. "You'd better go and change at once," he added, as he stopped in the back kitchen to leave the toboggan in a corner before going on to the barn.

Sarah was seated sulkily by the fire in the kitchen sipping some hot milk, and Louise looked round with a harassed frown as Joanna appeared.

"Do go and change at once," she begged.

"It's no use till I've fed the chickens," Joanna said shortly, feeling uneasily that all three of her elders were treating her as if she were in disgrace.

"Paul's gone to do it," Louise said, and Joanna gave a start of surprise.

"*Paul* has?"

"Yes. Do go and change. And then there's some hot milk for you."

Joanna felt strongly disposed to stop and argue, but remembering their complete isolation if anyone were ill, she meekly went upstairs and, with secret relief, changed out of her sodden clothes.

When she came down Paul had returned and was helping Louise to get the tea, while Sarah was still in a high state of sulks.

"Here you are!" Louise said, pushing Joanna down into a chair by the fire and giving her some hot milk. "Drink that at once. Are you sure you're quite warm?"

"Hugh didn't say I'd got to come in," Sarah remarked in an aggrieved tone, breaking her sulky silence when Hugh came in for his tea.

"I should have done if I'd been there," Hugh said promptly, and Sarah looked decidedly taken aback.

"But you wouldn't have *carried* me in," she protested.

"I certainly should," her cousin affirmed, with a wicked glance at Joanna, who looked quite sheepish.

"But you didn't carry Joanna," Sarah persisted.

"I should have done if she hadn't seen reason," Hugh declared, and Louise gave a gasp.

"You couldn't!" she exclaimed, with a glance at her fairly substantial sister.

"I certainly could," Hugh grinned. "Do you want me to demonstrate?"

"No, thanks," Joanna said hastily.

She would not admit it, but she felt shivery all evening, and when she awoke in the morning she was as hoarse as a crow.

"Johnny!" Louise wailed. "Oh, you are an idiot! Don't you dare to get up until the kitchen's warm! Oh—I could slap you," she finished.

To her relief Sarah was all right, but Joanna looked and felt very sheepish when she finally appeared at breakfast only able to utter hoarse croaks.

"No voice?" Paul queried. "This is a relief, anyway. Fortunately, Hugh, Johnny's colds always go straight to her voice. It's the only time we get any peace."

"You can't possibly go out," Hugh said, looking across at the invalid rather anxiously.

"Oh, I'll be all right," Joanna croaked.

"If you try to set one foot outside the door we'll tie you down," Paul declared, with unexpected firmness. "We had enough nonsense yesterday."

"But the chickens——"

"We'll look after the chickens," Paul said flatly. "Louise, if she tries to get out, hit her over the head with a blunt instrument. Johnny, you really do need slapping!"

"I suppose we should be thankful Sarah's all right," Louise frowned.

"If she hadn't been we'd have sent them both to bed in disgrace," Hugh said. "In fact I've half a mind to suggest that Joanna goes as it is."

"If you can make Johnny admit she's ill enough to stay

in bed it will be a miracle," Paul said. "No one's ever succeeded in doing that within my knowledge."

"I'm certainly not going to bed," Joanna croaked. "Except for my voice I'm perfectly all right."

"I'm glad to hear it, though I can't help thinking it's a good opportunity to practise taking temperatures," Paul remarked to Hugh.

"I—haven't—got—a—temperature," Joanna croaked as emphatically as she could, and Paul grinned as he got up.

"If so, that's no thanks to yourself," he remarked. "Coming, Hugh?"

The boys went off to get on with the outdoor work, but while Louise was upstairs making the beds Hugh's head popped round the door.

"Are you busy?" he queried.

"No, come in," Louise said, working quickly and expeditiously. "Is anything the matter?"

"No—at least, I wanted to ask you about Joanna."

"What's she doing now?" Louise asked with a sigh.

"Oh, nothing. At least, she's sitting by the fire making Sarah do some lessons. But I couldn't help wondering if she's all right, or if Paul was taking it too coolly."

"Oh, we all know Johnny's colds," Louise said. "They always take her in the same way, and usually sound worse than they really are. I'd be much more worried if it was Sarah. She was rather inclined to get bronchitis easily at one time. That's why Paul brought her in so unceremoniously. Of course, Joanna should have made her come in much sooner, but once Johnny gets excited about anything she never stops to think."

"So I've noticed," Hugh remarked, watching Louise curiously as she plumped up a pillow. "Then you think there's no need to worry?"

"I hope not." Louise looked at her cousin thought-fully as he leaned against the mantelpiece. "I shouldn't have expected you to worry like this."

"Well—it's not exactly Joanna, but I promised your mother to see that she and Sarah didn't get up to any mischief—and I feel I've failed. I knew they were out there tobogganing yesterday—and didn't do anything about it."

"Yes, but no one would have thought they'd be idiots enough to keep on when they were so wet," Louise said practically, and Hugh looked a little happier.

"Do you think so? It certainly didn't occur to me. It was you and Paul who thought about it."

"Yes, but we know Johnny's carelessness, and Sarah's weak chest," Louise pointed out consolingly.

Fortunately she proved to be right about Joanna. Kept indoors by the united efforts of her three elders—though not without difficulty—her cold responded to treatment and her voice gradually returned to normal, not without openly expressed regret on the part of Paul, who protested that those few days had been quite the most peaceful since their arrival at Long Barrow. In the meantime, being far too restless to sit and do nothing, she concentrated her energies on Sarah's lessons, and to atone for having to leave her work for the others to do, took over that young lady's education completely. At first Sarah's protests were loud and vehement, but Joanna's determination was too much for her, and after the first day Sarah submitted to the inevitable and, to the surprise of the others, made astonishing progress under her new and stern task-mistress.

CHAPTER SIXTEEN

MORE CHANGES

THE END of Joanna's cold coincided with the thaw. Louise, for one, had entertained secret fears that when the thaw came they would be flooded out, but fortunately the house itself stood on a slight eminence in the middle of the valley, so that although the ground all round was waterlogged, making them feel rather as if they were cast away on a desert island, the house itself remained dry.

"I'm going to ride in to the village and try to ring through to Uncle," Hugh said, coming into the kitchen after prospecting round. "Shamus can easily wade through the water in the lane. It isn't too deep."

"There's a car coming down now," Sarah exclaimed, running in, and they all hurried out to see the first fresh face they had set eyes on for a fortnight.

"It's old Davies!" Hugh exclaimed, as the car drew up on the far side of the flood and the doctor's round, bespectacled face peered out at them.

"Are you all right?" he called.

"Yes, thanks!" Hugh shouted back. "Our only casualty was a cold, and that's better now."

"Good!" the doctor called. "Glad to hear it. And I heard this morning that Joe is getting on splendidly. We've been cut off from civilisation, too, you know."

"Dr. Davies, would you mind ringing Uncle and telling him he can get through to us now," Hugh shouted, and the doctor nodded.

"Yes. What's the number?"

"I don't know. But if you ring Sir Robert Temple he'll get in touch with him."

"All right. Oh—Annie will be back later to-day. She's quite convinced that everything must have gone wrong here while she's been away."

The doctor waved cheerfully, and then slowly and carefully backed his car until he found sufficient space to turn.

"That will save me going to the village," Hugh said.

"But there are several things we need," Louise demurred. "Some of our food supplies are running a bit short."

"All right, I'll go," Hugh said promptly.

"Shall I come with you to help you carry the stuff?" Joanna asked, and he nodded.

"Perhaps you'd better. I don't think we ought to take the trap. It would probably get stuck in the mud sooner or later."

"I'll go and change," Joanna said, and ran into the house, leaving the two boys to saddle the horses.

"I was going to offer to come, but Johnny got in first," Paul said, with a wry grimace. "Anyway, I expect it's better for one of us to stay here with Louise and Sarah," he added with his new thoughtfulness.

Joanna was out again in a remarkably short space of time, and once they were safely past the floods they put the horses into a trot and proceeded briskly until they had to slow down to a walk for the steep hill down into the village.

"Hugh, while I've been stuck indoors I've been thinking," Joanna said abruptly.

"Then your cold has achieved something?" Hugh laughed.

"Don't start being like Paul when I'm trying to talk seriously," Joanna begged. "What I was going to say is, if Uncle's eyes are going to be all right, and he goes back to London, what's going to happen about Long Barrow —and us?"

Hugh looked at her quickly. He had been wondering much the same.

"I don't know," he admitted. "Uncle wouldn't make any plans until he'd heard the verdict, naturally, and I've no idea what he will have decided. I've been wondering myself."

"It's all right for you," Joanna said thoughtfully. "You'll go with him wherever he goes—but if he went back to live with Uncle Bob what would happen to us? You could hardly expect Uncle Bob to take us all in."

"I just can't guess. The only thing I do know is that Uncle will arrange everything satisfactorily. He always does."

They did their shopping, and, each wearing a well-filled haversack over one shoulder, began their homeward journey.

"We mustn't be any longer than we can help because Louise was worrying whether the horses would slip in the slush," Joanna remarked. "I know now how horrible it is waiting, since the night you took Joe to the doctor. I was quite sure the trap had turned over, and that you were all killed."

"If we'd had any sense we'd have rung you up from the doctor's," Hugh said.

"Well, for that matter, I could have rung you, but I just didn't think of it," Joanna said frankly.

They were unloading their haversacks in the kitchen when the sound of a familiar horn drew them out like a magnet, to see their uncle's car on the far side of the flood, and their uncle standing on the brink, gazing doubtfully at the expanse of muddy water.

"Dare I risk it?" he called above the chorus of excited greetings.

"I think so, if you're careful," Hugh replied. "Joanna and I rode Shamus and Jessamy through a few minutes ago, and it isn't as deep as it looks."

His uncle nodded and, getting back into the car, drove through with infinite care to their side, when they saw that he was accompanied by Mrs. Lister and Sir Robert.

"I've run away for a couple of days to see how you've all got on," Sir Robert explained, while Mrs. Lister proceeded to subject her family to a rapid fire of questions.

"Have you been all right?" Mr. Eldon asked above the hubbub.

"I hope none of you have been ill?" Mrs. Lister asked, casting anxious eyes round at their excited faces. "I was terribly worried when we found we couldn't even get through on the telephone. I wanted to come and stay as near to you as we could get, but John and Bob wouldn't agree."

"I rang through to Fontroy Magna, but when they said they were cut off, too, I realised that we might just as well stay where we were," Mr. Eldon said. "The Vicar sent us a wire as soon as there seemed to be the faintest chance of getting through."

"I shouldn't have worried half as much if Joe had been here," Mrs. Lister said. "We met Dr. Davies on our way here, and he says he's getting on very well."

"The doctor came this morning to find out if we were all right," Hugh said, at last managing to get a word in, "and we asked him to ring through to you, but I suppose you'd already left?"

"Yes, he told us he'd tried to get us," Mrs. Lister said. "And how has my baby been?"

"I've been all right, only Joanna's made me do lots of lessons," Sarah said. "But Johnny lost her voice, and Paul was awfully rude about it."

"Joanna!" Mrs. Lister sighed. "How did you manage that?"

"Oh, I got a bit wet in the snow," Joanna said casually, and Sir Robert, intercepting Hugh's quick glance at her and Paul's hastily suppressed grin, looked amused.

"Nasty wet stuff, snow," he agreed. "Isn't it, Sarah?"

"I like it," Sarah returned, "an' I'd have been all right if Paul hadn't carried me in."

"That seems to be rankling," Paul murmured with a chuckle.

"He was *most* offishus," Sarah went on. "Hugh didn't say I'd got to come in."

"As I've already pointed out, I wasn't there," Hugh said hastily.

"Well, what has been happening?" asked Mr. Eldon, when they had all trooped into the big kitchen. "Have you managed all right?"

While Joanna and the boys poured out an account of their activities for the past fortnight or so, Louise quietly made coffee for the whole party and produced a plate of home-made scones, and as she handed his cup to her uncle she seized the opportunity of a brief lull in the noise.

"Uncle, we were so pleased to hear your good news," she said. "Are you really all right now?"

"He will be if he remembers to go slowly," Sir Robert

said. "Hugh, you'll be able to give up your secretarial duties bit by bit."

As his eyes met the boy's they both laughed. Evidently he had heard all about Hugh's difficulties in trying to keep those duties a secret.

"I think the whole thing's been horribly mean," Joanna burst out. "We could all have helped you, Uncle, if you hadn't made such a mystery of it."

"It still makes me feel dreadful to think of the bare possibility," Mrs. Lister declared with a shudder, "but I do wish you had told us, John. Apart from anything else, Hugh must have had an awful time, skulking in corners trying to read to you and write your letters for you."

"I shall be glad to hand all your affairs over to you again," Sir Robert said, with a comical expression of deep mystery. "Especially as I'm taking on so much extra myself."

"What are you going to do?" asked Hugh curiously, as they all stared at Sir Robert questioningly.

"Well, I feel I've had rather too easy a time until now, so I'm thinking of taking on some new responsibilities," Sir Robert said casually. "Your aunt tells me it's time I grew up——"

"Mummy'll never grow up herself," Joanna said, looking puzzled. "She's the last one to criticise you."

"On the contrary, I'd say she should be the first," Sir Robert said with a laughing glance at Mrs. Lister, who was looking highly amused about something, but Joanna's mind had swept off at a tangent.

"Uncle, if your eyes are all right, will you be going back to live in London?" she asked, unable to bear the suspense any longer, and to her dismay her uncle nodded.

"Yes, I'm afraid I shall," he said, and Joanna's face fell, while Louise and Paul both looked taken aback.

"Then——" Paul broke off and turned to Hugh, "I suppose you'll go back to school for another year?" he said, trying to hide his anxiety about his own future, but Hugh did not answer. He was staring at his uncle in a puzzled sort of way. It would not be like Mr. Eldon, after offering his sister and her children a home, to go calmly back to London and leave them stranded. Then he turned to look at the girls. Joanna's dismay was too severe to be hidden, and Louise—Louise, who had declared at first that she hated Long Barrow—was obviously almost on the verge of tears.

A sudden wail from Sarah broke the silence.

"Uncle! You're not going to take Hugh away? What's going to happen to us?"

Mr. Eldon laughed as he swung her up into his arms.

"Cheer up! You won't lose him altogether," he said consolingly. "You'll be together here in the holidays— if you'd like that?—and——"

"But if you go back to London, what shall we do?" asked Louise, and her uncle laughed again.

"Well, I suspect the other three will go to school, but as for you—I thought you'd always hankered after town life?"

Louise looked at him in perplexity, and then turned to her mother.

"Are we—going back to Liverpool?" she asked, unable to hide her dismay.

"Do you want to?" asked her mother.

"No!" Louise's negative was almost as vehement as that of her sisters and Paul.

"Mummy, we haven't got to, have we?" Joanna wailed, while Sarah clutched at her uncle convulsively, and Paul turned to gaze at Hugh in dismay, for that would end all their plans of continuing to study together.

Mrs. Lister's face crinkled into its mischievous smile, and Sir Robert suddenly rose.

"No! You're coming to live with me," he said unexpectedly, and the young Listers gazed at him blankly, while Hugh, who had been looking at the three grown-ups in perplexity, gave a gasp of sudden comprehension.

"You don't mean——" Before he could finish, however, Joanna interrupted.

"But we couldn't! I know Uncle and Hugh will go back to live with you, but we can't *all*——"

"On the contrary, you're coming, and John and Hugh aren't," Sir Robert said, obviously enjoying himself.

"But——" Louise sought to find words to express her perplexity, but before she succeeded, Paul, after gazing incredulously from Sir Robert to his mother, suddenly gave an exclamation of astonishment.

"You—you don't mean—you're not——"

"Secretly I'm terrified at the thought of suddenly finding myself head of such a large family, but your mother seems to think I can fill the *rôle*," Sir Robert murmured, "and so——"

"Mummy!" Joanna gave a wild shriek and flung herself on her mother, nearly stifling her in the process. "Are you going to marry Uncle Bob?"

Mrs. Lister gasped helplessly for breath as Sarah tore herself from her uncle and also flung herself upon her, and Sir Robert turned to Louise, who was still staring in incredulous silence.

"Well, Louise? Will you have me for a stepfather?"

"I'd love it," Louise said warmly, her eyes glowing with delight, and Sir Robert turned to Paul.

"Well?" he asked with a smile, and Paul's hand shot out, to be gripped warmly.

"I—I just can't believe it," he gasped.

"I'm still a bit dazed myself," Sir Robert admitted with his very youthful grin, and then dived in to rescue Mrs. Lister, now helpless with laughter.

"Well, Sarah? Do you still bear a grudge against me, or will you accept me as one of the family?" he asked, drawing her out of the mêlée.

"Will we live near Hugh?" Sarah demanded cautiously.

"They'll be in a flat next door," Sir Robert promised, and Sarah gave a sigh of relief.

"All right," she said graciously, and then hesitated in sudden alarm. "Will Wogs come?"

"Definitely Wogs will come. Your mother specifically stipulated that she must bring her whole family."

Sarah gave a deep sigh of bliss.

"An' here in the holidays?" she demanded, evidently determined to go into everything thoroughly before committing herself.

"Definitely here," her uncle promised. "I wouldn't give the place up for anything. Joe and Annie can keep it going while we're in Town—I'll arrange for extra help for Joe."

Joanna gave a sigh of ecstasy that made everyone laugh.

"I'd hate to lose Jessamy and Sam—and Nero," she added, as the cat sprang up on the dresser beside her. "And the chickens."

"Joanna and her chickens!" Hugh exclaimed.

"Are we really going to be next door to you?" Louise asked her uncle.

"Yes. While we were in Town I heard that the flat would be falling vacant soon, so I jumped at the chance. It was obvious that if Bob was taking in the entire Lister family, Hugh and I would have to find somewhere else."

"You'll be able to come in and study with me," Hugh said, turning to Paul. "It will be quiet there."

"I don't quite like that innuendo," Joanna objected. "Anyone would think we were noisy." She turned and stared at Sir Robert approvingly. "I think this is going to be fun—but I do think you're brave to take us all on."

"I rather thought that myself," Sir Robert returned gravely. "What do you say, Hugh?"

Hugh smiled as both men glanced at him rather anxiously.

"I think it's splendid news. You'll be able to take Sarah off my hands sometimes——"

"I don't want to be taken off your hands," Sarah protested, and her uncle laughed.

"A born Mrs. Micawber, if ever there was one!"

"I'm going to come and help you study," Sarah declared, and Sir Robert turned to her mother.

"Ruth, I shall have to make one rule. Sarah is never to enter my consulting room. I have a feeling that if once she does——"

"You'll have to dangle Hugh in front of her like a carrot before a donkey in order to get her out before she starts helping you," Joanna exclaimed, going off into a peal of laughter as she pictured the scene, and only Sarah retained her gravity.

"I should like to help," she complained.

As they all bustled round getting the work done, Mrs. Lister and the two men noted several changes amongst the younger ones. To begin with, both boys treated

Louise with a new respect their elders were at a loss to understand. Paul, too, had altered considerably. Although for some time he had been doing his own work well, he now seemed more alert and reliable altogether, and kept a responsible eye on his sisters—a change not always appreciated by Joanna and Sarah—while he went out of his way to help Louise on every occasion. The two elder girls, for their part, for some unknown reason made repeated efforts to do some of the boys' work, though they were usually foiled by the boys themselves.

"What is this place? A Mutual Aid Society?" Sir Robert asked Hugh as they strolled out to the barn later in the day, and Hugh laughed.

"Not quite—only somehow while we were snowed up here we all seemed to get to understand each other better."

"I'm glad to hear it," Sir Robert remarked. "It might have had the effect of setting you at each others' throats."

"No!" Hugh shook his head. "You see, Paul and I were saying that we'd just got to do well because Uncle's giving me my chance, and Aunt Ruth can only just afford to let Paul go in for a profession." Sir Robert listened with interest, and forbore to remind Hugh that Mrs. Lister's financial affairs might soon be rather different. "And the girls got it into their heads to do all they could to give us more time to study," Hugh went on.

"That accounts for the girls' attitude," Sir Robert nodded. "But go on—I know there's more yet."

"Well, from something Sarah let out Paul suddenly realised that if he was given his chance there wouldn't be any money to help the girls, and so now he's trying to make it up to them a bit," Hugh said, and Sir Robert looked pleased. "Particularly as we've discovered that

Louise would like to have her voice trained, but won't say a word about it because she thinks Paul's future is more important," Hugh added. "He says he's going to talk it over with Uncle and see if something can't be done."

"So Louise, despite her passion for tidiness, has earned your respect after all?" Sir Robert said, looking pleased, and Hugh went red.

"Yes, I think she's been splendid about Paul. Don't you think something——"

"Yes, I do." Sir Robert did not wait for him to finish. "Don't worry any more. Ruth knew how she was feeling, and so Louise's future is all arranged. If she wants to, she can start her training in the autumn."

Hugh's face lit up, and he suddenly swung round towards his companion.

"You know, I think they're awfully lucky—if I hadn't got Uncle you're the one I'd choose——"

Sir Robert's hand rested for a second on his shoulder.

"Although you'll be next door now, Hugh, I want you still to feel that my house is your home, and that you can come in whenever you want—and that I'm just as interested in you as ever. Your aunt is very worried for fear you should feel——"

"I don't," Hugh said quickly, without waiting for him to finish. "Before they came—and for a while afterwards—I did feel as if I might be pushed out. But I don't now. I just feel that I'm one of them—in fact——" he broke off awkwardly, and as Sir Robert wondered what he had been going to say, Joanna came running up to them, followed more leisurely by Paul.

"Hugh! Louise and I think we ought to have some sort of celebration to-night. What do you think?"

"I'm in favour," Hugh said promptly.

"And Uncle's going to ride in to the village to ring up the hospital about Joe as our phone isn't working yet," Paul said. "He's suggested that one of us might like to go with him, so we wondered if you would."

"But before you go," Joanna said, taking her cousin's acquiescence for granted, "you might give us your ideas for to-night, because it's all frightfully short notice, and we'll have to start preparing at once."

"Yes, I should like to go—unless either of you wants to," Hugh said, and his cousins shook their heads.

"Not if you want to," Paul said.

"I shall be far too busy," Joanna declared with an air of mock importance. "But what about to-night?"

"Well, my suggestion is that Louise makes some of those cakes of hers that are so good—and that you get Uncle Bob to help you—he'll have to get used to your boundless energy some time," Hugh said, and bolted off to get the horses and find his uncle, leaving Paul chuckling.

"That's true. You don't really know what you're taking on, you know," he observed. "Mother and Joanna together are a handful. Personally I prefer to keep well out of the way when they both start rushing round."

Sir Robert laughed as he turned to accompany them back to the house. He thought he knew now what Hugh had nearly said. It was obvious that, far from leaving him out, the young Listers not only regarded him as one of themselves, but were even inclined to look to him for leadership, while he also noticed with pleasure that it was, apparently, tacitly acknowledged by them that Hugh had first claim on their uncle.

CHAPTER SEVENTEEN

AU REVOIR

As Mr. Eldon did not expect to be able to use his eyes fully for several months, the wedding did not take place until shortly before he was ready to return to Town, for Mrs. Lister refused to desert Long Barrow, until he was ready to leave, and they all revelled in the return of spring and early summer to the remote world of the downs. As the weather grew warmer picnics became the order of the day, and with Louise driving Jessamy in the trap and Joanna or one of the boys riding Shamus, they explored in every direction.

Sir Robert came nearly every weekend, and his presence invariably added so much to the merriment of the party, that even Sarah began to decide that she liked him *nearly* as much as Hugh.

"Fond though I am of her, I hope she doesn't transfer her affections completely," Sir Robert said in alarm one day, after she had announced this before wandering off with Woggles and Sam while they were picnicking on the downs. "I don't really think my patients would appreciate her assistance."

"I expect Hugh would be relieved if she did," Joanna said, lying stretched out at full length on the springy turf.

"I don't know that I would," Hugh said, thoughtfully biting a blade of grass. "I believe I'd miss her badly."

"I should have said *miss her gladly*," Paul said lazily, but Hugh shook his head. Apart from his uncle and Sir Robert—and latterly his Aunt Ruth—there had been

singularly few affections in his life during the last few
years, and Sarah's doglike devotion, comical—and even
embarrassing—though it frequently was, had meant
more to him than he would ever acknowledge.

"Where is she?" asked Mrs. Lister, looking round.

"I'll go and see," Hugh said, jumping up, but before
he could leave the group such an outcry of barking and
shouting arose that everyone leapt up and made for the
scene of the uproar without loss of time.

Down in a hollow, half screened by low bushes, lay a
pond, and in the pond, standing in the muddy water,
stood a terrified Sarah, clutching a wildly struggling
Woggles in her arms, while Sam stood on the bank,
barking furiously and holding at bay two loutish-looking
boys of sixteen or seventeen, who were roaring with
laughter and flinging stones into the water so that a
constant shower of spray was rising around their victim.

As Mrs. Lister gave an exclamation of horror, the two
boys exchanged a glance.

"Leave them to us!" Paul exclaimed. "You get Sarah
out!"

The slope of the down lending them impetus, the boys
were on Sarah's attackers almost before they realised
what was happening, and her shrieks of fear changed to
squeals of excitement as her brother and cousin each
selected an objective and hit out. In the meantime
Joanna seized Sam, who had already drawn blood judging by a thin trickle of red on the hand of one of the
boys, while Sir Robert, only a second behind her, grasped
a low bough of a tree and leaned over towards Sarah.

"Get hold of my hand," he ordered, and, tucking
Woggles under one arm, not without great difficulty,
Sarah caught his hand and was drawn to the bank,

where Louise reached out and took the dog from her, while her uncle seized her other hand and helped to pull her out. Then, leaving her to her mother and Sir Robert, he turned his attention to the fighting boys.

"Don't put Woggles down," Sarah wailed. "They threw stones at her, an' when I picked her up they chased me, an' I fell into the pond, an' then they wouldn't let me out."

Sir Robert shot a quick glance at the fighters. It was impossible to tell if Hugh and Paul had heard, but it was obvious that both were fighting mad, and their adversaries were by no means enjoying themselves.

Mrs. Lister and Louise both watched in horror, but, while she clutched Sam firmly round the neck, Joanna's eyes gleamed with excitement, and Mr. Eldon was looking curiously content as he watched to ensure fair play, but made no effort to interfere, for it was plain that his nephews were quite capable of inflicting all the punishment that was required, and were showing up as well as even he could have wished. Both had a fair knowledge of boxing, and Hugh had always been very strong for his age, while the last year had made a great difference to Paul's physique.

After making sure that, apart from fright, Sarah was quite unharmed, Sir Robert sat down on a fallen tree trunk as if it were a ringside seat and proceeded to watch, not only the fighters, but the spectators, smiling to himself at the sight of Joanna's excitement.

Hugh dispatched his adversary first. A shrewd blow on the chin sent the young hooligan down in an inert heap, completely done, while Hugh stepped back, breathing heavily and dabbing tenderly at his streaming nose. A moment later Paul's opponent, too, went down with a crash, and as he stood surveying his late antagonist a smile came over Paul's battered features.

"And now let's finish 'em off altogether by giving 'em first aid," he suggested, and his victim, who was slightly more conscious than his friend, gave a frightened whine, while Sir Robert laughed as he got up to examine Hugh's opponent, who was lying periously near the edge of the pond.

"Some water will bring him round," he remarked, and Hugh, with a painful grin, rolled his antagonist over and dipped his head into the muddy water.

"I didn't say drown him," Sir Robert pointed out, trying to keep his face straight, and the other boy, scrambling with difficulty to his feet, set off unsteadily without waiting for his friend.

"I regard that as a *quid pro quo*," Paul remarked, advancing to help. "Let's roll him in altogether, Hugh."

"I think he's had enough," Mr. Eldon protested, laughing as he stopped them.

"More than enough," Sir Robert said, watching the boy as he opened his eyes and blinked round fearfully. "He's all right now. You got some force behind that blow, Hugh."

"He does," Paul said ruefully. "I've felt it a few times."

Sir Robert pulled the young hooligan to his feet.

"And now go after your friend—and don't let us see you again," he said grimly, and the boy staggered off, only too relieved to get away without further punishment.

Mrs. Lister, who by this time had got Sarah's wet clothes off and had wrapped her in Louise's tweed coat, gave a sigh of relief.

"I'm glad they've gone. Do you know who they were, John?"

"No. I suspect they were gypsies," her brother said.

Louise was gazing at the boys with the same horror that had been depicted on her countenance the first time she saw Hugh, but he knew her now and only laughed.

"You *are* sights!" she exclaimed. "You'll look dreadful for the wedding."

The boys turned and inspected each other in startled horror. In addition to sundry bruises and cuts, Hugh's nose was rapidly swelling into most unpleasant proportions, and was still bleeding slightly, while Paul's right eye was almost closed, and his lip, which was split, was assuming a puffy appearance that certainly did not add to his beauty. Paul surveyed his damaged knuckles ruefully, and then looked again at Hugh as if he could scarcely bear it.

"Do I really look as bad as you?" he inquired in justifiable horror.

"Worse, if anything," Joanna chuckled. "But, oh! I wouldn't have missed it for anything. I've never enjoyed anything so much."

"The sooner we get her back to the refining influences of civilisation, the better," her uncle said, shaking his head severely.

"I enjoyed it myself," Paul said, in a tone almost of surprise. "I *must* have altered."

"I felt like murdering mine," Hugh grunted. "Is she all right, Aunt Ruth?"

Sarah, a quaint figure with Louise's coat sweeping the ground, spoke for herself.

"I'm quite all right." She gazed at him with adoring eyes. "You *were* brave, Hugh!"

"Hey! What about me?" demanded Paul, dabbing at his lip tenderly. "Wasn't I brave?"

Sarah turned to survey him as only a sister would look at a brother. "Oh, yes," she said calmly. "I s'pose you were brave, too."

"That's the last time I become a knight errant for any of my sisters," Paul said with a grin. "I say, do you think there's any chance of my eye getting back to normal in less than a year or two?"

Sir Robert laughed as he surveyed the two damaged faces. "You'd better take Sarah home and get her some dry clothes, Ruth, and in the meantime I'll do what I can to patch up these two—though I'm afraid they won't regain their lost beauty very swiftly."

To Louise's disgust the boys' faces still retained some traces of the battle when the day of the wedding arrived, though, thanks to Sir Robert's ministrations, they did not look as bad as some of the family had feared. However, as Paul philosophically remarked, the girls were such things of beauty and joys for ever that he and Hugh flattered themselves they passed unnoticed.

It was quite a quiet wedding, and when it was all over and Sir Robert and Lady Temple—her children could not get used to the idea of their mother's title—had departed, to the Lake District, Long Barrow seemed strangely empty. Sarah dissolved into floods of tears the moment her mother had gone, and refused to be consoled until Hugh took her out to catch minnows in the stream. Louise, too, was even quieter than usual, and felt so near tears that she did not dare to speak to anyone. Joanna gazed round despairingly, but her uncle had settled down with a weighty-looking legal volume—it still seemed strange to see him reading once again—and so she wandered out of doors, to find Paul leaning over the wall of a sty gazing reflectively at the pigs.

"I'm sorry this year's nearly over," she remarked as she joined him.

"It's been good fun," Paul agreed, leaning over to scratch the back of one of the pigs.

"I wonder how we'll like it in London," Joanna said thoughtfully.

"I've tried not to look at it selfishly, but from my point of view it should be wonderful. Fancy living in the same house as a specialist like Uncle Bob! He's promised to help Hugh and me a lot once we're settled there. And Louise is getting her heart's desire," Paul added with even more satisfaction. "I'd have hated to think that Uncle Bob was having to foot all the bills, but Mother says she's saved so much on school bills and other expenses this year that she can help quite a lot towards it—and Louise and I are both determined that some day we're going to pay back all he does spend on us to give us our chance."

"I've loved our lessons here," Joanna sighed. "I don't believe I'll like school half as much."

"With Louise studying music and practising scales all day you'll probably miss her so much that you'll be glad to go to school to meet other girls," Paul said consolingly. "Uncle Bob has arranged for me to go to Hugh's old school, so we'll still be together."

"It will be fun if you can go right through together—and be Drs. Dilly and Dally to the end of the chapter," Joanna agreed.

Fortunately they were so occupied in making the most of their last few weeks at Long Barrow before going to their new homes in London that the time passed much more quickly than they expected, and it did not seem long before, accompanied by their uncle, they were getting out of a taxi before a tall, Georgian house, while Joe and

Annie were left to hold the fort at Long Barrow. They were admitted into a hall of gracious proportions, and as they looked round curiously their mother appeared at the top of the staircase, and with a squeal of excitement Sarah made a dive for the stairs, tripped over Woggles' lead, and fell with a crash on to that protesting animal.

As her mother hurried down towards her, and her uncle and Hugh dived forward to pick her up, a door opened and Sir Robert looked out, a comical expression of resignation on his face.

"Not a casualty to start off with?" he asked, carefully closing the door behind him, and Hugh gave an exclamation of dismay.

"Oh! Have you got a patient there?"

"I have. But I'll be up to see you soon," Sir Robert promised, and vanished, while the newcomers went guiltily upstairs and into a most attractive drawing-room, where they received a most tumultuous welcome from the new Lady Temple, who was just as impulsive and impetuous as she had been as Mrs. Lister.

"My dears! You must be tired," she exclaimed. "I was coming to meet you, but my watch was wrong, and by the time I was ready to leave I discovered that you would be on your way here."

They were sitting having tea when Sir Robert joined them, and Joanna eyed him wickedly.

"I suppose we'll have to creep in and out in case we disturb you," she said.

"Well, I'd rather you didn't do acrobatic tricks in the hall," Sir Robert said, accepting a cup of tea from Paul.

"I fell over Woggles' lead," Sarah explained with dignity. "We were both so anxious to see Mummy."

"Well, I suppose this was an exceptional occasion,"

her new stepfather said. "Under the same circumstances I might have fallen over Woggles myself."

"Have you any patients here now?" asked Joanna, when they had finished tea.

"Not one. Why?"

"Then can we explore?" she asked eagerly, and Sir Robert laughed.

"Of course! Come on!"

The girls wanted to see the whole house, but Paul's entire interest centered on the consulting room, and the disgusted girls had much ado to drag Hugh and him away.

"Morbid, I call it!" Joanna said severely. "Wait until you've been practising for a few years. You'll be glad to get away, then, for a change."

To their huge delight they found that Sir Robert had booked seats for the whole party at a theatre for that evening, and after their year out in the wilds they felt quite strange as they sat listening to the orchestra tuning up and waiting for the curtain to rise. Sarah, sitting between her mother and Hugh, was all eyes, for this was a very unusual treat for her; Louise felt pleasantly grown up as she leaned back in her seat between her uncle and her new stepfather; and Joanna, sitting between the two boys, reflected that their new life was opening well, and might, even if in a totally different way, compare quite favourably with their life at Long Barrow.

As the curtain went up she gave a sigh of delight, and, feeling Hugh glance round at her, murmured:

"I believe I'm going to like it here—but I'm so glad we've got Long Barrow as well."

THE END